THOU SHALL NOT

By Tina Glasneck

Vie La Publishing House, LLC

Vie La Publishing House, LLC
Post Office Box 70011
Richmond, Virginia 23255

Special book excerpts or customized printings can also be created to fit specific needs. For details, please contact Vie La Sales Manager: Attn: Special Sales Department. Vie La Publishing House, LLC, Post Office Box 70011, Richmond, Virginia 23255

This is a work of fiction. Names, characters, places, and incidents are the products of the author's imagination or are used fictitiously. Any resemblance to actual events, locales, or persons, living or dead, is entirely coincidental.

ISBN-13: 987-0985416201
ISBN-10: 0985416203
First Edition: March 2012
Second Printing: March 2013
Printed in the United States of America

Dedication

I dedicate this book to my wonderful husband, who has encouraged me to follow my dreams and always believed that I could reach them. *Ich liebe dich bis in alle Ewigkeit*!

This book is also dedicated to my wonderful child, who has taught me the beauty each day can bring. Mommy loves you!

ACKNOWLEDGMENTS

An dieser Stelle möchte ich mich bei meiner Familie bedanken, die mir bei der Entstehung dieses Buches immer hilfreich zur Seite gestanden hat und diesen Traum real werden ließ. Mein besonderer Dank gilt Klaus und Ursula, die an mich geglaubt und mich unterstützt haben, Alex für seinen Rat und seinen Beistand und Tobi für seine Hilfe mit meiner Webseite. Ich werde dein Andenken immer in guter Erinnerung behalten.

Thanks to my family for their unwavering support and encouragement; I am forever grateful! I especially would like to thank Christian for his unwavering encouragement and for giving me strength to fly. I could not have accomplished this without you.

I'd also like to thank my mother for her nurturing nature and always having time for her daughter.

There are so many people who have assisted me in the creation of this book, through their kindness, listening ear and thoughtful words. I wish to thank them for their encouragement, patience and of course, laughing with me through this process, including, Baine, Justine and Colleen, thank you for your time, hospitality and laughter. Therese, Lori, Latrese, Mike, James, Lisa and Dawn, thank you for having an ear to listen and a smile; and also Ashley Shelby, Lexi Walker and the wonderful Lisa Lauer for their assistance over the course of my creating this story.

Also a special thank you to the Virginia Romance Writers for encouraging me to continue on my journey to publication.

To my fans, I am forever grateful for your support, and the opportunity to be able to follow my dreams in creating this book.

Prologue

Gray clouds hovered over Richmond, Virginia. A cold wind blew, chilling Alexandria "Xandy" Caras to the core. Bundled in her tan wool overcoat, she hastened from the police station to the historical mansion that housed The Law Offices of Hines, Gilbert & Woodstein.

Bypassing the office gaiety, she hurried onward, ignoring the office abuzz with its usual noises.

Dark shadows hung under her eyes, and remembering the mocking smirk of the officer at the police station did nothing to calm her.

The gun lay heavy in her purse; even heavier than the responsibility she carried on her shoulders.

Anxious, she dashed to Thornton's office.

Her Thornton.

Finding it empty, she slipped into his large wardrobe.

Tears streamed down her face. Tears for what could have been and what never would be.

Gripping the gun between her palms, she waited.

April 18

Her ankles ached.

The courtroom was filled to capacity. Xandy sat next to her attorney, Tom Doaks, at the defendant's table. Her once ruddy complexion was now pale. She stared straight ahead; her dowdy black hair masked her features. Wrinkled clothes draped her small frame and the too-often worn shackles chafed against her skin. Shivers of angst slid down her spine from the hostile glares boring into her back. She'd spent the last year in a cell, as continuance after continuance shoved the court date to another month.

"All rise," announced the uniformed bailiff.

Xandy sprang up with as much energy she could muster. Her heart galloped.

"Oyez, oyez," continued the bailiff, "the Circuit Court is now in session. The Honorable Judge David Nathaniel Henderson Scott, III, presiding. All those with suits to prosecute and claims come forth and you shall be heard. God save this Commonwealth and this Honorable Court. You may be seated."

"Madam Clerk, if you'll read the indictment," Judge Scott said. He turned toward the older woman to his left, seated behind an array of folders.

Xandy remained standing behind the defense table. She stared ahead at the clerk, bracing herself. Drawing in a ragged breath, she trembled. Sweat ran down her back, pooling at the base of her board-straight spine. She clenched her hands together.

"The grand jury charges the accused, Alexandria Caras, did murder by willful, deliberate and premeditated killing Thornton Aaron Gage. Virginia Code Section 18.2-32. How do you plead?" asked the clerk.

"Not guilty," Xandy muttered.

"You're going to have to speak up, Ms. Caras," said Judge Scott. His southern cadence echoed throughout the courtroom. "Can you repeat yourself?"

With strength she did not feel, she raised her chin and said, "Not guilty!"

The gathered crowd erupted at that news. Judge Scott's gavel slammed repeatedly against the dark wood until the buzzing ceased.

"Now listen, folks," the judge bellowed. "I don't know how they do things in other courtrooms, but here in my small kingdom, when I speak, you are to be quiet. Should you disregard my rules, I'm sure the jail has enough space to house you all."

"Your Honor, we would waive the reading of the additional firearm charge in order to expedite this matter," Tom said.

"This is in reference to the one count of use of a firearm in the commission of a felony?" Judge Scott asked.

"Yes, Your Honor."

"How do you then plead to this charge, Ms. Caras?

"Not guilty," Xandy said.

"Your honor if I may approach the bench for a side bar?" asked Gary Allen, the Assistant Commonwealth's Attorney. He walked forward, fresh-faced and astute, in his gray tailored suit.

"It's going to be okay, Xandy," said Tom. But his words brought her little comfort. He stepped from behind the table and stood next to the Assistant Commonwealth's Attorney.

The taste of bile rising from her queasy stomach increased as she heard their hushed tones and watched the judge's glances. Xandy tapped her foot. She tried to be still, but looking at the judge, who held her fate, garbed in his black robe, she felt the air being sucked out of her lungs.

Just as quick as the conference began, the discussion ended and the attorneys returned to their tables.

"Mr. Allen, I understand that you have a motion to present in reference to this matter," the judge said.

"Yes, Your Honor. We move to *nolle pros* the charges

against Ms. Caras at this time," Allen said.

Xandy gasped. The misery of the last 373 days came crashing out in tears on the well-worn carpet. She heaved and sobbed in relief. Today she could walk away free.

"Do you have any objections, Mr. Doaks?" asked Judge Scott.

"Not at all, sir," Tom said. His mouth cracked into a grin.

"Then, Ms. Caras, I would say you are free to go," Judge Scott said. Turning to the clerk, he then asked, "What's next on the docket?"

Tom turned to Xandy. "It is not a complete dismissal. It came down to the last minute to pound this deal out. Unless new and compelling evidence comes up against you, they are not going to bring the charges back up."

As Tom spoke those words, Xandy felt the world spinning on its axis. For though she was free, nothing would be the same. There would be no more 'I love yous' uttered from Thornton's lips. All of her hopes and dreams had been dashed by gunshots. Her freedom was tainted by the horrendous crime that would forever hang over her head.

Suddenly an incensed shout erupted from the back of the courtroom, followed by a booming male voice. "You'll pay for this!"

"I warned you all," shouted Judge Scott over the uproar, scanning the courtroom. "Who said that?"

Xandy's body continued to shake; her stomach churned. Her legs gave way. She collapsed back in her seat and stared stupefied at her hands.

The hands capable of murder.

<u>Chapter 1</u>

October 10

Sister Hannah Salem exited the car in front of the hotel. The cold air whipped around her, heavy with the smell of exhaust. Her thinning brown hair was pulled back in a messy bun. The colorful frock hung on her petite frame. Chilled, she pulled her jacket around her.

"Hans, what time are we to start tonight?" Hannah asked. Her voice was strained. She turned toward the man at her elbow.

"Service starts at 7:00, but we need to be there by 6:30," Hans said. Gripping his cane in his liver spotted hand, he shuffled forward.

"Humph," she snorted, "I guess I have to be quick about this then," she said while she walked toward her office. She had no desire to head out tonight, wanting to only curl up with a good book and get some much needed sleep, but the money wouldn't let her do it. With Pastor Byrd and through his congregation, she had a grand following, which meant money to fuel her smugness. "I'll be out in a minute."

"Do you need any help with anything?" Hans persisted.

"No," she shooed him away with the flick of her wrist. After primping, she picked up her phone and dialed the telephone number to confirm her after service engagement. Hearing the voicemail's beep on the line, she said, "I just wanted to confirm that we are on for tonight. I should be done around eleven. I look forward to meeting you then." The thought of meeting someone new excited her.

Hans and Sister Hannah drove up East Broad Street into the historic Church Hill district. The picturesque St. John's Church, with its black window shutters and high steeple, lay in the distance.

They hurried the short distance to the meeting room for the night's service, at Pastor Byrd's historic home. Walking up the red brick stairs, they entered the Victorian row house.

The renovated home resembled more of a small church with its folding chairs and make-shift stage. The sounds of the organ and hymns being sung greeted them. Rushing toward the stage, Sister Hannah grabbed the mic.

"It is befitting for us to meet in the shadow of St. John's, to declare our desire to be free," Sister Hannah said standing in the pulpit before the filled seats. "Patrick Henry stood in this same building and proclaimed what we, as a people, and individually want. To be free."

As she stood before them, preaching from the Gospel of Mark, Hannah stared out at the crowd. A diverse group gathered from poor to well off. Taking the Bible in her hand, she bellowed, "How hard it is for the rich to enter the kingdom of God!"

Sobbing, moaning and clapping reverberated throughout the room. Then one lone soul raced to the front and tossed his bejeweled chain on to the platform. One after the other came forward, tossing money, cell phones, and jewelry.

The service lasted for four hours. It was a mélange of praise, worship, clapping, yelling, sweating, and tears. As the music died down from the thunderous, rousing gospel music to a solemn hymn, and after the altar call, the crowd slowly dispersed. Hannah and some of her faithful started to repack the needed equipment for their next stop tomorrow evening on their travel circuit.

Having noticed a Rolex that was tossed on the stage, Hannah walked over to Pastor Byrd. "Pastor, do you mind if I keep that Rolex? It is such a lovely watch," Hannah said.

"Matter of fact, I had the inclination to give it to you myself. Let me ask the man who owned it though. He's still there in the back praying." Pastor Byrd walked to the back, as Hans walked over to Hannah's side.

"Are you coming, Hannah?" Hans asked. "I thought we'd go ahead and get a good night's rest and then be nice and fresh for our stay in King George County."

"Sister Hannah," Pastor Byrd interjected. "Praise God, I spoke with the gentleman, and he is fine with such a servant like you keeping his gift to God. He would be honored."

Hannah reached into the offering bucket and snatched the Rolex out of it.

"Hans, go ahead without me. I'll meet you back at the hotel. I just need some time alone." Hannah turned back to the pastor, dismissing Hans, who scurried away.

"Well, sister, thank you for participating in this special event. We were blessed by your words and hope you were blessed having been able to spend some time with us, as well."

"It was a pleasure being here," said Hannah with a simper.

"Well, I am going to close up shop here. Are you going to be okay, or is there anywhere I can take you?" asked Pastor Byrd.

"A friend of mine is waiting outside for me. Thank you again, Pastor, for having us." She offered him a dispassionate embrace and stepped out into the boisterous city with a smile on her wrinkled red lips.

Tonight she was a star.

He'd taped her perfidious mouth and silenced her deafening scream. Her once comely bun now frayed. Her makeup streaked, her perfection soiled.

On stage, he knew she felt at home. But not tonight. No, tonight, she lay petrified on the hard and dusty platform of the Mosque Theatre. Pancuronium coursed through her body, paralyzing her. He could almost imagine her throat constricting, her breathing lessening.

Silent and trapped in her own skin, tonight was her final act.

With a scowl, he loomed over her. Gripping his hunting knife, he lowered it to her warm soft flesh and carved into her delicate skin.

Groping, with gloved fingers, he pried the edges of the flayed skin apart, placing a cloth tag into the opening. The threaded needle punctured the taut skin surrounding the wound. The thick golden thread created a neat row of stitches.

He rose from her side, reached into his duffle bag and retrieved one of the large rocks he'd brought for the occasion. Palming it, he yelled, "Thou shall not" and swung his arm back. His voice echoed off of the rafters. He slammed the rock over and over into her skull until her brown hair was stained red and his arm was tired.

Waves of pleasure rippled through him with each hit. The sound of stone breaking bone was its own melody.

With a bloodied hand, he yanked the crimson-spattered watch from her lifeless arm and broke its dial as he had her skull. Placing the timepiece in a blue crushed velvet box, he cast one last careless glance at his scene and tossed the postcard depicting the Greek goddess Nemesis on the stage.

Let her bleed, let her die.

No one listened nowadays.

***

October 11

People hurried along the streets of downtown, bundled up in thick winter coats, scarves and gloves under the stabbing frigidity. It was only October; usually summer's warmth held firm against the cold until January. Instead of the sun's kiss, the dogwoods flailed and the wind howled. A storm was approaching, bringing with it snow, sleet and ice.

Xandy was one of those rushing. Her job as a file clerk for her trial attorney required it. The familiar chill of uncertainty crashed upon her, as she hurried out of the cold into the John Marshall Courts Building. Each time she entered the building, she remembered the faces of the deputies, their snide remarks, and taunts. Now, she stood in line with those that awaited their judicial destiny.

Xandy placed her small card holding wallet in the designated brown plastic bin. Today, Deputy Harlan Jacobs was doing the pat downs. The yelling of the lanky Deputy waving his metal-detector wand and its beeping vibrated throughout the old red brick and marble hall. He enjoyed taking the wand and holding it a little too long and too close to women's chests, she thought. But Xandy wasn't there to cause problems. All she needed was to pick up a file from the Commonwealth's Attorney Office, the very office that tried to place her in prison for an extended stay of five to forty years.

"I can't believe you have the nerve to be in this building," said Deputy Jacobs in a low growl, waiting for Xandy to pass through the line.

Xandy ignored his comments. He had told her repeatedly when being transported from the city jail a year ago that she deserved to fry for her transgression. It was the only thing that she might have agreed with the Deputy on, to fry for Thornton's death. To those in law enforcement, Thornton was a deity. He was a defense attorney with a prosecutor's heart and considered one of their own.

"You can ignore me all you want, but I know who you are, even if you try to hide," Deputy Jacobs called after her as she walked through security.

It was the usual day, Xandy thought. Each time she entered that building, someone reminded her that she wasn't welcome there, unless in handcuffs.

Detective Peter Lazarus's gut clenched as he saw Xandy scurrying down the brick stairs. She was guilty, but the goddamn Commonwealth had let her go. The evidence was there. He just had to find it.

Lazarus flashed his badge, and bypassed courthouse security. He strode to Constance Felmetzger's cubicle, his latest contact in the clerk's office. The telephones rang around him, as the array of assistants spoke in low tones. Locating the desired cubicle, he hung over the bluish half-cubicle wall.

"What do you have for me today, precious?" He asked.

"You are so sweet," Constance said with a half-giggle. She stood to greet him. Her freeze-curls bounced as she bent forward, flashing him with her deep cleavage. Her sweet perfume enveloped him like the arms of a long lost lover. Leaning over a little too long, she picked up a sticky note from her desk. Her eyes darted around the room. "I received a call today from someone asking about the Virginia Slayer Statute. I couldn't help but poke around a little bit while on the phone," she whispered.

"You called me down here for that?" Every time he came down here, it was a waste of time. Constance thought that helping him would make her more desirable to him. He could tell by her behavior that she liked him, but in this relationship, she only had one purpose:

information.

"The caller mentioned the Caras case." She batted her eyelashes.

"Now we're getting somewhere. I guess I owe you dinner for that little tidbit."

"I also got her phone number for you, just in case you want to check it out," she cooed. She offered it to him.

Taking the sticky-note, he flashed a perfect smile. "I'll call you," he said before he turned and strutted away.

The courts building always did it to her, Xandy thought as she dashed through the metal and glass doors out the building. Snow flurries and the abrasive wind slowed her pace. The panic was choking, but she'd learned how to hide it over the days and months. She fought to calm down. Her car, safety, and freedom were only a few feet away.

Reaching her car, she threw open the car door and collapsed into the leather seat. She closed her eyes and concentrated on her breathing. Inhale and exhale. Minutes ticked by as she grappled with her sanity. She knew the rhythm, just as she knew the fear, anxiety and angst.

For a moment, she thought of Thornton. She could almost catch a whiff of his cologne. She wished for moments that could never be, a time that they could never share. She wiped her hand over her dampened face, wiping away the tears she didn't know she'd shed. Reaching into her glove compartment, she retrieved her emergency bottle of Valium. Tossing one back in her mouth, she thought of other times, happier times.

Calmer now, Xandy turned the key in the ignition. She had one final stop, and then she could head home before the streets became impassable. Staring out the windshield, she saw a small sheet of paper between her wiper and the glass. Not another ticket, she hoped.

Reaching out, she grabbed it. It was still crisp. She read the words scrawled in black ink: WHERE IS MY MONEY? Blackwell.

Xandy gulped. Her day had gone from lousy to plain rotten. She knew it wouldn't be too long until he came looking for what Thornton took. Blackwell was a drug kingpin that believed in atonement and now he wanted his stolen money back; money he thought she had.

Back at her office with the needed documents in hand, she called Tom for further instructions.

"How was everything at John Marshall? Do you still think you're being followed?"

Xandy doodled on her yellow legal pad. "I know that I am. When I was leaving, I saw Lazarus walking up toward the court. Unless there's a recurring coincidence, he's everywhere I am 95 percent of the time..."

"Have you spoken to Captain Hawthorne about that yet?"

"No. Not yet. I can't seem to make that move. I don't want to ruin my friendship with him because of Lazarus."

"Right now, you have a huge boulder hanging over your head. You need to take care of that before something happens."

"I know..."

"Do you want me to give him a call?"

"No," Xandy almost shouted. The one word rushed out, expelled like a breaking dam. "This is my problem, and I have to take care of it."

"Then I suggest you do that."

Now the question was how to get rid of a cop who only wanted to see her behind bars.

<u>Chapter 2</u>

October 11

Jocelyn Tal looked at her watch. She paced the plush carpet in Brennan Tal's study, his recovery room. With her cell phone gripped in her freshly manicured hands, she cast a scathing gaze at its display. Still nothing. She'd been calling Brennan non-stop. Dialing his number again, it went straight to voicemail and his mailbox was full. They'd been separated for months, and her options were vanishing. It was now after 8:00 p.m. and she'd not heard a peep from him.

Jocelyn dialed Emily's number. Emily, her sister-in-law, was the only one who would still speak with her, and being the only female in a family of men, she was Jocelyn's best chance of getting a hold of Brennan.

"Hi, Joss. Are you coming to my party? You received your invitation, right?"

Emily was so innocent, so naïve, Jocelyn thought, "I'd love to, but if he's there, then I don't think it would be a good idea."

"Don't worry. I'm not even sure Brennan will be there. At least that is what Aden said. He seems like he's having fun being ... away."

Jocelyn sneered. "I'm sure he is. Well, if you speak to your brother –"

"Which one? You're sleeping with both of them."

"That is awfully rude of you, Emily."

"I'm not being rude, just honest."

Jocelyn didn't want to ruin the only friendship in the family that she had left due to her own bitterness. Exhaling, she said, "When you speak with Brennan, please tell him to give me a call. I'd hate to have to keep coming to our house –"

"His house!"

"Thank you for the correction. I'd hate to have to keep coming to *his* home to speak with him, when it could all be resolved with a simple conversation. I'd hate to pop up when he doesn't want me to, you know what I mean?"

"I don't think you have to worry about him hooking up with anyone soon. It seems like you've turned him off women for a while. He hasn't been with anyone since you two separated, and in spite of everyone trying to get him over you –"

"You're saying I might still have a chance with him?"

"Jocelyn ... I'm only eighteen, so what do I know? But since you asked, I don't think so. What about Aden? I thought you two were into each other."

"Things are complicated, Emily, very complicated. I would love to tell you everything, but I don't think it's meant for your ears."

"You are not a prude. I said I'm eighteen, not dumb. I knew, just like everyone else, even Brennan, something was going on between you and Aden. But why couldn't you two have done something about that without hurting him? He treasured both of you and now ... now he has no one but me."

"You're not no one."

"I don't mean it like that ... but you both could've saved us a lot of problems if you'd just run off before getting Brennan involved in this."

"Emily, we are very close, but I am not going to

explain it to you."

"You just did. I got to run. I'll let them both know about you, though."

"Only Brennan, not–" Before Jocelyn could continue her sentence, the line went dead.

Damn it to hell. Jocelyn snatched up her coat and left. She didn't want to see any of the Tals at the moment. Thinking about them was enough.

Lazarus stared at the yellow sticky note with the name and number scrawled across it in thick black ink. His gaze drifted to the parking deck and the Mini Cooper in spot 97. From his position on the street, and in spite of the wintry weather mix that was falling, he waited for her to come out. His gut was always correct, but for some reason no one could see behind those doe eyes. She mesmerized them or something, but not him. For him, she was Judas's child. She'd made a deal with the devil and killed his friend.

She was still at work.

Lazarus should have been running down other leads for other cases, but he couldn't. Nothing else mattered but getting that bitch where she belonged. He clenched his fist.

Everyone who knew Thornton knew what sort of man he was. Cut from the cloth of honor, and straight as a nail. With the smoking gun still in her hands, and a lousy excuse, she'd wiggled out of the charges, but not this time. This time he'd make every single letter stick to her lily ass.

The squawking of his radio told him to return to the station. Finally back at the precinct, Lazarus could only stare at his reflection in his small mirror in his locker. His spinet was military neat. Everything had its place. It was only the essentials: an extra change of clothes, toiletries and that one clipping.

The clipping showed her face in black and white under the headline which read, *Woman Arrested and Charged with Attorney's Murder.*

Murder.

It was a long shot of a charge then; Lazarus knew when the paperwork was filed. But since Thornton had been so prominent, the Commonwealth knew charges were going to have to be filed. Shame that Xandy had killed him while defending herself, *supposedly*. But then again, Lazarus knew that her mask of vulnerability was only that, a mask. She wasn't a sniper, a former cop or even military, true. But she knew her way around a gun.

He rubbed his temples. Lazarus pulled out the folded piece of paper from his left front pocket and removed a copy of a wrinkled receipt for a Lady Smith purchased by Xandy only a couple of months before the shooting. If luck was on his side, he might have found something that could prove that Xandy was no novice. He'd find out, as soon as he paid the local shooting range a visit.

"Lazarus, the Captain wants to see you," Bob, the desk officer, called out to Lazarus.

It wasn't what Lazarus wanted to do. He was supposed to meet with the manager in another forty-five minutes, but it looked like his *fun* would have to wait for later.

With a strut, Lazarus made his way to Captain Victor Hawthorne's office. The middle-sized office was a luxury, positioned off the large open area of the Major Crimes division. The office, decorated in fine dark fabrics with accolades posted, gave the air of intimidation, just like the man seated behind the large, solid desk. Lazarus imagined that was what his captain was going for – intimidation in every way.

"I'm going to recommend a little time off for you, Peter. I've been reviewing your performance over the last few months, and I believe you can use the time to get over your obsession with the Caras case."

"Did she call you?"

"No. I know you are still actively following her, although you are supposed to be working on other cases. The Caras matter is closed," Victor said. He leaned his brawny frame forward. His almost omniscient gaze bore into Lazarus.

"But, Captain," Lazarus said, "she's hiding something, I tell you, and the Commonwealth said they'd bring the charges back up if we got any new information. That's what I'm doing, trying not to make this case go away,"

"We've spoken about this," Victor said. "Hell, I've even ordered you not to do exactly what you're doing. You've already been on desk duty because of your actions. Do you want me to suspend your ass based on a hunch?"

"I'll admit I'm pushing the boundaries here, but something is there," Lazarus said. He squinted as if he were trying to solve a difficult math problem.

"You've been following her for six months. What do you have?" Victor asked as he leaned further forward.

"You're sort of putting me on the spot. She'd purchased a gun before the murder and I'm on my way to find out more from a contact I have at the shooting range. What I really need is to get into her apartment. I think I'll find something, a journal or whatnot that could substantiate my belief. She's been too perfect while she's out. Always blending in, or at least trying to, but I know, I know …," he rambled.

"You want to violate her constitutional rights?"

"I see what you're doing, Captain. You're a liability. This isn't about me, but you! Everyone knows that you fucked her, and that's why she got off. You're trying to say that you're concerned about due process, but you're just trying to protect your whore."

Ever since the case had been dismissed, Lazarus had been unwell. Victor had heard of suspects saying in lockup that Lazarus had even planted evidence on them, charges which had to be dismissed. This was the last of it. Victor could not continue to hold the hand of a man-child who had the right to shoot in the name of the police.

"Well, even if I had considered your buffoonery, that, in and of itself, is enough. I'm suspending you for ten days, pending an investigation and disposition by IA!" Victor shoved the written notice toward Lazarus.

"You've grown weak, if you're taking the word of a killer over your own officer!"

"Detective, I am also admonishing you to stay away from Ms. Caras."

"I'm going to take this up with Internal Affairs and the Chief."

"Do what you have to do, but in the meantime, hand over your badge and gun."

Removing his gun, Lazarus slammed it on Victor's desk, while tossing his badge on the wood. With one last cold look, he turned and stomped away, leaving Victor with more than an impression that a hell-storm was brewing.

<u>Chapter 3</u>

October 11

It was the end of an already long day. Seated in his office in front of the computer, Brennan Tal read the email assigning him to another investigation. He paused. He was to head the internal affairs investigation regarding another insubordinate officer. Although far from his liking, checks and balances were necessary. Being in Internal Affairs was often divisive between him and the other men on the force. Not too many wanted to be friends with the one policing them.

He needed a break for the night, but going home to a cold house wasn't an option. Instead, with phony ebullience, he strode through the precinct, greeting his comrades in blue. The atmosphere was its usual cacophony, with women weeping, telephones ringing, people shouting, and dispatch squawking. He walked to Major Crimes Division and poked his head into Victor's office.

"Taking a break and thought I'd stop by," Brennan said.

"Not trying to head home again, I take it," Victor said, as he stared at Brennan. After a moment's pause, Victor continued, "I know you're in IA now, but do you want to do a little police work with me tonight?"

"What do you have in mind?" Brennan asked with a

grin.

Victor chuckled, slapping Brennan on the back. "Come on. Let me take you down to the morgue. We just got a body in. She was discovered at the Mosque Theatre."

If Brennan hadn't taken human anatomy and been around dead bodies for years, then the sight of the woman lying on the stainless steel table would have caused him to vomit. The white surgical mask did nothing to dilute the stench of death. It smelled like two-day-old road kill on a hot Virginia day. The suffocating stink permeated the room.

The sight of the recently found woman proved evil existed. The face was unrecognizable. Bone showed through the deeper depressions of the cranial wounds.

"What do we have here, Doc?" Victor asked.

Brennan glanced at the medical examiner, Ashley Reynolds. Holding a clipboard in his aging hands, Dr. Reynolds raised an eyebrow at Victor's question. "Have you come to the dungeon to observe me for the next five hours, Captain?" Dr. Reynolds asked. Making a notation on the chart, he continued, "I heard about your promotion, Detective Tal," Ashley said. "Didn't think I'd find IA down here so quickly though."

"Me neither," Brennan confessed.

"It's by my invitation," Victor said. "The case has yet to be assigned to the new guy and I thought it might be good for our old friend to have a look."

In a voice that belied no emotion, Dr. Reynolds said, "From what I can tell you at this point, the deceased died from multiple depressed skull fractures. This is of course preliminary until I am able to perform the autopsy."

"You mean she was bludgeoned to death?" Brennan asked.

"That is still to be determined, but from a cursory exam, I would say that is the case."

"Have we been able to identify her yet?"

Dr. Reynolds glanced at his preliminary paperwork. "Yes. Her name is Diane Smith aka Hannah Salem."

"Let me know as soon as you're done about your findings," Victor said.

"Yes sir."

Taking one last glance at the motionless body, Brennan couldn't help but wonder about the criminal mind behind the deadly and bloody crime.

"Excuse me. Is Victor Hawthorne in?" Xandy asked for what seemed like the trillionth time. She stood in front of the police precinct's help desk, self-conscious as several men and women in uniform turned and stared her way. They recognized her, Xandy thought.

Breathing, she tried to concentrate on the man in front of her, and not those dawdling by. She was there to stop an overzealous cop from following her. That was it, nothing else, and when it was all over, she'd be able to walk out, still free.

If she were the old Xandy, she could have sauntered over to the officer at the nearest desk with a provocative swing of her hips, tossed her hair over her shoulder, and slid into the unoccupied seat, dazzling him with a radiant smile. Setting his coffee cup to the side, the officer's slouching form would have straightened as he ogled her.

But that was then.

"I'm waiting to see Captain Hawthorne. Is he in?" Xandy's face reddened as her anger grew. "I'd like to speak with him."

The officer leered at her, sending a chill of fear down her spine. Don't show your weakness, she thought. His badge gave her his name and number. She'd complain about Officer Thomas, too, if she had to. What is one cop over another?

"What's your name?" he asked as he reached for his pen.

"Alexandria Caras," she sputtered. Her name always brought up animosity, especially since hers had been the only case to use the precinct's Captain to rebut grand jury testimony and eventually helped in the negotiations to get her charges dropped; something that not even a desk cop could forgive.

"Caras...Caras...why does that name sound familiar?" Seeing Xandy's flushing face, he averted his glance back to his papers. "I guess you were lucky." Turning on his swivel desk chair, he then yelled, "Hey Captain, you got a visitor."

"Let me see what Bob wants, Brennan, before he yells my name again across the station instead of using the goddamn phone," Victor said loud enough for Bob to hear.

Rising from their chairs, they walked toward Victor's door to exit.

"That's my cue. We'll have to get together for beer next time. Thanks for the evening." Brennan ducked out of Victor's office.

Victor turned his attention toward the woman with the dark brown eyes he would never forget.

After impatiently waiting, Xandy finally took a seat on the couch in Victor's office. Wringing her hands, she tried to calm her knotted stomach.

"I take it from the pissed-off look on your face, you're not here this time for pleasantries?" Victor asked, falling into the seat next to her.

"I wish I were, and I know that I said I would let Lazarus calm down, but he's still following me. Ever since the verdict was announced, he's been my constant companion. I hate to ask for this, but I need it to stop." Breaking eye contact, she looked down at her hands.

"Has he done anything?"

"No, but I can't continue like this. He's the shadow that is always behind me. I've been cleared of the criminal charges! I can't keep dealing with his issues..."

"I know that, Xandy. I'll take care of it."

"Just make it stop, please."

"I will. Things will get better." Victor placed his arm around Xandy's shoulder and pulled her closer. She leaned into him. He smelled of musk and citrus with a hint of wood. It felt perfect. If she could've, she would've bottled that one moment up to reopen on rainy days.

"I hate to see you so nervous," Victor continued, "I think you need a good distraction. It'll help the situation. I need you to do something for me."

Xandy batted her eyelashes at him and beamed. "Victor, after all that we've been through, I think you could ask me anything."

"I know you may be reluctant to the idea, but I have this buddy of mine who I think you should meet."

She pulled away. "You're starting to sound like Tom."

"I know, but he's a great guy!"

"Does he know?" she asked, rising. She turned away and glanced at the busy officers, who kept glaring at Victor's door.

"Know what?"

"My history."

"That shouldn't matter."

"It always does," she whispered.

Xandy drove westward down snow-sprinkled Monument Avenue. Traffic crept by the Stonewall Jackson monument. All she wanted to do was take a hot bath and soak away the worries of the day. Maybe she could even try to get some sleep tonight. She yawned. The insomnia left her exhausted. When she did sleep, it was always the same dream. She heard angry voices and gunshots.

She saw Thornton's face: first his joy, his pain, and then his last breath. Nothing made it better. Distraction could never ease her sorrow. She chased ghosts, caught in between the way things had been then and the way things were now.

Her gaze kept sliding to her rearview mirror to see if she was being followed. Since leaving that courtroom, she kept watch, waiting for the promised revenge. Now agitated, the usual thirty minute drive home took ninety minutes, as traffic lights flashed yellow and careless drivers clogged up the intersections.

Finally pulling in to her parking lot, she spotted her roommate's car. Jonathan was one of the few bright spots in her life at the moment. They'd been living together since her return to civilization. Although the apartment was the same that she used to share with Thornton, he was welcomed companionship. His warmth, flattery and wit appealed to her. It made her ache for life again.

Soft music played as Xandy entered their apartment. Her cat, Amarillo, greeted her at the door with a meow and rubbed against her. Xandy placed her things to the side and picked up the striped orange tabby cat, holding her tightly to her. After a couple of seconds, the cat jumped down and switched away.

The scent of roses hovered in the air, along with a hint of cheap perfume. Looking down, she saw a trail of pink rose petals on the carpeted floor. Her favorite. Candles cast a warm glow about the apartment.

Had Jonathan finally realized through her maddened little world that she still wanted to want him?

But couldn't.

This was what their evenings used to be like, she

thought, as she removed her heavy overcoat and snow-covered boots.

She walked farther into the apartment. Xandy heard voices. She rounded the corner, following the path of petals, only to find two bodies intertwined on the chaise she'd picked out.

Xandy waited for one of them to notice her standing there, gawking. As their moans of pleasure increased, she knew she could not just stand there like a fool. But she couldn't tear herself away. Envy coiled like a snake ready to strike. Jonathan's lips and hands moved along the blonde's bosom; she leaned into his caress and moaned.

Xandy's vision was seared by the scene of their bodies, naked flesh on naked flesh. The sounds of lovemaking grew ever louder. She forced herself to turn away. But before she could make a graceful exit, she heard the woman say, "Johnnie, it looks like we have company."

Reddening, Xandy turned back to face them again and stared into the hateful gaze of Lauren Donovan, a blonde beauty with whom she shared a history of animosity They had similar interests in men and lifestyles, even with Thornton. Until him, she and Lauren were two sides of the same coin. Thornton changed her, and in lieu of the girl looking for only a good time, she became a woman in love with a man who loved her. Xandy stared at the woman who'd been a constant pain in her backside. She'd continued to play, while Xandy chose to quit the game.

"Don't pay me any mind...I'm just heading to my room," Xandy said.

Hearing Xandy's voice, Jonathan unburied his face from Lauren's cleavage. He stared wide-eyed, and jaw gaping, jumped up and bumped into the lamp next to the chaise. His erection, which was wrapped in a condom, was pointed her way.

"Oh." Ashamed, he tried to shield his member from her sight with his hand. "I...I didn't think you would be home now. I...I wasn't expecting you to be here so soon."

Forcing a smile, Xandy said, "Don't worry about it. I'll go and give you both some time alone...just next time, remember to let me know when...you know." She nodded at his waning salute.

Turning to leave, throwing back a glance, she saw Lauren's smirk. Xandy rolled her eyes and shook her head in disbelief as she fled to her Mini Cooper. Her mind warred with her yearnings. Seeing them together made her miss Thornton even more.

Maybe he was the only one who would ever love her... the only one who would ever care for her. Thoughts that she couldn't control whirled like a ravenous tornado. Her embarrassment had turned into self-pity and self-doubt twinged with a little self-hate.

The day had gone to hell in a gasoline doused hand basket, Xandy thought as she tried to speed away in the slow traffic. Beethoven played in the background to calm her; however, in such a frenzy of frustration, it did little. All she wanted to do was escape.

Chapter 4

October 11

A fire roared in the large marble fireplace, warming the two story library with its mahogany book shelves and vaulted ceilings. The library's picturesque window overlooked the grounds of Brennan's estate, as well as the James River.

Brennan sat behind his massive desk unable to concentrate on the papers before him. They could have been a treatise on world peace for all its relevance and interest. He'd read the same sentence at least five times and had gotten no further.

Brennan heard his younger brother, Aden, approach before he saw him. Brennan felt his gut somersault, his jaw tighten. He wanted to beat the shit out of him, be a man of action and fists. Only his dead mother's memory stopped him from doing it.

"Why does it seem I constantly have to clean up after your messes?" Brennan asked as he flung papers across his desk.

Irritation oozed throughout him. Once again, his brother's carelessness had caused more than a couple of problems. He'd have to be more decisive in his dealings with Aden or take the risk of losing everything due to his nonchalance.

"I finished reviewing the company's books for the last

quarter," Brennan continued. "And I am not impressed by how much has been wasted, due to your *hobbies*." Brennan picked up the ledger, shaking it in his hand. "Can you explain these charges?" He could feel his temperature rising; the testosterone pumping through his already tense body.

"I don't know what you're complaining about." Aden said matter-of-factly with his ever present smug smile. "The figures are solid and we're experiencing exponential growth. I reviewed them with the accountant. I may like to play, but I am also quite capable of pulling my weight in this family. The firm is doing well. With your main focus being charity cases or rather down at the station, you need to let me do my job!" Aden paused. "In all honesty, I think you need to go out, meet someone and have some fun." He tilted his head slightly and adjusted his tie.

"Checks and balances are the key to a successful business." Disgust tinged Brennan's words. "This is all coming from my hard work, energy and time, not yours."

"You're a workaholic. I've told you this before."

"Have you forgotten that no matter what, you work for me? And I pay you handsomely for your expertise. But don't forget that you're here because I want you to be."

"I need you to trust me."

"Trust is not given, but earned, or rather in your case re-earned." Brennan stared back at the stack of papers he still needed to review. He'd wasted enough time on his childish brother and only half-heard Aden sulk away.

Now alone, Brennan huffed. Things were perfect, as always, under Aden's careful eye. Yet his betrayal was unforgivable. If it weren't for their united monies, he would have let his brother rot. Brennan pulled the stopper from the Scotch decanter and poured himself a liberal glass.

No apology could ever undo what Aden did. The image of his and Jocelyn's tangled bodies in the guest bedroom flashed before Brennan. His marriage to Jocelyn ended because of the fulfilled smile he watched form on his wife's face; a smile he'd never been privy too.

It still made Brennan want to cut off Aden's head and shove it down his fucking throat. His knuckles turned white as he continued to clench the glass in his hand, tighter and tighter.

That night, he'd walked upstairs, pulled out Jocelyn's suitcase, and began throwing her things into it.

Wrapped in a sheet and still smelling like a mixture of sex and his brother, Jocelyn followed him. "I'm sorry. I never meant to hurt you. We can get over this. Don't do this!"

Brennan stared at her unkempt hair, flushed cheeks and bruised lips. He'd been fooling himself all along. She didn't love him. For her, he surmised, he was just a walking meal ticket. "He's my brother," he said.

"It was his doing," she simpered.

He whirled toward her. She pouted her lips and tried to appear sorrowful, he knew, but to him she looked like a deer about to be struck by a Mack truck. "It takes two to fuck," he shouted.

She blanched. "At least he knows what he is doing," she said. He watched her shoulders straighten as she tightened the sheet around her. Her scowl disappeared and her lips turned up into a haughty smile.

He felt as if she had hacked into him, cutting him open. Every emotion was raw. Snapping her suitcase shut, he said, "You have fifteen minutes to get all of your shit out of my house."

"If I don't, then what? You're not man enough, Brennan. You never were. You're not half the man your brother is."

He tossed the suitcase to her. "You now have fourteen minutes."

Dr. Reynolds raced into Victor's office. His usual neat appearance was disheveled, his eyes bloodshot. "Captain, I wanted to get this to you as soon as I could. In reference to the Hannah Salem autopsy, my first impressions were correct. She died from penetrating trauma, but before that, she had been badly bruised. Contusions covered her body, varying in size. I discovered something interesting in her mouth. The victim had a two inch laceration on her tongue that had been stitched closed. I was able to retrieve a piece of cloth. It's been sent to the lab."

Victor stared at the autopsy report with its sketch. His mouth went dry as he tallied up the number of black and blue marks. "Anything else?"

"I sent the blood work to the lab, as well. I did locate what appeared to be a needle mark on her neck, which could have been used to inject her with something to immobilize her. There was not any bruising on her arms to suggest that she was restrained or on her hands suggesting that she fought back."

Victor cleared his throat. "Did this piece of cloth have anything on it?" Victor asked.

"Yes. 'Thou shall not 2023'."

Flipping open the dossier he'd received from Victor, Detective Benjamin Monroe pulled out the NCIC criminal record for the itinerant preacher, Hannah Salem, also known as Diane Smith. Her fingerprints came back with a match in the AFIS database.

Monroe sat at his desk across from his new partner, Detective Ed Hobbes, inundated with work at his desk. Monroe was new in the city and to the department, having moved to the area from Houston, Texas.

Things were a little slower here, at least he'd been told so when he had applied. The move was to make it easier on his wife, so she could sleep a little better at night, but that was the least of his immediate problems. Even with all his experience from the academy and active time, he needed to make some friends soon or risk being ostracized. Many within the department had been hoping for his position before he stepped off the plane.

Still, Monroe knew the city. Years ago, it was called the 'Murder Capital of the World'. With the new sheriff, police chief, and the reorganization of the housing projects, crime had gone down. But now, from the snippets he'd picked up on so far, the newest body caused waves.

Scouring the page, he read Sister Hannah's list of convictions, which included fraud, petty larceny and several warrants for failure to appear on her court dates. Monroe shook his head. She had been released seven years ago from the Department of Corrections. Having satisfied the conditions of her probation, she then rechristened herself to her stage name. Until 2007, she'd stayed out of trouble.

Thumbing through the papers, he found the police report for her most recent charge of felony embezzlement, which was recently dismissed. He perused its contents. Monroe flinched as he read how Ms. Salem promoted herself as a deity and provided miracles for money, promising healing for worship. Monroe wasn't sure how deification could be used in an embezzlement case, but for the Commonwealth's Attorney's Office to step in, there had to be some evidence, physical or circumstantial, to the alleged crime.

Monroe typed up a note to give the prosecutor a call in the morning to find out why the charges were dismissed. He shook his head, as he thought of her recidivism. She'd changed her name, but not her lifestyle.

He still needed to piece together the shards of her last twenty-four hours. Maybe then, he'd be able to come up with a suspect and not just some circumstantial bull.

It's one thing to kill someone, another to tag 'em like cattle, he thought. He heard the shuffling of heavy feet thudding toward his desk. Glancing up from his paperwork, he regarded a man with deep wrinkles etched into a sunburned face; thinning white hair covered his head.

"Are you the detective working on the case with the evangelist?" the mystery man asked.

"Yes, I am one of them. I'm Detective Monroe." Monroe ushered the gentleman down in the seat across from him and formally introduced himself. "How may I help you, sir?"

"When Sister Hannah didn't show up, I knew something had to be wrong," said Hans Kampf. His tenor voice trembled. "She was always diligent about her prayer time and the congregations' needs, you know."

Detective Monroe arched an eyebrow. "What do you mean?"

"Well, last week, we received a call about a camp meeting, and usually we don't entertain last-minute changes, but Pastor Byrd, one of her faithful followers, wanted to have a cleansing, for his flock to become more ascetic, like Martin Luther. He wanted to be rid of the trappings of this world—that's not my term for it, but his."

"And what usually happens at these services?" Monroe asked.

"It's a time of praise and worship followed by Sister Hannah's teaching on getting rid of worldly trappings. Often people will then give things away and the service can last several hours, depending on how the Spirit moves."

"Was there anything unusual that happened during

the service?"

Hans's face twisted. "No, not really. It was wonderful, and there were so many signs of God's presence there. Many were saved...everything happened like usual.

"Like what?" Monroe asked, trying to understand what could have possessed someone to kill a preacher.

"There was a part of the service when the congregants decided to throw away the things that held them back – things that they thought were their idols and what kept them from worshipping God completely."

"Well, you had some throwing cigarettes, jewelry, money, you name it. After Sister Hannah saw a watch that was thrown, she asked for it after the service, and if it would be okay for her to have it. The only reason this stands out is because it wasn't the normal type of thing for someone to get rid of – neither for God or country, from my experience. I'm not an expert, but it had to be worth thousands."

"Where would the things go once tossed on stage?" Monroe asked.

"They would go to the sponsoring church and they would then provide us with a check to cover our fee. I'm not sure what Pastor Byrd did with all the items. Sister Hannah asked for the watch though."

"Did anyone have a problem with that?"

"I really don't know, but no one seemed to have a problem with how it happened. Whatever was given was for the glory of God and His ministry."

"Who tossed it on the stage?" Hobbes asked.

"I really don't know," Hans said, as he looked down at his hands and back to Monroe and Hobbes. "A man."

"Can you describe him?"

"Lanky – well to do, I guess, with brown hair, maybe around sixty or so. He seemed ill though from what I remember. He coughed a lot. He was just one of the congregants there. Pastor Byrd would know. I can give you his telephone number." After giving Monroe the telephone number, he continued. "Afterwards, she put it on and glowed. She was like an angel and a lovely woman."

"And what was your relationship with her?" Monroe asked.

"I was her mentor, and friend," Hans said, his words heavy with meaning.

"I take it you also loved her," Hobbes said.

"Of course I did, but she loved God more. I couldn't help but respect that choice."

"Do you know what the watch looked like?" Monroe asked.

"Of course I do. As my young niece told me, I needed to become tech savvy, so I took a picture with my cell phone. I wanted to send it to everyone." Hans then retrieved his phone from his coat pocket and passed it to Detective Monroe. "If you'd like, I can have my niece email it to you."

"That would be nice. And when was the last time you saw or heard from Sister Hannah?" Monroe asked.

"After the service, she told me to head back to the hotel because she had to meet someone. She never said who it was, though."

"Was it normal for her to stay away from her group so long without getting in contact?"

"Normally no, but with this benefactor, things were different."

"Benefactor?" Hobbes asked.

"About a month ago, someone had gotten in contact with Sister Hannah. Information regarding this person and all details about their meetings, contact, and calls were not shared with me, but I can guess that for her to change her calendar so abruptly, that whoever was willing to pay handsomely to make sure she was in

Richmond."

"Was she not supposed to be here for the camp meeting?" Hobbes asked.

"Initially no. But around that time, during our morning planning session, she told me that we were now heading to Richmond, a city she usually avoided."

"When she didn't show up, why didn't you notify the police she was missing?" Hobbes asked.

Hans shook his head. "I don't know. I kept waiting for her to show up. We were supposed to check out of the hotel this morning, and there have been times before when she'd shut herself away to prepare, but I never thought it could be something like this." His eyes then started to well up with unshed tears. "I'd like to see her now if you don't mind. She doesn't have any family. She was really a great woman."

Detective Monroe recognized that pain too well. He'd seen it with so many people left behind as their loved one went on.

Hans stood and stared at Monroe. "Just make sure you find out who did this to her."

Monroe glanced at the picture of the watch, when he noticed Hobbes hovering over his shoulder.

"Texas," Hobbes said watching Hans' retreat, "next time someone comes in to make a witness statement, you make sure that I am the one asking the questions and not you. Don't forget your place around here. Until you learn this city, it belongs to me."

Monroe stayed still. He wasn't going to be backed into a corner just because the cop who wanted his pay grade didn't get it. "Let's get this straight. I am the lead investigator on this case and you are my partner. If you don't like it, then take it up with the Captain."

Monroe flipped open the Salem crime scene file, the taste of bile thick on his tongue. Before he'd left Houston, the last case he worked on dealt with the victim's being branded. That sick prick had worked methodically like their current perp. He shook his head. They'd caught that guy, but not before he'd gotten too close to his family. He had no reason to assume that this case could be the same. He shook his head to escape the mental cobwebs trying to fester.

Monroe scanned the list of items recovered until he read the words *woman's wristwatch.* From what Hans had said, a man tossed the watch in question on stage.

It didn't take long for Monroe's inbox to receive the promised picture from Hans. He downloaded the photo the old man had sent to him and printed one for the file. With a quick click of his mouse, he pulled up the crime scene pictures. He zoomed in on the broken-faced watch on the decedent's wrist. It didn't match what he'd been emailed. Instead, it looked like a bargain store watch – cheap.

Studying his notes, Monroe circled two words: *watch* and *benefactor.* Where was the watch, and who was the benefactor?

The meeting left him with more questions and few leads.

Suspended or not, it didn't make a difference to Lazarus. He walked through the gun store's glass door and wiped his feet on the black mat. The dinging bell signaled his arrival, but with the number of people present in the showroom, no one paid him any attention. The glass cases displayed everything from ammunition to hand-held pistols, while on the walls hung the larger rifles and shotguns. Peeping at the schedule hanging on the wall, he knew why the place was so busy. He'd chosen the time for one of the handgun training classes.

With a strut to the counter, catching the eye of one of the salesmen, he asked for the manager.

"You must be Detective Lazarus. I'm Keith. We spoke

over the phone." Tall with silver hair, a round belly, and suspender pants, Keith stretched out his large hand and clasped Lazarus's in a warm greeting. "Well, come on back to my office. We'll have a little more privacy there."

"Awfully neat back here," Lazarus said. Keith's office was pristine, more so than any office he had ever seen. Everything had its place. Even the pin board with all the latest class offerings hung neatly, as if premeasured.

"Yeah. My wife has a tic. Woman comes in and makes sure that I can find everything," Keith said with a grin.

At the mention of a wife, Lazarus's gaze fell upon the silver frame on his desk. The stilted department store pose of Keith and his missus in Hawaiian shirts stared back at him.

"Please have a seat. After we spoke, I pulled up all the information I could find about Ms. Caras from my records." He opened a manila folder on his desk. "She had a range pass here, and did all of the classes, particularly the handgun retrain." He passed the folder over to Lazarus.

"What can you remember about Ms. Caras?" Lazarus asked.

"She's a lovely woman. I'm not sure how she was introduced to bull's-eye shooting, but she had the talent of a high master. With a ninety-seven percent accuracy, she could outshoot a lot of our regulars."

"What was her caliber of choice?"

"For target practice, she always chose a Buck Mark .22, but I think she owned a Lady Smith .357. At least I know I always tried to sell her one."

"How long and often did she regularly come here?"

Keith leaned back in his chair and rubbed his chin. "Now, I don't keep records like that, but she was a regular. Now, what is this all about?"

"Her name came up in an investigation and I – "

"You don't have to worry about her. She's a great

shot and tested with a handgun, rifle, shotgun, you name it. I always joke that I'd have liked to see her face off with good ol' Annie Oakley with a Gun." Keith chuckled at that.

"Well, thanks for your time. If I have any more questions– "

"Maybe you'll make it back out here. On Wednesdays, we have our law enforcement night, and you guys get to use the range for free. Our way of saying thank you for all of your service to this community." Keith patted Lazarus on the back and shook his hand.

"Thanks again. One last question before I go. Did she ever hesitate when shooting?"

"Ms. Caras didn't know the meaning of hesitating. If it was a good shot, she took it."

The passing scenery blurred as tears fell down Xandy's face. She beat the wheel, honked when drivers were too slow to react; she changed the radio station looking for a song, just as she was looking for herself. Right was left and left was right. She found herself pulling up in front of a familiar building. She needed to feel something. Anything. She needed to feel alive!

Pulling into the parking garage, she found a guest parking spot. Her head hung low. Sobs racked her body.

Xandy wasn't sure if he was home, but she had to at least try. She had to jump over her shadow, she knew. Opening the car door, she allowed the cold air to force her to focus on her goal – why she was there.

Taking the elevator to the ninth floor, she found Victor's apartment and knocked.

Victor ran harder on the treadmill. Xandy's perfume was stuck in his nose; the scent of lavender kissed skin. It beckoned him. Only a cold shower was going to ease his rising discomfort.

Stopping the treadmill, he swung the sweaty towel around his neck. His day had been long at the station, and instead of working twelve hours, he'd been there for fifteen hours, making sure to get the new detective up to speed. He padded toward the bathroom, when he heard a knock.

"Who is it?" Victor asked. Interestingly enough, the concierge hadn't buzzed him about someone coming up.

"It's Xandy," he heard muttered through the door.

Peeking through the peephole, he saw her standing there, and his heart skipped a beat.

"Hey Xandy. Is everything all right?" Victor asked opening the door.

"I come bearing gifts," she said lifting up the smiley-face plastic bag. "Dave saw me on my way up, and since your food had just arrived, I told him I'd bring it to you."

He backed up and let Xandy pass. The open floor plan gave her an overview of his apartment with its large living room picture window that overlooked the city below. Sparsely decorated, except for a black leather sofa with matching glass tables, matching lamps and a flat screen TV that hung over the fireplace, everything had its place. No pictures hung on the white walls.

"Hope you don't mind me stopping by without calling. I sort of ended up here."

"What do you mean?"

"Jonathan had company, and I *didn't* want to stay there for that, so I sort of got in my car and ended up here."

"I'm fine with that. Let me clean up. I'm a little sweaty."

Xandy leaned forward and took a whiff. "I don't mind. You smell like a man should."

"You don't have to flirt with me to get part of my eggroll," he said with a laugh.

"But I do, if I want duck sauce on it."

"Let me freshen up and you make yourself at home. You know where everything is."

"You mean nothing has changed since I was here last time?"

"Besides a refrigerator filled with beer, not much. I'll be right back."

Victor turned the knob to hot, allowing the building steam and soothing water to flow over his tight muscles.

Humming under the water's cascade, Victor closed his eyes: *Xandy's hands gently touched him. She leaned into him, placed her hands on each side of his face and pressed her lips to his. Creating a trail of kisses down his neck to his broad chest, she continued downward until she knelt before him. Then taking his–*

The lights in the bathroom suddenly flickered and then went completely out.

He quickly turned off the water and wrapped his towel around his waist.

He heard Xandy calling his name from the living room, but having not even a smidgen of light to help, he fumbled through the bathroom, back to his bedroom, until he saw her holding a small penlight.

"I'm fine, Xandy, let me get my flashlight and then some candles lit," he said. He padded to the kitchen and retrieved his flashlight out of the cupboard, as well as several candles.

With the candles lit, and the room once again illuminated, Xandy's gaze fell on Victor wearing only his towel. She watched his muscles flex. His broad shoulders and v-shaped torso were bare and his biceps bulged with every small movement. He was chiseled, but not bulky like the pumped up gym type of beefcake, but from years of hard-work.

Her eyes were drawn to the sex lines that disappeared beneath the fluffy towel.

She cleared her throat. "I should ... should go ahead and set the table." Making her way to the kitchen, she removed two glasses, flatware and plates while Victor disappeared back to his room. After only a couple of seconds passed, she heard the rustle of clothes, followed by the sound of wood being placed in the fireplace.

"With the lights off, it is going to get cold in here fast," Victor said. His nakedness was now covered. In spite of the potential coldness, she would've liked for him to walk around the way he was before– but of course, that made no sense. Following her own thoughts, she shook her head, mentally wrestling with the idea of what did she do now.

Chickening out on her original plan wasn't palatable, but no matter how much she wanted to seduce him, she wasn't the type of woman to storm into a man's apartment, bare her body and soul to his rejection, and ask him to pounce on her.

No. not even a sudden blackout with a handsome man was going to convince her that now was the best time to jump over her shadow.

"I...I should be going," Xandy said.

"Like hell you are! The city just went dark and you want to head out there. Wait until the lights come back on. I'm not going to bite."

Unless I want you to, she thought.

With the warm fire lit before them, she brought over the Chinese food and drinks. "I saw you had some beer in the fridge and thought you might like one." She instead sipped on cold sparkling mineral water.

Seated and with the wood crackling and popping, they ate in silence.

"Okay, what's going on?" Victor asked.

"I told you. I...I just thought I'd stop by since Jonathan was *occupied*. He and his girlfriend were a little too loud and busy in my living room."

"Why not head to Rebecca's? I thought you two were inseparable?"

"Sometimes we are, but tonight I preferred your company."

"There is not a lot of entertainment I can provide though, since the power is out."

"We've never had problems, and I don't think tonight will be any different. Even if we end up playing the *question game*, we'll have something to talk about."

"I haven't played that in over twenty years."

"You're not that old, *Captain*! You're only what, thirty-nine, and if I remember correctly, one of the youngest captains in the department."

"You're going to make me blush," Victor said. "Okay, since you brought up the question game, I'll bite. What's your favorite location, beach or mountains?"

"Hmmm, I think it would have to be the beach. When I was younger, we used to head to the beach, play in the sand, build sandcastles and run along the surf. I loved the feel of the sand between my toes. You?"

"I love water too, but my all-time favorite was whitewater rafting in West Virginia."

"I'd love to do that. Guess I should put it on my list."

"We should go when it gets warmer. I've wanted to do it again." Victor took a swig of his beer. "Okay, now it's your turn."

"Well, since you are stuck with me here, I can't help but ask. If you could be anywhere now, where would it be?" Xandy knew her answer. If she had enough courage, she'd already be seated on his lap, but she wasn't sure how to make any sort of move to move from friendship to friendship with benefits.

"I've always wanted to take a vacation and head to

the Caribbean for a month or two. Someplace where I can relax near the water, maybe on a boat and watch the night sky. You?"

"I'm happy right here with you," Xandy whispered, not looking at him but staring into the red and orange flames.

Xandy moved into the crook of his arm. She tilted back her head and gazed into his beautiful honey eyes. Raising her hand, she gently touched his face, leaned in and kissed him.

With each lingering taste, electricity rushed through her. Her heart pounded in her ear. With one move, he gathered her into his strong arms and dipped his head down to her neck. Her skin tingled from his warm breath as his fingers caressed her, inching down her back.

The only sounds heard were their panting between hot kisses and the crackling fire. She wanted to crawl into his skin to be closer. Her hands roamed until she felt his arousal.

Suddenly, emotions slammed into her. She saw Thornton's face– his love then betrayal. Hesitation popped up like a cork out of champagne bottle; it foamed and overflowed, leaving behind a sticky residue of doubt. No matter how much she wanted Victor, she couldn't continue.

Xandy pulled away. "I don't think I can do this?" she whispered.

"What's going on…Buttercup?" Victor asked.

I'm scared. I'm scared of getting hurt by you. I'm scared of giving you me and being disregarded…I'm scared! She wanted to scream those words at him; for him to see and hear what she couldn't utter. Instead, she rose from her spot on his lap and moved back to the cushion beside him.

"I'm fine… but you have to explain the Buttercup pet name," she said. It was easier to focus on that then the polka-dot elephant in the room: what they'd almost done and how it could change everything.

"Because when I look at you, I see a beautiful wild woman." He reached out and stroked her back.

She smiled.

It was a grin that to the less informed spoke of silent promises. She'd learned to read his smiles, but he couldn't read hers. For behind it lay the complicated and convoluted.

Her heart was playing Russian roulette and his words had just pulled the trigger.

Chapter 5

October 12

Metro News
Early this morning, police released the identity of the body found at the Mosque Theatre as evangelist Hannah Salem of Proverbs Global Ministries. The cause of death has not been released at this time. If you have any information, please contact...

The light pierced Xandy skull. She winced in pain. Her head ached. With her forearm covering her eyes to dull the incoming light, she sighed and stretched out. Her hand came in contact with warm flesh and masculine muscles. Alarm rose. She grabbed the covers, pulled them over her clothed body and discovered his body hidden under the sheets.

Seeing Victor's sleeping form, she wanted to leave, but her heart lurched. The idea that she could even entertain wanting anything more from him horrified her.

Thornton had taught her well: there was no room for fairytale endings.

Xandy eased out of bed and glanced at Victor's sleeping form in the disarrayed sheets. Some things were better not dealt with, especially questions that contained the word 'us.'

Closer to the front door, her exit in sight, the sight of a

woman's picture on the front page of the newspaper caught her attention. She knew her. In large letters, the headline screamed, *Evangelist murdered.*

The pages crinkled as she snapped it open. With each passing word she read, her mouth grew dryer, her palms sweated, and her heart smacked harder against her ribs.

She knew Sister Hannah. Her hand flew to her mouth – for she knew her intimately.

Together they were a part of her cellblock family.

A family better forgotten.

Victor heard Xandy leave, but what could he say? Don't go or better yet, we need to talk. He couldn't do it. *What had he almost done with her? If she hadn't pulled the plug...* He shouldn't get involved with her, he knew, but he'd desired just a small taste of her since their friendship had started, all those months ago, and last night that low burning flame had almost engulfed him.

He didn't know what had come over her yesterday to make her throw herself into his arms, and sure, he didn't mind being there to pick up the pieces, but it wasn't enough. Touching her once made him want to do it all over again, every day and every way.

Now having tasted of her, he had a craving to know her even better. And that scared him worse than just desiring her. Sex he could find anywhere, but a woman who somehow made him wish for more. She'd kissed him and in that one move, she'd broken down his ice cold shell.

Rising from his bed, shortly after her departure, he padded around his apartment searching for clarity. The city was still asleep at four in the morning and he had another twelve hours before his shift started.

His cell phone lay heavy in his hand. Finding Xandy's telephone number, he stared at their picture together. She beamed. He remembered their joking around; her leaning in to him and snapping the picture.

"Damn. How am I supposed to be just her friend?" Victor said aloud. Staring at the picture he sighed.

"Every woman likes flowers, might as well send some," he said. As soon as the words were uttered his cell phone rang. It was dispatch.

"Captain, you're needed at the station."

Responsibility called, which meant his personal pining would have to wait.

Lazarus hesitated before making the call. After hearing the feminine twang on the other end of the line, he identified himself as a private investigator and asked about Ms. Caras.

"It's about time someone called me about her," said the anonymous woman. Anger laced her voice. "I just received word that she was the beneficiary of Mr. Gage's life insurance policy, which gives her motive. The Virginia Slayer Statute determined that if one was involved in murder then they should not profit. Ms. Caras profited from it."

"Ma'am, she was cleared of that."

"Yes, but there are things about Ms. Caras I know that you don't."

"Like what?" Lazarus asked.

"If you're interested, I'd like to hire you. I'll give you more dirt than you can handle. Let's meet to discuss the details."

Intrigued, Lazarus wrote down the woman's address. "And what should I call you... Miss...?"

"Donovan. Lauren Donovan," she said.

Pulling up to the office complex, Xandy parked her car. The hair on the back of her neck rose. She scanned the corner parking lot and the nearby road.

She gripped the steering wheel. Her muscles tensed. Her eyes danced from left to right, searching for a threat. Taking one final look around, she spotted Lazarus's blue Chevy Impala parking behind her.

Grabbing her purse, Xandy hurried into the warm, plush doctor's office. The scent of lavender overpowered her senses. It was supposed to calm her, but instead, she thought of Lazarus outside.

Grabbing a magazine off the oak coffee table, she tried to distract herself. The words blurred. The pictures of models parading around in the latest fashions seemed irrelevant to her life. Self-conscious, she wrapped her right hand around her left wrist, remembering the feel of the cold handcuffs that Lazarus had put on her, the sound of the cell door slamming behind her, and the smell of human waste.

Xandy closed her eyes. She strained to hear every noise, to hear her own heartbeat. She could hear the leaves of the plants rustling from the heat, soft music playing in the distance, and a man nervously tapping his foot on the hardwood floor. She heard magazine pages being ripped out, the crinkling of the paper as it was shoved away, and all the while the telephone rang and the water cooler blub-blubbered. It was the usual office visit, with the usual noises. It was what she was used to, no surprises awaiting her, nothing but the normal doctor's appointment.

As the door opened, Xandy opened her eyes. A small auburn-haired woman plodded out of the doctor's office; her shoulders slumped as she held a Kleenex to her tear-stained face.

"Ms. Caras, the doctor will see you now," the receptionist said.

Composed, Xandy sat across from Dr. Irvin Edwards. His dark hair was combed back, and parted to the side; glasses framed his penetrating gaze. She could smell his sweet pipe tobacco emanating from his tweed-patched elbow jacket.

"How are you doing, Xandy? How was your week?" Dr. Edwards asked.

"Okay," Xandy said. She didn't want to tell him about the scene back at the apartment or her reaction to it.

"Well, we both know that is not a good answer to my question," Dr. Edwards said. "So how is everything?"

"Things are difficult at the moment." She sighed. "I need to see something different. I'm frustrated and I feel stagnant. Cursed to relive what I can't change," Xandy said. It was not what she wanted to say.

"During our last visit, we established a plan for you to move forward. Are you ready?"

She'd been in counseling since the day she'd overcome her undiagnosed agoraphobia, which was almost six months ago. Here he sat across from her in his tweed jacket with patched elbows, safe in the confines of his office. He had no idea what it felt like to deal with life– her life. She needed to feel safe.

Instead, each morning she awoke with the thought of inmate counting about to happen and the threat that the other person in her cell was more likely to carve her with a shiv, than to speak of pleasantries. Even the thought of *her* still sent chills up her spine – as well as a wave of shame.

"What do I think? I think that it would be better to just bury me six feet deep and forget about me...there is no more me. I just... I can't get over what happened. Neither the meds nor the sessions are helping me. I can't sleep, eat, read...the only thing I can still do is run. I'm good at it. I can still do it, but I'm no good at living now!" She looked down at her fisted hands.

"Thornton would want you to live your life," Dr. Edwards said.

"How would you know that?"

"Because he loved you."

She couldn't respond. Thornton didn't love her; love didn't plot to destroy the object of one's affection. He'd only used her. Tears of frustration trickled down her face. Sobs tore through her.

"You have to remember that. For next week, I want you to tell me something positive about your life. Let's not concentrate on Thornton, but on the good that he must have seen in you. Do you think you can do that?"

Xandy slowly nodded.

Xandy walked away from her appointment with her head low, and her shoulders sunken.

Lazarus waited in his car for Xandy to come out. He'd been sitting there for the last hour. It was doctor visit number fifty or so since he'd been following her. He was starting to lose count. She'd gone daily and now it was down to once a week. It didn't matter. She was seeing a quack seeking peace after what she did.

His cell phone interrupted the monotony.

"I have the Caras file you wanted a copy of. I'll give it to you when I see you tonight," Constance said, "but I also did some more digging during my break yesterday. I spoke with one of the secretaries in the Commonwealth's Attorney's office and was told that this Caras lady started working for attorney Doaks right after her charges were dismissed."

"What's your point?"

"Well, I was just wondering, if this woman has been through so much, why would she continue to put herself through all that? I mean, from the rumors going around, no one likes her, and even I can't understand it."

Lazarus chuckled. "Maybe she's trying to improve her reputation or gather information to keep the charges from coming back up, for all I know."

"Sounds like you have a personal vendetta against

her, though."

"No. In this line of work, when one of us takes a bullet, we all do. I'm going to figure it out and make sure she ends up as close to hell as she can get."

Dr. D. James, police psychologist, sat on one side of the desk, tapping her *Lamy* pen against the latest issue of *Psychology Today*. With her hair in tight pencil curls, her almond brown eyes glazed over in tedium.

According to her calendar, she had an appointment with Detective Lazarus. It was to be her first officer session with the detective, but as of yet, she was dealing with a no-show.

She'd reviewed Peter Lazarus's dossier last night after the other things that required her attention, sleep not being one of them. Lazarus was a decorated officer until 2007. After seven years on the force, he'd moved up to detective and now with fifteen years under his belt, he was considered one of the toughest young cops in the precinct. His reputation was well deserved, and he'd accomplished a lot and was only 35. His file was loaded with accolades, Medal of Merit receiver, Mayoral citations, and commendations from the public and senior officers. If he continued on that route, he'd one day even be a lieutenant, if not captain or major.

After thirty minutes of waiting, Dr. James heard a knock on her office door. Lazarus stepped reluctantly into the room, his shoulders straight and his back rigid. He resembled someone headed more toward the electric chair than to a simple counseling session. She wondered what he wished to hide.

"You're late," Dr. James snapped. Her octave voiced her dislike. She stared at the decorated officer like a hawk did a squirrel that it was about to swoop down and have for lunch.

"What a greeting. Traffic." Lazarus pulled out the chair and plopped into the seat.

"Let's make something clear. These sessions are required for you to return to your post. Until I am satisfied that you are indeed fit for duty, you'll be on suspension. As you are aware, Internal Affairs has set a date for your review as well. Captain Hawthorne stepped in, though, and asked them to wait until these sessions are completed before they comment."

"Why is that? Is he scared that I'll tell them every damn thing that I know about him and that girl?" Lazarus slid down in his chair.

"We're not here to talk about Captain Hawthorne, but about you."

"Captain Hawthorne is crooked, and that is why I'm here. If you IA ball sacks could get your heads out of each other's asses, you'd see it. She got off with all the evidence against her by one of our own going to the Commonwealth and vouching for her—"

"You are not here to discuss that. You are here for me to determine if you are fit for duty. You're here because of insubordination! The FFD test will decide if you are fit for duty or not. The recommendations that I can provide will either be that you will need counseling and then reevaluation at a later date; or that you are not in need of counseling; or that you cannot be reined in, or remediated."

"Sounds like you've already decided," said Lazarus.

Dr. James pulled out the stack of papers. She handed Lazarus the testing materials.

"Let's get started."

Xandy pulled up to Rebecca Quijada's house. Despite the chill in the air, Rebecca sat bundled up on her porch.

Checking her reflection, Xandy saw the pale streaks that stretched down her cheeks toward her lips, and her unruly hair. She dabbed her face with a tissue and took a pensive breath. She tried to muster up a smile, a grin, a bit of cheerfulness, but it wouldn't stay.

Her mask was slipping.

"Come on in," Rebecca said. She stood and pulled her orange wool sweater tighter around her. "I just made some tea."

With a subtle smile, Xandy followed her inside. They headed to the living room, decorated in a warm and relaxing terracotta.

"Why don't you run?" Rebecca said after a few moments of silence.

With a warm cup of chamomile tea between her palms, Xandy watched the steam rise. In the silence she waited to find her voice – to explain. Clearing her throat she took a sip.

"It depends how you mean it," Xandy said. She gripped the mug's handle.

"Get out of here."

"And go where? I can hardly pay my bills."

"Didn't you receive Thornton's insurance money?" Rebecca asked.

Xandy's brow furrowed. "No, his parents did. They gave me his car, though, and some of his personal effects that I couldn't bear to part with. I was just his fiancé. If I had money, I would not have needed to get a roommate and ..." A blush rushed up her neck to her face, casting it in a bright red. Xandy looked away and took a sip of her tea.

"What happened between you and Jonathan? Did he hit on you or something?"

"No," she sputtered, coughing up the hot brew. "He had someone over and I caught them... together, you know."

"Well, at least you saw him naked, right?" Rebecca snickered.

Xandy picked up the pillow next to her on the couch and threw it at Rebecca, missing.

"I'll take that as a yes. I was trying to make you laugh a little."

"Doing a horrible job of it," Xandy replied with a short giggle.

"You aren't really into him, are you?"

"No ... I don't know. He's male and offers me some attention at a– "

"Distance. That is what you like about him. He lets you believe there could be more, and there is no pressure of it becoming more," Rebecca said.

"That's not my issue though. I did something last night that I'm not sure if I'm going to regret."

"I'm all ears." Rebecca leaned forward.

Taking a deep breath, Xandy squeaked, "I made out with Victor."

"What?" Rebecca giggled. "You tongue wrestled with the Captain? I knew that was going to happen sooner or later as much as you gush over him with your Victor this...Victor that. Has he called you?"

"No. I don't know what I'd say if he did call."

"How was it?"

"That I am not telling," Xandy feigned zipping her lips.

"Are you going to call him?"

"That is his role. I'll hear from him."

"And if not?"

"Then I'll have to remind him why he should like having me around," Xandy laughed. All the thought of Thornton and the shed tears were erased by the hope of something new and fresh blooming.

"Sounds like we need to go shopping for some nice lingerie then," Rebecca chuckled.

"I think a yoga class would be better," Xandy said. She then rose from her spot on the couch. "I should really head home."

"Are you sure? You can stay here tonight."

"Thanks for the offer, but I can't just leave Amarillo home alone again." Amarillo, her cat and sometimes confidant, would be waiting.

"You and that cat, I'll never understand."

"Thanks again. I needed this," Xandy said, giving Rebecca a hug.

"That is what friends are for."

Watching the questions session with Dr. James and Lazarus through the video feed, Brennan sat back and took notes on any points of contention and possible leads for his IA investigation. Although there were a million other ways he could imagine spending a work day than watching the banter between a doctor and a reluctant cop, it came with the job. He was only halfway through the expected six-hour testing and questions session, when his cell phone rang. Before he could consider who he was speaking to, he'd answered her call.

"You're such a know-it-all and you really don't know a damn thing," Jocelyn screamed at Brennan over the phone. From her shrieking in his ear, Brennan knew she'd read the divorce complaint.

"If you have anything else to say, have your attorney contact mine," Brennan said.

"Is this your way of getting back at me? By dissolving our marriage like this?"

"If I were caught up on revenge, I would have figured out something worse than this. We've been separated for the last six months. For years, you've shown narcissistic tendencies– "

"Don't try to analyze me, Brennan. Don't you dare think you have the right to even think you know me!"

Before he could respond the line went dead. Looking at his cell phone's display, Brennan could only chuckle.

The best way to end a conversation with Jocelyn was to make her end it first. It always proved his point.

Twenty-four hours gone, and Monroe's case was going nowhere fast, until Pastor Byrd called him to ask for a meeting at the gym around the corner.

The stench of sweat and chlorine from the gym's pool permeated the air. Men and women pranced around in their exercise clothes, and the sound of pop music, grunting and metal hitting metal from the weight machines intermingled to create its own chorus. Having located the indoor basketball court, Monroe saw that it was almost empty, except for two guys playing one-on-one.

"What time was he supposed to arrive?" Hobbes asked. He leaned against the white wall staring at the men at play.

Monroe could almost smell Hobbes's irritation. It was like a bad case of halitosis – always there when he opened his mouth. But then again, it was the only emotion Hobbes ever showed. Monroe could only hope to not get stung while dancing with a hornet's nest.

Monroe recognized the tall clergyman from his description. He was carrying a large duffle bag and garbed in a purple and gold jersey with matching shorts. With his bald head and chestnut complexion, he resembled a shorter Kareem Abdul Jabaar.

"Sorry about making you come here to meet with me, but the boys that I mentor are scheduled to show up soon. From what you said, it seemed important to do this today, and from my guess, in person," Pastor Byrd said.

"Thanks for agreeing to meet with us," Monroe said. "We wanted to talk to you about Hannah Salem." He took out his small note pad from his coat pocket.

"Yes. Her death ... but God's plans are not our own. How can I assist you?" Pastor Byrd asked.

"I just have a few questions. Do you mind telling me how you knew Ms. Salem?" Monroe asked.

Pastor Byrd chuckled. "Until recently, I had no idea who she was. Through word of mouth, I was introduced to her ministry and her movement to return to a less commercially driven society. Asceticism leads to increased spirituality. I felt the message she could impart would be beneficial to my flock."

"And the part of the service where those in attendance threw their belongings on stage?" Hobbes interjected.

"I've seen a lot over the years, but the zeal she was able to impart such truth with was amazing. People were breaking free, and that is what I knew God needed her there for."

"And the watch and other items that were retrieved after the service?" Monroe asked.

"In reference to the watch, it belonged to a man who I had never seen before. I saw him place it on the stage during the service though. The other items were retained by my church, and we cut a check to cover the costs of the guest speaker."

"Do you remember anything about the gentleman with the watch?" Monroe asked.

"There was something a little odd about him. He walked with an exaggerated limp. He had bottle-top thick wire framed spectacles and shaggy black hair. He was a little shorter than me. About average build." Pastor Byrd said.

"What happened after that?" Monroe asked.

"I asked Hannah if she needed a ride, and she informed me that someone was coming to pick her up."

"Do you know who?" Monroe asked.

"No," Pastor Byrd said. "I never got to see the individual or the vehicle. I had wanted to ask her one additional thing after she'd said her goodbye and I walked out after her. But it was almost like she exited the house and then vanished.

Just then the gym door opened up, and two teenage boys entered wearing their basketball gear. "Hey Pastor," one called.

"What did you want to ask her?" Hobbes asked.

"Oh, nothing really, just if she was interested in receiving additional support for her ministry. Prior to showing up, Hans, one of the men in her party, was asking about sponsorship and if my church was interested. I wanted to discuss it with her though."

"Did you ask Hans about that before she'd left?" Monroe asked.

"Yes. He said he'd speak with her about it. I did see them talking and whatever she said didn't go over too well since he sort of sulked away."

"Did he come back to talk to you?" Monroe asked.

"Not about that."

"Do you know what they were discussing?" Monroe asked.

"She informed me that she had plans with someone and Hans was going to return to the hotel. I guess he didn't agree with her going out alone."

"What did he do after she left?" Hobbes asked.

"Hans, some from the congregation and me headed to Denny's for a late dinner. We stayed there until around midnight, and then we all went our separate ways."

"How'd you hear about Sister Hannah?" Monroe asked.

"Hmmm. I received an email about her ministry. I remember it being a mass email— almost spam-like. Not sure how we were contacted or put on her mailing list, but it worked out."

"Do you still have the email?" Monroe asked.

"I believe so. Give me your email address and I'll forward it to you." Pastor Byrd retrieved his Blackberry and with the punching of a few buttons, he said, "You should have it by the time you return to your office. I just emailed it to you." He then shoved his phone back into the gym bag.

"Well, thanks for your help. If you remember anything else, please let us know."

Pastor Byrd nodded his head. He then walked over to the two kids and grabbed his basketball.

Unlocking her front door, Xandy's gaze cut across her apartment. A grimace marred her face. Her stare rested on Jonathan's door. She could only think of the woman he chose to spend his time with; anger slapped against her like stormy waves on a beach. Jonathan had to know what Lauren was attempting to do to her. He knew her situation and he still chose to bring that bimbo to her house!

Of all the women in the world, it had to be the splinter in her heel. Lauren was like a fatal disease–sucking the life out of anyone she called a *friend*. Maybe it was the exaggerated way she found them together, but maybe, just maybe, Lauren's dealings with Jonathan had nothing to do with him, but her? Lauren was calculating, manipulative, and did everything for one sole purpose – herself. The filing of Lauren's frivolous lawsuit against her was evidence enough of that, Xandy knew. Still the question of Lauren taunted her. What could she be after? At that thought, Xandy fingered the gold locket around her neck.

Xandy entered the kitchen. She snatched her mail off the counter and sorted through it. A glossy postcard from the Mosque Theatre stood out in the stack of bills and sales papers. Picking it from the stack, she turned it over. *Loveliness is to be held* was scrawled across the back.

Panic slapped her. She already knew the answer. Releasing the postcard, it floated to the ground. She wasn't crazy or paranoid– instead someone really was following her. Retrieving her cell phone, she punched in the number on speed dial.

Seeing Xandy's photo pop up made him think about their night together again, Victor hesitated. They'd crossed into new territory. In a perfect world, he'd be able to drive by her place, calm any fears. Yet, the more he analyzed their current situation, he couldn't figure out a good way for it to end. But that didn't keep him from desiring to have her beside him again, for him to be able to touch her again.

There was more there though than just physical attraction, he knew. He wanted more than just a good lay. He felt as if he'd waited so long for her to come along.

"Everything okay, Xandy?" Victor asked.

"No. Maybe I shouldn't have called, but I just got a strange piece of mail."

"What do you mean?"

"I mean someone just sent me something that is giving me the heebie-jeebies."

Victor could hear the panic in her voice.

"Are you home alone?"

"Yes."

"Okay, I'm going to send an officer over to you to take your statement and for you to file a report."

"You can't come?"

"Work called me in earlier, but I'll try to come by after work, if that's okay. I think we need to talk."

"Uh-oh. Talk?" Xandy was quiet for a moment. "I guess I have to understand that. Then I'll see you tonight."

Waiting for the officer, Xandy curled up with a thick comforter, but was unable to calm down. Only one thing would help: she needed to hit the pavement and feel the cold air propel her forward. With a loud sigh and much effort, she kicked the thick comforter to the side and got up from the couch.

Splashing water on her face, she caught a glimpse of her reflection in the bathroom mirror. Her face was pale. She didn't recognize the haggard woman staring back at her. Distressed, she slipped on her running clothes, laced up her Nikes, and rushed out of the door. The worst of the storm had passed, leaving only masses of melting brown snow in its wake and puddles of murky water. Xandy needed to run.

Not jog, but run.

She wanted to exhaust herself. She wanted to be free. She wanted to be herself again. Just for a moment.

As Xandy's feet battered the blacktop, her heart thrashed in her chest. Her lungs forced air in and wind out, whooshing. The sound of her soles against the asphalt was her melody, the tune she followed.

She ran until it hurt. Then she ran some more. The stench of the city blasted her nostrils. The odor brought her out of her comatose state. As her feet slowed, she found herself alone as traffic bustled by, and college students hurried to class. The sun's rays shone brighter, making the darkness and cold of yesterday a distant memory.

She glanced at the homeless man on the park bench, the new burial plot being dug out, and the couple arguing with their newborn resting in its quasi-new stroller. Her demons gave chase.

The images somersaulted over and over in her mind. She stopped running and walked back to her apartment.

Others lived. She too had to move forward and away from the guilt of Thornton.

There were no more tears left to cry, instead her shoulders straightened.

***

Ilene Kernbach yawned as she put the final touches on the painting, her forged Michelino. She'd been staying late at the museum for the last few weeks to get access to the biblical painting on loan from Florence, without the glaring lights. With the ploy that the original binding needed restoration, she'd been able to move it to her studio in the building.

Setting the brush aside, Ilene stepped back and scrutinized her work. After getting the composition perfect, she'd worked on the colors and textures. The hues were too bright, still wet. With a skillful hand and painstaking detail, she'd come as close as ever to pulling off her greatest forgery.

With a smile plastered on her face, she removed her soiled apron and tossed it next to her workbench. There was still a small detail that needed to be changed, she noticed. Her eyes burned, but then again it was time for her scheduled break.

Opening her studio door, she stepped out into the hallway, pressing the button for the elevator. Like every night, the need for caffeine drove her to plunder the director's stash.

As the elevator door opened, she came face-to-face with the man she wasn't scheduled to meet until tomorrow, for he was to buy her newest piece.

"What are you doing here?" She asked the man standing in front of her, taking a step inside.

His dark-clothed arm reached out and seized her, pulling her toward him. He turned her around and covered her mouth, silencing her rising scream. She tried to kick him, claw at his gloved hands, his face, but he was quicker.

Feeling a slight prick in her neck, paralysis slowly began.

The dark shoes walked the carpet of the museum toward the Paolo Veronese exhibit, which was undergoing renovation. The security cameras had been disabled and the clear plastic tarps made for a great hiding place.

Now, he carried his cargo, hog-tied and gagged toward the painting he determined best for the scene. As the killer snuck up the corridor, locating the painting, endorphins rushed; synapses fired; and excitement built to a point of orgasmic frenzy. Her labored breathing echoed in his ears.

Anticipation was building.

Just like with the prior victim, death needed to linger, life fading minute by minute, precious drop by precious drop. Hope would seep away as the wounds bled.

Setting her carelessly on the new carpet, he saw her cat eyes staring at him. Incapacitated, she could do nothing— not even scream.

He grabbed her unwilling hand with his left hand, and with a scalpel gripped in his right, he pressed it to her upturned palm. The scalpel cut deeply into its meaty flesh. Parting the edges of the fresh incision, the killer eased the tract into the newly formed folds. The needle pierced her palm. He pulled the suture until her skin puckered.

Towering again over her small frame, with crocodile tears, he ogled her. He watched her chest rise and fall and could almost imagine her sobs. Removing his homemade hand-held spear from his pack, he raised it above his head.

With a forceful thrust, he plunged it into her beating heart.

Chapter 6

October 13

Monroe was overcurious. Murders didn't usually happen in art studios or museums. It didn't fit the normal motives or patterns. Instead murderers usually chose to hide their victims and not display them.

Kernbach's studio smelled of oil and acrylic paint, combined with a hint of turpentine, lemon cleanser, and a pungent scent he couldn't place. The studio was organized, for an artist's space. Her desk was separate from her easels, brushes and array of paints. Dry paint splotches covered the floor in blue, red and yellow hues, and what once was a white smock hung over the back of a wooden stool placed in front of two paintings that looked, initially, the same, except one was unfinished.

Monroe stared at the paintings on the easels. It stood beside an identical painting, which appeared aged, dry and the original, he surmised. From the skills shown on the canvas of the replicated image, he knew what they were dealing with, an art forger. He wouldn't be surprised to find out that she'd done it before. People usually continued what they were good at.

With his notebook in hand, he walked over to Kernbach's desk. It was littered with papers and all organization seemed to be lacking. From what he could tell, Kernbach would have written down everything, and maybe even a viable clue could be somewhere in that mess.

With a gloved hand, he flipped over paper after paper until he discovered Kernbach's datebook. Turning through the pages, he discovered that she had been scheduled to meet with a Johannes Mensch today. A telephone number was written down beside the name in a flowery penmanship. He quickly scribbled down the name and telephone number. Maybe this Mr. Mensch would be able to provide a clue or two.

"Detective, sorry for interrupting, but the night guard would like to talk to you," said officer responding to the scene.

The guard walked forward, still wearing his black slacks and matching black sweater with a white business shirt popping forth. His timid gait told Monroe what he already knew. The poor kid was working and studying full-time, probably using the down time to listen to a lecture through a podcast.

"So tell me," Monroe said, with pronounced authority. "What happened? You discovered the body?"

"Yes, sir. I was on my rounds around three this morning and discovered Ms. Kernbach. But I didn't see anything on my cameras. As soon as I found her, I called 911."

"It wasn't odd for her to be here so late?"

"No. For the past few weeks, at least during my shifts, she'd been holed up in her studio. She would usually leave between three and four, and then, from what I've heard, come in first thing in the morning when the museum opened."

"Did you see anyone enter the building or walking around after hours?"

"I come in around eleven and leave at seven. I saw only the normal faces, and they all work here," he said, pointing at the floor.

"There was nothing suspicious about their behavior?" Monroe asked.

"It was the usual night, except for this," he said.

"Is there anything that stands out to you about the last time you saw her?"

"She seemed hurried." The guard looked around, down as he tried to remember. "She'd been down in her studio and rushed by with three large coffees. She looked exhausted too, but she'd been working for the last few weeks late, until 3:00 a.m. I kept to myself though. She always let me know that I was just the security guard and was to stay out of her business."

"What do you mean?" Monroe asked. His brow furrowed as he continued to scrutinize the guard's twitching, eye movements and gesturing.

"One time, I went to check on her. My relief had come in, and while making my last round, I dropped by to see if she was alright around seven or so. She told me to mind my business. That's what I've done ever since."

"Was there anything odd or suspicious about her?"

"She always smelled like turpentine," he said.

That could account for her working on pieces for the museum, restorations, or working on her own forgeries. That would make sense, thought Monroe.

"Thanks," Monroe said. "If we have any more questions, we'll be in contact."

"Monroe, come here, I might have something for you," called Hobbes.

Those were the friendliest words he'd heard since his inception in the force, Monroe thought, as he excused himself and headed to Hobbes's side.

"This is Robert Lee. He lives out back in the bushes. He's been kind enough to tell us about what he saw."

In the former Capital of the Confederacy, where heroes of antebellum Virginia are still celebrated, meeting a man by such a name wasn't much of a coincidence. It was just as common as seeing the Confederate flag.

Robert Lee was nothing more than a dirty vagabond who stank of feces, alcohol and sweat. As the scruffy-haired man's muddy eyes darted back and forth between him and Hobbes, Monroe tried not to breathe.

"Ah seen him too!" he shouted. He flailed his arms up and down. "Ah know what he looks like."

"Describe him," Monroe said. He took out his pad again.

"He was lahk a devil on ho'seback. Pure evil if you ask me. Ah tell you, he was it."

Aden glimpsed at the evidence of his betrayal. The candles still flickered, the bottle of champagne sat empty in the silver bucket, and two flutes rested on the bedside table. The sheets lay in disarray, evidence of their sexcapade. He could smell Jocelyn on his skin, still taste her hot Delilah kisses.

He watched Jocelyn's reflection in the glass pane of the penthouse window as she dressed. She wasn't supposed to be there. They were never to see each other again. The price of their deceit was grinding his conscience. He had sunk deep. How was he ever to get back into the graces of his brother? He sighed. He'd messed up again, allowing his penis to decide his course of action.

"I'm leaving," Jocelyn called to him as she headed toward the door.

Aden continued to stare out at the city, refusing to look at Jocelyn. "Joss, I can't do this anymore. I can't keep doing this to my brother. He's all I got."

"You're being melodramatic."

Silence was his reply.

"You desired me, Aden, remember? You wanted to know what it was like to lay beside me, hold, kiss and caress me. What now? Having second thoughts?"

"I don't know what I want..."

"You made me lose everything to be with you and now… now you're getting rid of me?"

Pain shot through him, but he didn't know what else to do. He could hear the exasperation in Jocelyn's angelic voice and everything she said was correct, but now having her, he wasn't sure if he wanted her.

"What did you expect? You screwed over one brother for another. You're tainted. I can't have something with you, even if I wished to."

"Don't call me again!" Jocelyn snatched up her purse. "You always were a goddamned prick." Jocelyn picked up the crystal vase on the table nearest her and threw it at his head. "Fuck you, Aden!"

The crystal crashed into the wall next to him. It shattered. The brilliant shards reflected the candlelight.

"You already did," he responded, turning away. He didn't want to see her go, but as the door slammed, he did nothing to stop her.

Dr. Reynolds snapped on his white plastic gloves as his diener, Daniel, rolled the newest body into the white and stainless steel room. The body bag's contents were always a surprise – sort of like the toy in a Happy Meal. Dr. Reynolds unzipped the black bag to reveal the almost peaceful looking face of a young woman. As the opening revealed more, he saw the wooden spear-like object stuck in her chest, surrounded by reddish-brown blood, which had soaked through her once-white blouse.

"What do we have here?" Dr. Reynolds asked.

"This is the body they recovered from the museum." Daniel grinned. His jet-black hair and alabaster pallor sometimes seemed to be more at home in these walls. Gothic and obsessed with death, his work was exceptional, thought Dr. Reynolds.

"Well, let's get started. They are going to want the report of whatever we find." Turning her hands up, Dr. Reynolds spotted the fresh cut across the meaty-part of her palm. Sticking out from the neatly sewn stitches he noted the tag. Grabbing his forceps, he straightened it and stared at the typed print, 'Thou Shall Not 58'.

The transcript was thick. What they'd missed then, Lazarus knew was between those pages. A hint of it. He flipped through until he reached the testimony of Lauren Donovan. She'd hired him, but he also wanted to find out who she was. Her name was more than familiar. Since then he'd had tons of cases, many days in court, but reading her words, it was almost as if he were there again.

One line sprang out to him: "Thornton was to meet me in Hawaii. We were lovers, and together. I knew once she found out about us, that she'd kill him. He was her way into high society – upper middle class living. She killed him for what he had. She killed him for the money."

Lazarus pulled out Xandy's bank statements. He checked each of her three accounts. There was nothing odd about them; no strange purchases or anything that stood out, but what did one person need three accounts for?

A knock interrupted him. She was at least punctual.

"I hope you've been doing your homework," Lauren said spotting the paperwork on his table. "I want her to pay for what she did."

"What are you trying to find out?"

"I've filed the wrongful death suit and I need the information to prove she was behind his death," Lauren responded. "Time is running out."

"When did you do that? I haven't heard about it through the press or anything."

"On October 1st. You see, before Thornton died, he told me about a safe deposit box that he had. And if anything should happen to him, then I needed to open it."

"What of the safe deposit box then?"

"I don't have any information about it."

"Huh?" First she was told to get the box, but she didn't have anything.

"It's simple. He told me about it one night after too much wine. Before he died, he was paranoid about her finding out about us. He babbled a lot. He gave me a key, though."

"A key?"

"Yes."

"Why haven't you been there yourself?"

"I don't know where the safe deposit box is. I need you to find that out for me." She removed a white envelope from her cashmere coat pocket. "Let me know what you find out. Since this is not an active investigation, I expect that my hiring your services means that what you find in that box comes to me…and only to me."

Lazarus smelled a snake and sneered. She knew where the box was. She just couldn't get into it.

Detective Monroe could not come to terms with the investigation. The bodies were adding up, but none of the facts. The recent crime scene at the museum left a lot of evidence to be shuffled through. He wasn't sure how long it would take to build a reliable case. With the pressure coming down from above, he needed something.

The witness called himself Robert Lee Jefferson Davis. Maybe it was because of his love of the South, but if they had to build a case on this guy's statement, the case was beyond screwed. Monroe had questioned him several times, and each time he came up with a different tale. There was nothing concrete about anything he said, besides that the person they were looking for was male. Out of a city with a population of over one hundred ninety thousand, forty-nine percent were male. They needed more to bring to the grand jury.

The killer wouldn't be so easily caught, Monroe knew. Was there anything that connected the two homicides? These crimes weren't your typical holdups or carjackings. They didn't seem to be drug-related or the result of robberies. These two women didn't appear to have anything in common. The only things linking the murders, besides the mutilation, were the broken watches, tags and the line: *Thou Shall Not*, followed by a number.

In fact, the evidence collected included a postcard depicting the Greek goddess Nemesis from the first murder, along with the numerous rocks and blood spatter samples, and now the painting of Cephalus and Procris. The body was posed, right under that painting. It too had to be connected in some way. He had to wait for it to be processed to see what the technicians could get off it. The murder weapon had nothing on it that could be traced. It was simply a hand-made oak and steel hand-held spear.

With Dr. Reynolds's report, they'd figured out that the perpetrator would debilitate the victim with a "roofie" of some sort; toxicology was still trying to figure out exactly what. Then, the individual would be killed in a dramatic manner. The scene was bloody, but only the victim's blood. There was no additional DNA residue under the victim's nails, no videotape surveillance.

Nothing.

They knew about two murders so far. The first had been discovered roughly two days ago. The first victim was estimated to have died approximately one day before she was found, due to the state of rigor mortis, and the second one just last night. Monroe's gut churned. This had serial killer written all over it.

No kill was perfect. Better yet, no killer was perfect and although the best crime was committed alone, these victims told a tale. Everything was there. They just needed to read the signs.

Monroe flipped open the file and queried Ms. Kernbach's NCIC criminal record. Mere seconds passed by until his suspicions were confirmed, for she had been previously convicted of art forgery. He wasn't sure how she'd gotten the job at the museum with such a criminal history, but he did note that the most current charge was recently adjudicated. Doing a cross check, he found her case file.

He perused the report and called Hobbes over.

"I may have found something, maybe even a motive," Monroe said. He watched as Hobbes came and stood straight at his side with his chest puffed out like a robin on a spring day.

"What do you have?" Hobbes asked.

"I just finished reading Kernbach's prior case file. Do you remember a story a few months ago about the Berkley family?"

Hobbes scratched his bald head. "They claimed that the museum stole their painting and exchanged it for a new one, why?"

"It's the same artist that was being copied last night," Monroe said. "The Berkley Michelino was brought to America by her great-great-grandfather after the Franco-Prussian War in 1871. When it was appraised for a new insurance policy, it was determined to be a fake, after having been authenticated just months before."

"You think the victim was doing the same thing?"

"The prominent Berkley family had filed a criminal complaint only eighteen months ago, and the charges dropped six months before she died. Not only do I think it, but since Kernbach's charges were dismissed due to lack of evidence, and she continued to work for the museum, maybe someone was trying to set her up."

"There was lack of evidence for a million-dollar painting? That could be motive for murder," Hobbes said.

"I'll get the car. I think we need to see what Ms. Berkley has to say."

The killer's predatory gaze watched as the final stragglers headed out for fall break, leaving the professor alone. The once-rambunctious students and their joyful screams had dissipated, leaving behind silence, the crackling of the lights. The only thing left was an unattended housekeeping cart with its strong ammonia-like smell.

Hiding behind Professor Walker Gentry's cracked office door, the killer watched each steady step toward him. His hungry stare never faltered as she sashayed down the dark hall of the history department. She clutched the written exams to her ample bosom while her sandy brown extensions fell into her oval face with its hint of mischief. A mischief he knew about. With slender fingers and a puff of air, she swept her hair forcefully away.

Only a few steps from her office, Gentry's cell phone rang. She cradled it to her right ear.

"Conrad, fall break can now begin!" she said.

The killer was acquainted with Conrad, even though he couldn't hear his responses. He was Gentry's student assistant who'd just turned eighteen last month. Gentry had the reputation for hiring based on peens and pecs.

"If you've graded all of my papers, we can now go on the trip," Gentry said. "I'll bring the new ones from the late class with me. We just finished." After a pause, she continued, "No, it was not meant for anyone else, just you."

The killer could hear Gentry's vulgar cackle, as it caused a wave of excitement to wash over him. Alone with her, he'd have time to play with his feral cat.

"You are such a good stud...I can't wait to see how you let me ride," she whispered as she pushed against her cracked office door, opening it. "Let me go, and I'll give you a call as soon as I'm on my way. It'll just be the two of us."

Putting the cell phone back in her pocket, Professor Gentry entered her office. She flicked on the light switch. Nothing happened.

Gentry reached over to turn on the lamp on her desk. She set the exams on the light wood. The killer reached around her neck, pumping the pompous professor with his poison.

The professor fell to the carpeted floor. The killer could almost see the word 'scream' on the professor's face as she stared up at him, her pupils dilating. Her heart's bump bum was almost loud enough to detect. He watched her hands' nervous tremble and quickly stuffed a cloth into her mouth. Removing cable ties from his pocket, he restrained her arms.

It would take up to five minutes for the paralytic to work.

The killer hurried to close the door. He turned his attention back toward his goal for the night. He heard her moans and turned his head to the side as if seeing someone else, as if trying to understand, solve the puzzle set before him. All he wanted was to rip out Gentry's beating heart and shove it down the sick bitch's throat, but that wouldn't serve his purpose well.

It was even worse than the killer thought it could ever be. Instead of saving others from her, he'd made the mistake of reacting too late, and now, someone else bore his burden. The killer usually saved his violence, never allowing the scene to possess him, to take the lead, but having overheard her conversation, it made him want to hurt her even more.

"Tell me your sins and receive forgiveness," he said.

Silence.

"Then death is your reward," the killer whispered.

Gentry's eyes glazed over as if looking into the distance.

The killer switched on the lamp and turned to the

professor's bookshelf and removed the Works of Seneca. Flipping to the Tragedy of Phaedra, he ripped the pages from the leather binding, and then carefully placed all except the first sheet into the professor's balmy hand.

The whole campus knew what was happening in Professor Gentry's lecture hall, but no one did anything.

Until now.

Kneeling next to her immobilized body, the killer placed a satchel on the carpet. He removed the required tools for the job and laid them on a dark, crushed velvet cloth.

With scissors he cut along the seam of the professor's garments, revealing hairless and aged skin. Setting the scissors to the side, he grabbed his preferred tool. The scalpel now light in his hand, the killer carved into the professor's flesh, making a large, deep vertical incision into the professor's womanly mound with his surgical steel. Digging into her pubis, the killer excised the bean-like clitoris with his blade.

The killer looked into her pain-filled eyes with pure satisfaction.

And smiled.

Using dissecting forceps to force the folds of the skin apart, the killer placed the tag into the wound. With expert precision and steady hands, he moved the needle in and out of her skin, sewing it neatly shut.

He picked up the scalpel again, slicing into the professor's arms vertically. His blade followed the blue line, tearing open the arteries, veins and the plastic ties. Blood splashed upon her diamond-encased timepiece.

Waves of anger crashed against him. He grabbed the scissors off Gentry's desk and thrust the black-handled scissors into the professor's chest.

And twisted.

He waited for her last breath as she stared back, gasping. Then he removed her watch and placed it in a plastic bag, and swung it against the door frame, breaking the glass's face, marking the time of the kill. Removing the other timepiece from his satchel, he snapped it on her opened wrist and pocketed the cut ties.

With his hat pulled low over his face, he yanked the locked door shut behind him and walked away, leaving only his offering for atonement and a commandment.

Thou shall not 519.

<u>Chapter 7</u>

October 14

The morning arrived before Xandy wanted it to. She spied the white glow of the DVD's clock. The officer had come and gone, but no Victor. Instead of the moonlight of last night, bright sunlight streamed into her living room.

"Why did the morning have to come so soon?" Xandy asked Amarillo, who perked up her orange striped ears and sat purring. Retrieving her cell phone from the coffee table she read Victor's message, which he'd sent sometime during the night:

Sorry, swamped. Can you come down to the station during your break?

The idea of airing out their relationship at the station made her queasy. But if she had to do it there, then she was going to be as presentable as possible. Taking extra care, she found the one business outfit that gave her style and made her feel like a woman. The matching two piece pants suit was tailored to fit her slim frame. The notched collar of the jacket accented her long neck. The Italian material felt nice against her skin. Primping, she rubbed perfume behind her ears and put in the pearls from her mother. She pulled her long wavy hair back into a French twist. Lastly, she applied red lipstick to her plump lips.

Today, her plan was to show him what he was

missing.

"Brennan," Victor said standing over Brennan's desk, "I have someone coming by in the next few minutes and I know you're in IA, but can you meet with her?

"Meet with her?" Brennan asked. His brow wrinkled at the question.

"Yeah, issues about a potential stalker. She's already filed a report. Could you give her some insight as a personal favor to me?"

"I do have an appointment with Dr. James in thirty minutes, but I might be able to squeeze her in."

"Just make the introductions and then you can head to your meeting. Since this is on the private side."

Brennan wasn't sure what to make of the issue. Bells and whistles were blowing for him. Victor wanted him to use his time to do him a favor? Sure, it wasn't anything criminal, just a talk about stalkers, and since he'd done more than his share before IA, he understood the reasoning behind it, but still, he didn't know Victor to ask a personal favor from anyone.

"We can meet in my office then. What's her name?" Brennan asked.

"Alexandria Caras. I'll let her know to meet us here."

That name was coming up too often and with Lazarus' allegations, it piqued Brennan's curiosity. Who was she and why were two good officers involved with her?

Taking the first break available, Xandy grabbed her jacket and purse and rushed out of her office. She was only one of the many crowding the streets, as other women in business suits and tennis shoes bustled alongside those who sashayed as if on the catwalk.

Xandy entered the station, with a dry mouth. Her

heels click-clacked against the gray tile floor. It echoed the sound of her anxious heart. She entered the elevator and was whipped along to her destination, as the numbers of the floors beeped by in rapid succession.

When the doors parted, she was greeted by the hearty receptionist. "May I help you?"

"Yes, I'm here to see Captain Hawthorne. He left word for me to meet him here," Xandy said, taking a seat. The waiting area was inviting with its décor, dark floor and warm colors, nothing like the sterile area she was used to around the bull pen. She didn't want to be there, but she also didn't want to walk away. However, there was only so much comfort to be had considering the reason for her presence.

Removing a pen from her purse, Xandy started to doodle. It always helped for brain storming.

Her doodles morphed into a name: Blackwell. He had caused her a great deal of pain, although she had no proof, besides suspect journal entries. Blackwell didn't work that way. Someone was harassing her, maybe even following her. If Blackwell could arrange for an office massacre, he could also get rid of the lone woman who survived it all.

But why now, she wondered. The criminal charges had been dismissed. Nothing about Blackwell had come out since then, and maybe he wanted to make sure it stayed that way. Maybe she had the possibility of causing collateral damage, especially if he thought she knew more about his and Thornton's illegal activities– money laundering, buying public officials, and fraud. A list full of maybes!

Her breath caught. Should she tell Victor what she thought, or hold this new revelation close to her chest? Was Blackwell's wrath coming hell-bent upon her? Xandy flinched at the thought.

Setting down her pen down, she saw Victor in the

distance.

She stared dumbfounded at him rounding the corner, taking in his swagger, his muscular build. When he came closer, Xandy caught a whiff of the scent of his cologne, a woody fragrance, combined with the man wearing it. He wasn't alone though. Another man followed.

"Xandy, thanks for coming," Victor said, clasping her hand in his. "I'm sorry that I won't be able to meet with you, but my associate here will gladly speak with you to discuss your safety concerns."

"Ms. Caras," Brennan said, extending his hand. "It's a pleasure to meet you."

Xandy attempted to regain her composure at hearing Victor pass her over to someone else as if she were a used rag. "Well, please call me Xandy." She tried to smile, but found it difficult.

"I'm sure you're in capable hands and Detective Tal will take great care of you. We'll talk later," Victor said. Not waiting for her response, she notice, he retreated out of her view.

"Any friend of Victor is a friend of mine," Brennan said, leading her to his office.

Taking a seat behind his massive desk, Brennan looked down at his watch, knowing he had better things to do. She eased into the chair across from him, crossing her legs.

Victor had been too eager to arrange her coming in, in order for her to alleviate her anxiety. They'd discussed it in detail. Yet Brennan was hesitant at best and more than skeptical at her stalking suspicions. He'd promised Victor he'd give her a minute and in spite of his attraction to her, it was almost up.

"So how can I help you?" Brennan asked.

"Did Victor tell you anything about me?"

Catching his sigh, he said, "He mentioned that you feel you're being stalked, but I'd like to hear the details from you."

After listening to her story, he asked, "Did anything precede these events?"

"I've been receiving strange mail ... from nice and supportive to threatening Bible thumpers. It all just depends on the day of the week and the moon's alignment. The crazies seem to come out during the full moon."

"And I understand you live with someone," Brennan asked.

"He's hasn't been home in a couple of days."

"Oh, the foreboding quasi end of a relationship can be hard. How long were you together?"

"It's not such a relationship." Her voice dropped. "That's why I asked if Victor told you how he knew me."

"Victor is my friend and all, but I don't dig into his personal life. Just out of curiosity. How does Detective Lazarus fit into this?"

Brennan watched her every movement as she looked down at her feet, at the rug, and then back at him. "It's very difficult for me to talk about this, but...almost two years ago, my fiancé died."

His face softened at that piece of knowledge. He had heard bits about it around the station, but it was different hearing it from her. This was too much personal drama for him to deal with, and her answers weren't getting him any closer to figuring out who could be after her. He snuck a glance at his watch.

"But he didn't just die; he was killed and I was charged with it." Her voice lowered to a whisper.

He leaned forward and looked at her as if understanding. "How are you coping?"

Tears gathered in her eyes, "I've been cleared of everything, but Detective Lazarus is not making my recovery any easier, to say the least–"

The ringing of Brennan's office telephone interrupted

her before she could answer. "I'm sorry, Detective Tal, but your appointment has arrived," the receptionist said through the speaker.

"I'll be right with her. Thank you," Brennan said. "Sorry about that. Please go on."

"Since my charges were dismissed, Detective Lazarus has been following me. To me, it borders on harassment."

"Do you think he is the one who sent you the letter?"

"I don't know. I can't dismiss it though."

Brennan half-smiled. This was all Victor's ploy in setting him up ever since he'd said something at the station. He didn't have time for Victor's shenanigans.

"With everything you've been through, with a high-profile case like yours, it is easy to think that people are after you. It's been my experience that some backlash from the public is to be expected. I don't know the details of your case, and the fact that many believe you got away with murder is not helping in your progress. If you want my advice, toughen up. Your uber-paranoia is creating a sense of dread, drama and circumstances that are only imaginary." He stood to usher her out of his office.

Xandy stared at him, her mouth hanging open.

"I hate to be abrupt, but I do have someone waiting." He paused looking at her. He didn't know why, but maybe at least giving her his card would be enough to get her out of his office and maybe even get Victor to find someone else that could deal with her baggage. "Ms. Car—Xandy, I promised Victor I would help. Please take my card and give me a call should you need someone to talk to, okay?"

Brennan sat back down at his desk. He watched her stomp briskly away. His next appointment was waiting, but he needed a moment. He'd been an ass to her. He'd never treated someone like that in a professional environment, who just wanted to talk to him about something that seemed so real to them. His life didn't afford him the time and room to deal with another set of issues. He had more than enough with what life had vomited on him.

The insistent buzzing broke through his cloud of contemplation, like a child bursting from the forest with poison ivy; now, he was free of the leaves and darkness, but stuck with the itch.

Dr. James floated into Brennan's office and took a seat. "I wasn't too sure how long you were going to keep me waiting out there, especially since I'm squeezing this meeting in."

"A last minute appointment, sorry about that. Let's discuss Detective Lazarus. He's officially being charged with insubordination."

"After reviewing his personnel file, I think we can only take issue with the order from Captain Hawthorne. However, Captain Hawthorne did follow protocol, and he did give Detective Lazarus several warnings regarding his actions. I'm almost surprised the suspension didn't come earlier."

"What is your recommendation?"

"I feel that the suspension is warranted, but I believe he has received too many days. His actions are at the most a Class B offense for his repeated failure to follow a direct order. At the most, he should receive five days."

"Thanks. I'll take your recommendation into consideration before I forward anything to the Chief."

"Off the record, I think Detective Lazarus needs some serious counseling. He's still grieving the loss of what he called his friend, and I believe he is acting out, looking for a scapegoat where none really exist."

"If counseling is something that could make him a better officer, then it is something I will include in the final recommendation, as well."

Dr. James glanced at her watch. "I hate to cut this

short, but I need to get going."

"No offense taken. We'll be in touch," Brennan said rising.

Brennan knew he still had one last piece to fit together before he could close Lazarus' file. What was it about the Caras criminal case that made him obsess over it?

Victor flopped back into his office chair. He groaned. The audible sound did nothing to lessen the feeling of being a dog running away with its tail between his legs. He'd seen the disappointment as it passed over Xandy's lovely face; her lip's slight pucker and her eyes squinting. But work called. He'd have to make it right later on, but right now, the investigation required his full attention and not the woman who was distracting him from his first love.

He turned to his computer to type up his notes from his last session. Victor stared at the screen and an email alert he'd received from Detective Monroe. Opening the email, he read the short summary of an impromptu witness interview and clicked on the picture attachment. The image of Hannah Salem, all smiles, caused her dead face to boomerang in his head. To see what she looked like alive and then remembering her dead body on the slab was a brutal reality. Knowing Monroe was out of the precinct, he dialed Monroe's cell number.

"The watch belonged to a Donald Higgins. I contacted him and he told me that he gave it to Sister Hannah. We need the watch."

"We find the watch, we find the killer," Victor said. "Do you have a preliminary profile as of yet?"

"Although the circumstances surrounding their deaths are similar, there is a difference in the rage exhibited. I am unsure if this is significant enough, or not. I'll jump on it though and see what I can get to you as soon as possible.

"We'll get this bastard off the street before it gets any worse," Monroe continued. "Every killer makes a mistake sooner or later."

"For this city's sake, let's hope it's sooner than later."

Attorney Randall Grimes waited for Detective Monroe to arrive. He couldn't help but check the time. The precinct's clamor, combined with the late hour caused his head to hurt more than it had already. With cotton mouth, he craved another swig of something strong to get him through the night. Even though he was on retainer with the Berkley family, to be called out in the middle of the night to inform a detective to cease in the questioning of his client was bothersome. His hands shook, red and splotched. He needed to head back to the hospital to check on Marie, his wife, and not this. Not this, not now. He couldn't afford to play babysitter over a dismissed criminal case with a dead defendant.

"May I help you?" Randall looked up. The cop across from him looked even worse than he did. His eyes were bloodshot, and he couldn't even stifle his own yawn.

"Yes. I'm here on behalf of the Berkley family. And I am here to remind you that they have an attorney. Any questions that you may have will need to go through me." Randall stood, allowing his 6-foot-7-inch frame to tower over the 6-foot officer.

"This is an investigation, not an interrogation." Monroe said, setting his large cup of coffee down on his desk.

"Quite frankly, I don't care what you're trying to do. If you have any questions, then you contact me and only me!" Randall's voice hardened.

Monroe stared at the man across from him. He stank of old alcohol, worse than a back-alley wino, and there he was making demands. "Let's cut to the chase. I am investigating a string of murders. Should your clients fail to cooperate in this investigation, I will arrest them personally for obstruction. If you want to be present, then do so, but I really don't care what you have to do. I want them here first thing tomorrow. If they don't show up, I'll make sure to have the patrol car waiting to bring them in."

"I see I need to speak with someone with experience here. You don't know who the Berkleys are, I take it."

"I guess they are not the Kennedys. If you want to complain about the way I am handling this investigation, the Captain's office is straight back." Monroe turned away and leaned back in his chair. He could only hear Randall's sigh.

"There has to be more information than this," Monroe said. His voice rose, as he spoke to the customer service agent on the phone. His day was going downhill. First, Ms. Berkley called her attorney on him, and now he was being blocked by someone in a call center on the other side of the world.

"I'm sorry, sir, but this is all the information available for this number. As I've said, the number you provided is from a prepaid phone, and there isn't a contact name or address."

"Thanks," Monroe muttered. He slammed down the phone. It would have been too easy just to get what he needed. Whoever had called Hannah Salem had used a number that was registered to no one. After that last call, no more information was listed. Cross checking her records hadn't helped either. It was the same number she had dialed.

"Damn it," Monroe said, as he rubbed his temples. The one lead he had was a dead end.

***

Lionel Blackwell tapped his fingers. He sat in his Italian leather chair and stared at Xandy's black-and-white picture.

Cash.

He needed his cash. It was the only reason she still lived, but even that reason was disappearing. No one told him what to do. He told them.

He was trying to be patient. He didn't like being nice any more than he liked begging. It was beneath him to do that. There were men whom he killed who'd responded quicker to his threats than she did, but she had what he needed.

He could see through her charade. She was waiting for the right time to skip town with his money, and the only thing stopping her was the recently filed civil suit. Once she walked away from that, she'd be gone with his millions. His folder was filled with her pictures. Up until she saw Jonathan with that other conniving bitch, he knew what she did every moment of the day. Now her routine was changing. She was spending more time at the station.

Lionel cracked his knuckles. "Tom, I expect that you have something to tell me on why she's behaving this way. You told me the case is expected to be dismissed."

"The decision is supposed to come down by the end of next week," Tom said.

"Good. I think until then, I'll send her another message. Maybe one that isn't so diplomatic."

"I don't need to know about that." Tom shook his head.

"I pay your bill. You report to me about any change. Got it?"

Tom nodded.

"You're dismissed, then."

Webbie hurried into the space emptied by Tom, almost knocking him over as he entered Lionel's office.

"I have something that I need some muscle to take care of. I think you'll like it." With a manicured hand, Lionel passed Webbie the address and a picture. "This is the one. I want you to wait for an opportunity though, and then seize it."

"Is there anything I should tell her?"

"Yeah, that Xandy sent you."

Xandy didn't want to slosh around in the rain, even if it had turned into a drizzle, but when Rebecca called, she couldn't think of a better excuse to not head home. Victor still hadn't said anything to her and the thought of waiting for his call was not what she wanted to do tonight. She didn't want to be alone after he'd made sure to push her off on someone else. Rebecca rounded the corner and entered Xandy's office, in all her grandeur.

"Are you ready? I sure as hell hope not, because you are not looking it," Rebecca said.

"What's wrong with what I have on?" Xandy asked eyeing the suit that cost more than her bi-weekly paycheck.

"We are going to a club. Not a board meeting. Let's go to the bathroom so I can at least make you a little more presentable for the evening."

"I'm not too sure–"

"Don't worry. Let me work my magic."

Xandy smirked and slowly rose. How was it that in their early thirties, Rebecca could still try to make her feel ten years younger?

In the bathroom, Rebecca pushed Xandy into a stall. Hanging on the inside hook was an array of clothes.

"What's this? I am not going to leave here looking like a…"

"Either you put the DKNY blouse and mini skirt on or I'll make you wear what I'm wearing. We are not going to a nursing home!"

The idea of a second skin made of denim appealed to Xandy about as much as a lobotomy. Begrudgingly, she slipped on the low-riding, mini, and a black leather and lace décolleté corset. Her hair was transformed to a messy coiffure.

"The corset is too tight," Xandy said.

"You can still breathe." Rebecca chuckled. "Now just a little make-up."

With the heavy black eyeliner, mascara and purple eye shadow in place, Xandy stared at her reflection. It was better than a makeover at the MAC counter in the mall. She thought she was breathtaking.

However, the familiar chill of panic hit her. Her mind raced. The make-up would make people look at her twice, which was not something she wanted. No one needed to take a second look at her; no one needed to scrutinize her more. Snatching a paper towel from the metal dispenser, she blotted at the colors.

"There goes all my hard work."

"It's not me."

Rebecca sucked her teeth. "At least keep the outfit on."

Xandy had the sudden urge to rip off the tight and revealing clothes and burn them. If it meant she wouldn't have to walk around with her ovaries almost on display.

"Please…pretty please," Rebecca pled and batted her eyelashes.

With a forced chuckle, Xandy said, "We better leave then before I change my mind."

"You sure you don't want to wear just a little lipstick?" Rebecca asked with the lipstick in her hand. She leaned forward ready to apply it to Xandy's uncolored lips.

"No, I think I'm fine just the way I am." Taking her purse, Xandy disappeared back into a stall. Retrieving the bottle of pills, she shook it until one landed in her palm. Tossing the pill into her mouth she swallowed.

"You alright?" Rebecca asked. Xandy could hear the worry in her friend's question.

"It's just been a while since I've put myself on display like this and then Victor hasn't called–"

"Girl, don't go worrying your head over him. He'll call."

"I saw him today and besides a handshake, he didn't even act like I existed."

"A handshake? Ouch."

"That's not helping, Becca."

"The best way to get over one guy is to find another one."

"I don't want a new guy, I want–"

"I keep forgetting you haven't done this in so long. Men are weird and half of the time, they aren't sure which head to follow. Now, come on out of there. You can't be my wing woman if we are stuck in the bathroom at your office. Just give it some time. He'll come around."

"And if he doesn't"

"Then, you'll have to find someone else and break it down for him what you're after."

"I don't even know what I want."

"If you don't know, then how is he supposed to know?"

Sitting on the black rimmed toilet seat, Xandy stared at the burgundy stall door. She was worth it, she knew, now she just had to show him she was.

Lazarus watched Xandy head into the club. Shockoe Bottom was packed with pedestrians. With stop and go traffic and groups of young men and women carousing, music blared from the different nightclubs. It had taken a while for her and her friend to find a parking spot. He stayed behind them, blending into the crowd of twenty- and thirty-year-olds looking for a good time. Tonight was the first time he'd seen her so made-up. Maybe she was starting to get careless.

It didn't matter. If she was here for the night that gave him the chance to find what he needed at her apartment.

Inside, the club was packed, leaving only wiggle room. Laser lights flashed an array of colors as bodies moved to the rhythm of the music. Hairs on the back of Xandy's neck stood. She felt someone watching her. Not just a casual glance, or even a thorough ogling, no, the feeling was of scrutiny. Xandy turned in every direction until she saw his face.

She located Jonathan across the room.

For the past couple of days, they'd been avoiding one another. He was rarely at the apartment any more since the living-room sex scene. After a few minutes, she found him at her side.

"Hey, X. What are you doing here?"

"What?" Xandy asked cupping her ear. She could only hear the DJ's announcing the latest booty-shaking contest.

Taking Xandy's arm, Jonathan led her over to one of the walls, and leaned against it, shouting into her ear. "Can you hear me now?"

"Yeah, I didn't expect to see you here," Xandy said glancing at the crowd of gyrating bodies.

"Me you either. You never used to be one for the clubs. This is a surprise."

"I guess it was time for me to live a little."

"Look, I'm glad I ran into you. I found a new place. I'm going to be moving out."

"When?" Xandy asked. She could feel the panic rising like a snake slithering up her leg. She swallowed and concentrated on his words, not what it meant to be alone.

"I'll come by and pick up my stuff. Let me get back to Lauren before she loses me in this crowd."

While scanning the area earlier, Xandy hadn't seen Lauren, but then again, she hadn't been looking for her. "She hates me. Her ridiculous case is proof of that."

"I don't know. I mean, Lauren is a good person. I think you two just have some sort of misunderstanding. She thinks you were after me." He said with a charming chuckle.

"I liked having you around, but besides a friendship, there could never be anything between us —'

"Because of Thornton? How long are you going to mourn him? He's not the god you've made him into." He reached out and grabbed her arm. "Forgive me. I didn't mean … hell, I don't know…" He shoved his hands in his pocket and looked to her like the apologetic school boy she imagined him once to be.

Xandy watched as Jonathan was swallowed up by the crowd, leaving her leaning against the wall like a wallflower at a sixth grade dance.

"Let's have a drink," Rebecca said, coming up to her. "Are you all right?"

"Just one round of drinks. Then I have to head home …."

Lazarus eased the metal tension wrench and pick from his coat pocket. With a couple of quick moves, he heard the deadbolt give. He didn't know how long he had before she'd be back. He turned the knob and was greeted by warm 25-watt light.

He closed the door silently behind his large frame and moved slowly down the hall into the open living room. The apartment was still. Taking off his backpack, he removed the outlet transmitters. One by one, he exchanged the electrical outlets and installed the outlet transmitters throughout the apartment. If Xandy tried to plug anything into them, they'd work.

Maybe the bugs would give him the information he

needed.

As he was about to walk out the door, he saw the stack of unopened mail on the kitchen counter. He fingered through it. Included in the stack was a bank statement. With one smooth move, he pocketed the envelope and left the way he came.

"Detective Monroe?"

Monroe stared at the woman standing across from him. Her heart-shaped face demanded his attention, and her lips caused him to stick out his chest. The sound of his name on her lips made him feel stronger, as if electric currents rushed through him. She reminded him of the woman he had waiting at home, only a few years younger.

"How may I help you?" Monroe asked and ushered the woman down into the wooden seat across from him. Having caught Hobbes's eye, he saw him ease up from his seat and walk toward them.

"I'm here because of the murder." She stared at him, through him. "I saw the man who killed Professor Gentry."

Monroe grabbed a pad and looked around the room. "Why don't we head to the conference room? I think we will be a little more comfortable in there."

"I don't have a lot of time, and if Tony hadn't told me to come, I wouldn't be here," she said.

"Tony?"

"He's nobody. Listen. I only saw the back of him."

"What can you tell me about him then?" Hobbes asked. "How do you know about the murder?"

"I was late for the exam, and I stopped by the professor's office to speak with her about a makeup exam. And that is when I saw him...working on her. The door wasn't completely closed. He was ... was leaning over her ..." Her voice hitched. Silent tears streamed down her face.

"Why didn't you call the police then?" Hobbes asked.

"I did. I mean, I called, and because I was on campus, the campus police tried to respond, but they wouldn't listen to me and ... and ... I didn't want to get wrapped into this even more than I already am .... There was so much blood. So much blood ...."

"What's your name?" Monroe asked.

"Marilyn. Marilyn Feife."

"I'm going to call down the sketch artist so we can get a better description of the guy you saw. You've been a great help so far."

This could be the break the case needed, Monroe thought. It could be the information he needed to stop a murderer.

Xandy arrived home late. The loud music still rang in her ears, and exhaustion racked her body. She felt as if she'd been gone for weeks. She'd broken the rule and mixed the alcohols and had too many shots of tequila and ice teas. She could feel them revolting in her stomach.

As she stood in her kitchen, she flipped through the stack of mail she'd left unsorted from yesterday. She placed the bills to the side and the advertisements in the recycle bin. It was then that she noticed the blood-red envelope. It was postmarked as presorted business mail, with a black stamp bearing the zip code of 23219. That was the downtown area, where her former company was located.

Curious, she opened the envelope and pulled out a piece of torn paper. It looked like it had been ripped from a book. Xandy scanned its contents– it was the opening scene of the *Tragedy of Phaedra*. She'd read the play in high school, what felt like eons ago. She tried to remember the plot line; it was something about the forbidden passions of a stepmother for her stepson. Why would someone send this to her?

Her heart slammed against her chest. Dropping the page on the table, she stared at it: its font; the coloring of the paper, the violently ripped edges and a smudge of blood on the page's edge.

With a mixture of dread and nausea, she called Victor.

"Captain, I have a Ms. Caras on the line. She says that it's urgent that she speaks with you," the dispatch officer said.

Victor had ignored her direct calls to his cell. Seeing her picture on his display only distracted him from the task at hand. He sat alone in his office pouring over the most recent update from detectives Monroe and Hobbes. With three bodies lying on ice in the morgue and his detectives being no closer to solving the crimes, he didn't want to deal with Xandy too.

He said he'd stop by and he meant it, but somehow his intentions and actions just weren't aligning.

"It always is," Victor muttered. His work day had officially ended two hours ago. For the last two hours, he'd been able to concentrate on paperwork with little to no interruption. There was nothing keeping him in the office. His relief, Captain Cox, was already taking care of any brush fires that might pop up.

"Hi Xandy," Victor said. "I really can't talk now. I'm...I'm in a meeting."

"I guess I should have called 911 then!" Xandy snapped. "Here I am with some bloody mail that I've received and you can't talk to me–"

"Calm down. Now what's going on?"

"Don't tell me to calm down," she slurred.

"Are you drunk?" Victor asked. Patience was something he didn't seem to have tonight.

"I guess you'll stop by to check out the mail when you get a chance." With a click she hung up.

Victor stared at the phone. How the hell was he supposed to juggle it all? He didn't think she'd lie to him about having another threatening letter. The lab was still running tests on the last one. And over the past few months, he'd never known her to even have a drink, let alone get wasted.

He'd make the drive there and deal with her. There was no reason for their— whatever it was— to continue like *this*. He wasn't a little lapdog to come every time she ordered it. His thoughts were filled with resentment. They hadn't even slept together, and although he couldn't stop thinking about her, she was putting the gun to his chest.

Pocketing his keys, he headed to his parked car and then toward the west end.

Emotions and thoughts ran free. For a moment, Xandy thought she saw a fully garbed Native American chief standing at the end of her sofa. She waved and he waved back. His skin sagged and it was night and day simultaneously. The wind blew, alleviating the sun's heat.

"Xandy, open up!" Xandy heard banging on her door followed again by cursing and more banging.

Shaking her head, the vision disappeared and she was once again in her apartment, sitting on her sofa, hearing Victor at the front door.

"I'm coming," she called out.

"What took you so long? I've been calling you and banging on that damn door for the last five minutes. I was about to break it down." Victor stared at her.

"I'm sorry." Xandy said and pushed up on her tiptoes and pressed her lips to his. She'd failed to change after getting home and still had on the revealing, tight outfit

Rebecca had squeezed her in to.

"Whoa," Victor said and pulled away. "I didn't come out here for that. What is this about a letter?"

"I know you didn't come for that. I'm really sorry about what I said on the phone, that's all." Xandy rubbed her arms, as if fighting off a chill.

"I've just had a long, hard day." Victor wrapped his arms around her. She collapsed into his embrace, and it felt right.

"Me too," she said.

"Where are my manners? While you're here you might as well sit down. Can I get you something to drink?"

"There is something you can get me," he said.

She gazed into his brown eyes, hypnotized by him. His lips brushed across hers; then he paused.

"Have you been drinking? Maybe this isn't such a good idea," Victor said pulling away.

"I'm fine." Xandy said trying to pull him back closer to her.

"I don't know about this." Xandy could see his trepidation through his crinkled brow and the ever increasing distance between them.

"I know what I'm doing and what I want," Xandy said. With one quick move, she unpinned her hair and placed her hand on his muscular chest. She reached out and started playing with the buttons of his shirt. Taking his hand in her own, she placed it on her heaving breast. "Can't you feel how much I want this?"

He moved his hands slowly down her arms to her neck, décolleté and hips. Each area he touched fanned her wanton flame. With little prodding, Xandy kissed him. She opened her lips to his tongue's silky invasion.

Jumping up, she straddled him. He inched up her short skirt and squeezed her derriere. "The kitchen table," she said breathless between kisses.

With one quick swipe, Victor shoved the wine glasses and mail out of his way and sat her on the mahogany wood. She gasped when she heard the glasses thud on the carpet.

"I didn't break them," Victor said, kissing her again.

"I don't care about that right now." Her hands reached for his shirt. Fumbling with it, she ripped it open, watching the buttons fly across the room.

"I don't have another shirt here," he said staring down at his gaping shirt.

Xandy appreciated the view of her cop with his muscular chest, sprinkled with black hair. "Don't worry. I'll keep you warm." Her hands reached for his belt. Unbuttoning the button and unzipping the zipper, his pants fell to his ankles in a heap. Seeing him in all of his excitement, Xandy licked her lips.

"Lean back and enjoy the ride," Victor said with a wicked grin. He stepped out of his clothes and removed a condom from his wallet. Xandy's eyebrow shot up at his preparedness. Did he come there expecting this to happen?

Seeing him sheathed and ready to go, she focused back on him and the task at hand. Planted in between her legs, his large hand caressed her chin and tilted it up. His soft lips brushed against hers. It was different from the prior kiss – tender, sweet. She sighed into his mouth and reveled in the sensation of him.

She felt his palm pressed against her moistness, and cooed. Finally, she welcomed him as he entered into her depths. His hardness stroked her, as he moved in and out. She didn't care that her movements were limited on the table or that the hard wood wasn't as comfortable as she'd always imagined. Instead she scooted forward and raised her legs higher.

Xandy screamed his name between moans as he pushed her beyond passion to pure euphoric pleasure.

Billows of bliss blew over them.

As he stood there planted between her legs, Xandy's stomach started to churn. She could feel the margaritas on the rise. She gently pushed Victor away. Jumping down, she ran to the nearest bathroom.

The cramps pushed her to her knees, as her stomach regurgitated its contents. There, she spewed her liquid courage into the toilet. All of her nine-dollar drinks came back up to greet her.

Too weak for words, she rested her head on her arm on the edge of the toilet. Oh hell, she thought, when her stomach started to cramp again. What had she done? The mixing of the alcohol and the pills was a mistake.

She felt as if she'd been smashed by a semi. Still her mind wandered to the man waiting for her. She knew what she'd done and for a moment the loneliness was gone, but what if this made him react even worse than last time? How many emergencies would she have to have for him to show up willingly? Exhausted, she drifted off into drunkard's bliss.

Victor patiently waited. He heard Xandy puking up her night's merriment. When the sounds came less often, he called out, "Xandy, you okay in there?"

He was greeted by complete silence.

Victor walked over to the bathroom, cracked the door to check on her, and found her passed out on the toilet's rim. Retrieving and wetting a washcloth, he reached over, and wiped her mouth. She'd have a killer headache in the morning, he thought.

He picked her up and carried her barely clad body to her large bed. Gently, he placed her down on the smooth cotton sheets and covered her up with a blanket.

Back in the bathroom, with the used condom still covering his deflating member, he looked down to see that the condom was torn. Panic gripped him. He felt his heart in his throat. *What the hell happened?*

"Oh shit! Shit."

The fates decided they had to throw a little extra spice into the scenario.

Damn.

Chapter 8

October 15

Victor stood at the front of the capacity filled conference room. Scruffy and with dark shadows etched into his face, he absently stared straight ahead. His night had been shorter than usual, and leaving Xandy alone in bed so he could head down to the station was not the way he'd imagined their first time having sex to go.

The fresh image of the body of Professor Gentry hung on the white dry erase board, next to the prior two victims. They were running against the clock, and every day that they didn't have a trail increased the risk of another body bag arriving at the morgue. Another homicide victim on his ever lengthening list of unsolved crimes. The serial killer wanted nothing more than to wreak havoc on his city. He tightened his fist around the podium's wood where he stood, looking out at the already tired faces of his officers.

"Although I would like to deny what we all have been thinking for the last few days, the newest deceased has cemented our beliefs. The total body count now numbers three– three victims, three locations and three professions. I'm sure you've noticed the pictures of the victims pinned to the boards. I know we are currently undermanned, and more hours are going to be spent on this, but we also have the duty to keep this city safe.

"We need to comb through the last twenty-four hours of their lives, and maybe figure out a pattern for why they were chosen, and ultimately find a suspect. Run their DNA in the system, socials, whatever it takes.

"I've assigned Detectives Monroe and Hobbes to work on this case. This is top priority. Everyone else will do the needed research, look in the files for any clues and report back. Are there any questions?"

"Why haven't we called in the FBI?" asked a recent recruit to the force.

"We ask them in, only when we need them," said Hobbes. "We usually don't take kindly to outsiders fiddling around with our city." He glared at Monroe.

"Sure makes for a turbulent partnership," Monroe said.

"Are there any more questions?" asked Victor. After a moment's pause and no questions, he said, "Good. Let's go catch this motherfucker."

"What have you done?" Rebecca screamed into the telephone.

Xandy was still feeling the remnants of last night's partying and her memory of last night was foggy at best. Her mouth was dryer than the Sahara, and her head ached as if drums were being played inside it. "What are you talking about?"

"What am I talking about?" Not giving Xandy a chance to respond, she said, "Some man was here and tried to attack me. But he didn't know he chose the wrong woman to attack. The only thing he said was that this shit was from you. I don't know where he got your name from, but I opened up a can of whip ass on him, and then called the cops on him. Talking some crazy –ish to me because of you. So I'm going to ask you again. What have you gotten yourself involved in?"

Xandy gulped.

"I'm waiting for an answer."

"Okay. Okay. I think it's something that Thornton did. He stole some money from some drug dealer."

"Do you have it?"

Xandy forced a laugh. "If I did, don't you think I'd be living better than I am?"

Rebecca paused. "I don't think you're telling me everything, and considering I just got into a fight about it, you owe me the truth. But I'm willing to give you time to tell it to me."

"I'll get this worked out. Do you want to stay here with me for a couple of nights?"

"Hell no! They are after you, and if he comes back, I got something for him. No one is going to scare me out of my house. No one!"

"We have a new order of business today," said Mayor Carey from his seat at the head of the City Council's conference room table. "The contents of this meeting are not to be released to anyone outside of this room. I have conversed with the relevant authorities and the best we can do is try not to alarm the citizens of this city." He paused seeing the other council members turning to one another and hearing their hushed tones.

"Three bodies have been discovered over a period days. State and local officials are already involved in trying to apprehend the individual responsible for this, but should we release this to the public, we take the risk of ending up with a copycat and a lot more victims. So until we hear more from the authorities, we will just have to sit on this. Chief Zimmerman is here to answer any of your questions."

The police chief slowly approached the podium. His gold badge gleamed, as if freshly polished, and his white and blue uniform sat perfectly on his tall fit frame. "As you all are aware it isn't only the number of victims that's alarming; it is the way they had been mutilated and killed. This information has been leaked to the media, including details of the killer's calling card. Additionally, I have my officers, sector lieutenant and major crime detectives on the case. They are reaching out to the community for leads. The purpose of this news conference is to calm the populace. Due to the prior media leaks, details released are to be kept to a minimum. Nothing is to be said that could cause panic in the city."

Donald Johnson, one of the newest members of the city council, shook his head. "This is doomed to fail! Are you telling me we have a confirmed serial killer on the loose, and you plan on doing nothing but letting this monster run around to find his or her next victim?"

"Councilman Johnson," Chief Zimmerman said, "You are not looking out for what's best in this situation. If we inform the public, we are looking at mass hysteria, pandemonium. I am not saying we shouldn't advise the population to be generally careful, but in no terms do we mention a serial killer." The Chief stared at the politician, for he recognized in him an opportunist ready to use this situation for his betterment. Scowling, he turned to the others.

"This is completely ludicrous. You are being an accessory!" Johnson blurted out.

"Thank you, Chief Zimmerman," Mayor Carey said. "So let us go as a united front with the chief of police and get this press conference over with. I will warn people to be aware of their surroundings and to take care."

"If there are any other questions, please say something at this time," Mayor Carey said.

No questions came.

They headed in to the conference room where the reporters, cameras, and microphones were gathered. The reporters' cameras flashed. It was a feeding frenzy. Flies out for blood.

At the lectern, Chief Zimmerman, like a marionette, did as he was told.

No one contradicted him.

They were too close. A witness? Someone had seen him leave? His disguise might not hold up under close scrutiny.

Someone might recognize him? The killer brooded over his coffee. His hand fisted the white ceramic cup; the cooling robust scent brought back the reason why. The command that it gave.

That one memory.

It made him feel more like a man, more alive, more than anything else, like he existed and that in his world, they still existed together.

He thought of her. Her pale skin. The feel of the blade running against her flesh. His first victim.

The detective was getting too close to finding a smidgen of truth. It required something new. And he knew just what it was. Everything changed.

He would have to change, too.

Chapter 9

October 15

Teary-eyed, with bed head and wrinkled clothes, Troy Gentry sat across from Monroe. "I can't believe she's gone," Troy croaked.

"I'm sorry for your loss," Monroe said. He observed the young man with his almost frat-boy appearance.

"Don't be. She was conniving and self-serving. When she stopped having sex with me, I knew she was seeing someone else. This confirms it even more. She didn't like them older than twenty-five. When I hit the quarter-century mark, she started to look for a new conquest."

Monroe could hear the resentment in his remark, as the tears he'd been trying not to shed fell down his youthful and suntanned face.

"What do you mean?" Monroe asked.

"She was a cougar, always on the prowl, and being a professor with power did nothing to rid her of her need for fresh meat."

"How do I know you didn't do it? You had the anger and opportunity."

"Because I was with my girlfriend, Chastity," he said. His face reddened with the admission. "She's ... she's in the lobby. She cheated, and the only thing I share with her is my last name. We are ... were separated. The last time I spoke with her, she wanted me to water her plants.

She told me that she was leaving on vacation for fall break. I could only assume it was with her newest toy."

"Do you know who he is?"

"I'd assume her teaching assistant," Troy said. "That's how I met her."

The sight of Professor Gentry's mutilated body was heinous. He could only imagine how excruciating the pain must have been for her.

"Sir, I know what you may think of me, but I still loved my wife. I was her second choice, though. She'd think of the newer, tighter body she'd seen in the corridor and say she wished I still looked that way. She missed my naiveté. She saw only my age, nothing more."

"You had motive to kill her, though."

"I had motive, but I still had hope she'd come back to me. I thought she loved me, I really did. Now, I can never get that back. I can never get her back." Troy's voice cracked.

"Do you know how I can contact the student assistant?"

"Her cell phone. Everything was in there."

"Was there anything else missing, that you are aware of? Can you identify if this is your wife's jewelry?"

Monroe pulled out a picture of the watch recovered from the scene and passed it to him.

"I've never seen it before and to tell you the truth, she wouldn't wear something like that. It's too common."

"Is there anything else you can think of that you like to add?"

"Yes, actually. When I picked up my wife's car, her license plates were missing."

Monroe made a note of the missing license plate number: UNIPROF. It was one more thing he'd have to relay. "Thanks for coming in," he said. With Gentry's departure, he couldn't help but wonder now if the killer also took the plates.

Monroe glanced at the list of items taken from the scene. Like the others before her, Professor Gentry's watch had been broken. And compared to the cheapness of the one on her arm, it meant that the killer took the real one and replaced it, but why? What was the message he wanted to send?

"Start from the beginning!" Blackwell ordered. He stared at his black and blue private investigator across from him.

"I was doing what you asked me to do. I didn't know she would be able to do some kung fu shit on me," Webbie said. His eye was swollen shut, and blood still crusted his nose. "She was worse than a ninja!"

"You still gave her my message?"

"Of course I did! But, instead of my hand staying connected to her neck, she sort of gave me a good kick to the groin. Once I let up, all I remember is her pounding on me with her fist and feet. I got out of there as quick as I could. I'm sure she called the cops, though. I saw blue lights not long afterwards."

"Why were you still there?"

"With the blue lights, the neighbors came out and everything. I couldn't just speed away. No one saw me though." With that, Webbie grinned like a fifth grader after a game of baseball – he'd taken a base even though he took one to the face. "What now? What do you want me to do?"

"Sit tight. I need to find out if that worked. If not, then I'll find a better distraction. What you couldn't do, he can."

Marilyn Feife jogged at Byrd Park around Swan Lake. The cold chill of the day was left behind, as sweat poured down her dancer's body. The winter hours left the city covered in darkness, and the glow of street lights was sprinkled throughout. The tennis court lights shone in the distance.

Officially, the park closed at dusk, but she had only one more lap and then she could head back to her apartment a couple of minutes away. Normally the lack of people didn't disturb her, but since she'd seen what happened to the professor, she'd made an extra effort not to jog alone.

"Marilyn, I have to head back," Honor said.

"I only have one more lap."

"It may be one, but for me, it is going to feel like 20. I like the idea of jogging, but I am still not at your level yet."

"Can't you wait for me? Or I can even go slower. We can walk the last round."

"It's almost dark out here, and Jay is coming to pick me up. How about this, I'll wait for you here."

It was a better compromise than being completely alone.

"It won't take me long. I'll go extra fast," Marilyn said and grinned in relief.

"I'll call Jay and let him know I'll be a little late." Honor retrieved her cell phone from her jacket pocket.

"Thanks you're the best!" With a quick wave, Marilyn started her final lap.

Music from her iPod blared in Marilyn's ears. She jogged toward Boat Lake and tried not to think about the night the professor was murdered. Feeling her muscles, she slowed her pace.

Suddenly a man approached her. He could have been attractive in that older-man sort of way, if he hadn't had such a wolfish stare. It was almost as if he looked through her, she thought.

Marilyn knew that face, but wasn't sure from where.

He reached out to grab her arm. Marilyn jerked away

and ran back toward where Honor waited. There were no other pedestrians in her area of the park, and no houses close enough to run to. It was the one spot on her run where she was truly isolated.

Marilyn screamed!

The images of death, her death, burst before her eyes like light bulbs being turned on and off. Her heart stampeded against her ribs. Her lungs burned. Her muscles ached. Her momentum was slipping. Her pulse thudded in her ears. She could taste the bile in her throat.

She felt him upon her before she saw him.

His gloved hand snatched her to him and covered her mouth, muffling her scream. She kicked and clawed like a feral cat.

All to no avail.

The needle filled with succinylcholine pricked her.

And suddenly she was trapped in her own skin.

Metro News

Mayor Howard Carey and Greater Richmond Police Chief Sidney Zimmerman assured residents that the city was still safe. Despite these claims, sources have speculated that a serial killer, whom they call the 'Thou Shall Not' Killer, has struck again. The body of Professor Walker Gentry was discovered in her office on the Morris Stuart Community College campus early on the morning of October 14. A preliminary autopsy is scheduled within the coming days.

This year has been especially tough on law enforcement with budget cuts, additional man-hours required and the falling numbers of officers, as surrounding counties offer both higher pay and better benefits.

This marks the seventy-ninth homicide this year.

Monroe leaned back in his desk chair. His fifteen minute break was almost over. It was hard to escape news of the so-called 'Thou Shall Not Killer,' but at least the newspaper wasn't releasing too much information about the victims or causes of death. Reluctantly, he tossed down the newspaper and opened the Gentry file that required his immediate attention.

The investigation notes, autopsy reports and the list of evidence recovered he placed to the side. Instead, he first focused on the crime scene pictures. His trained eye studied the blood spatter and pools, the angle of the scissors' entrance into the chest, the stitching.

Turning to his computer, he double clicked on the Crimtech software shortcut on his desktop and entered the data from each of the crime scenes, ranging from the blood-soaked rocks, the trajectory of the victim's blood, and the lack of defensive wounds. After the entry of the parameters, Crimtech began to search the databases for cases, solved and unsolved, that fit the current crime spree. Did a prior victim already fit the description when the first body was discovered? Monroe wondered.

Grabbing the crime scene pictures from the third murder again, he scrutinized them. The brown carpet was soaked with rust-brown colored blood.

The killer wasn't playing with his victims, but was intent on killing them painfully. Two of the three murders suggested the release of pent-up rage. The murderer almost seemed to vent. Yet for the second murder, something was different. Maybe it was that it was a death of one quick thrust. There wasn't a lot of blood, nor was there an unleashed passion. What was the reason for the difference?

With this in mind, Monroe scanned Gentry's criminal history. She was previously charged with raping a college freshman during a professor-student "meet and greet." It didn't help that the victim was barely eighteen.

Shortly before eight, Monroe dialed Gary Allen's telephone number. He tapped his pencil and hoped the

Assistant Commonwealth's Attorney wasn't already scheduled for trial. He'd already left a couple of messages and had yet to receive a call back.

"Gary here," Gary said in a chipper voice.

"This is Detective Monroe."

"Monroe, yeah sorry about that. My case load has been outrageous. How can I help you today?"

"I'm calling to find out a little about my victims, Diane Smith, Ilene Kernbach and Walker Genrty."

"I had my paralegal pull their files and was just about to put together an email for you. All three of them were charged with different crimes, as you are aware. Their outcome was also similar. All three had their charges dismissed."

"Why would that happen usually?"

"It is used in our discretion and taken on a case by case situation. In these three cases, when several charges are present, we offer a plea deal. For Smith and Kernbach they had restitution, court fees and if they completed their court ordered counseling, then the charges were to be dismissed. Often we will also reduce the sentence from a felony to a misdemeanor if certain terms are met."

"And Gentry?"

"For Gentry, the victim rescinded her complaint and refused to testify. Without a victim, you can't have a case. Gentry's charges were completely dismissed and I believe she went straight back to work and received her full salary for time missed."

"She was able to walk free with no strings attached?" Monroe asked. He could hear the hardness creeping into his voice.

"Detective, sometimes that is how the cards fall."

"Thanks for your help." Monroe ended the call and attempted to find the killer's catalyst. Each of the three victims had money, status, and a criminal record.

Three predators walked free with the court's blessing.

A homicide investigation usually required looking into the victim's immediate circle, but Monroe knew a serial murderer didn't always need a connection. The motivation as presented at the crime scenes and observable behavior would present the most reliable information to determine the identity of the killer. The murders took place during the night, and discovery was usually in the morning hours, by either cleaning crews, security staff, or in the case of Gentry, the unlucky student assistant wondering where his meal-ticket went.

"Sorry to interrupt, Detective, but I wanted to give you the toxicology report, since Captain Hawthorne was unavailable," Dr. Reynolds said. He handed Monroe the manila folder. Opening it, Monroe scanned the reports. "Pancuronium was found in their systems?"

"Yes. Considering that we located injection sites on all three victims, I believe it was injected and used to debilitate the women."

"It's a paralytic?"

"It is one of many, but this one is used so often that there has been a shortage recently. It's called the 'Pink Juice' in vet circles but isn't really a street drug. It is most often used in lethal injections."

"If that's the case, I wonder how he'd get it."

"I'd check the weakest link: vet offices. Since it requires a prescription, check and see if there have been any recent veterinarian clinics that have been burglarized."

"Thanks for the tip, Doc."

Pulling up the Crimtech program again, he typed in his new query, and waited for it to spit out what he expected might be his second solid lead.

Vaginal mutilation could also be evident for a misogynist or could it be a crime of passion? Monroe wondered. It was certainly uncommon. Gentry's vaginal mutilation embodied a hate that in itself could only be regarded as torture, but for what? Did the professor confess to something? Could that be the key of what made the crime scenes of kills one and two different from number three?

Victim one was found after a church service, victim two had been painting, but victim three was not associated with anything that could connect her to a crime for which she had previously been charged. Could that be the reason for the overkill?

The software's output confirmed his conclusion. Although the cases had similar patterns as those exhibited by prior famed serial killers, the method of killing was new. There was no record of one convicted for a crime of this nature with this methodology. Additionally, in the prior case files, a sedative or tranquilizer was used to assist in the transporting of a victim; however, there was no evidence to suggest that the victims in the present spree were tranquilized for only such a purpose. The current murders took place where the bodies were discovered, suggesting that they were never moved from one location to another.

Unless she was strong and agile, Monroe assumed that no female could have done all of this by herself, the lifting of a woman on stage, the carrying of one as well. They were looking for a man. A man confident enough to kill wherever the opportunity presented itself, even if it was not in a place prepared for his purpose.

Monroe looked at the stitching. There was nothing unusual about it, besides the fact that it was in human skin. Could that point to someone in the medical field, someone with medical training?

Then he looked at the tags. Each said the same thing or a variation thereof. The first tag cited 'Thou Shall Not 2023,' while the second tag said, 'Thou Shall Not 58.' The third tag read, 'Thou Shall Not 519.' What was the number in reference to? The Ten Commandments? And if so, weren't they indicative of a universal code of moral conduct?

Googling 'Thou Shall Not', Monroe came across the King James Version Bible. Many Protestants regarded the King James as the authoritative translation, but those commandments read "Thou shalt not." For the overzealous, to change even one letter meant to change God's word. Could this small change be indicative of the killer's desire to live outside of the commandments – saying they applied to others, but not to him? A total disregard?

The file also contained photos of a postcard depicting Nemesis from the first murder, the painting of Cephalus and Procris from the second scene, and the bloody pages of the Tragedy of Phaedra from the professor's office. As if a light went on, he understood: the message was Greek, but it contradicted everything from the tags. The crime scenes pointed to someone interested in Greek history or mythology. Could this be a coincidence? What was he trying to say?

Monroe found an online mythology primer. With the tags, the killer wanted to give them a message. Even if he stayed up all night trying to find the code to decipher the message given, the message and answers were in the crimes themselves.

He needed to look at the qualities of the killer and how they would fit the scenes. As far as the reports stated, there were no fibers, video surveillance, or even defensive wounds. The carpeting at the theatre, museum, and office had been walked over often. There were numerous footprints of multiple sizes, and since neither location had been vacuumed before the murders, it was more difficult to even gather a potential footprint.

Between the reaction time of the drug and their full loss of movement, there had to be time that they could have reacted. That was the only thing that could explain the duct tape. It kept any of them from calling out, from screaming. Whoever was doing this was acting with premeditation, and a calm rage, until the unsettling act.

All the victims had committed crimes in the city and been in the city jail as a result. Their crimes were committed within six weeks of each other. Could they have been in the same pods? If they were in the same pod and knew each other; who else was in the pod? Dialing the records department, it was time to find out if his hunch had credence. Maybe this was the link they were looking for. Right now, it seemed to be the only probable link available. But wouldn't that mean the perpetrator wasn't killing randomly but by a common scheme?

From the profile Monroe had created, the perpetrator was killing according to the Ten Commandments, but killing out of order. The numbers were corresponding to the two locations of the Ten Commandments in the Decalogue – in Exodus and Deuteronomy. He typed in the tag from the first murder in the search engine. The Bible verse of Exodus 20:2, 3 came up. Could it be that the murderer was telling the police why he was killing?

The cited verse specified that no other God was to be worshipped. The main principle of monotheism. Monroe picked up the file for the first victim. Flipping through the pages, he came across the statement as taken down by the magistrate for the original embezzlement charge. He underlined the words: miracle for money, bow before me and I will heal you.

Monroe wasn't a theologian, but he could understand the comparison. Her acts, her self-deification, desire to be worshipped, and egocentrism were the force for the charges. Could the murderer be part of her congregation, or maybe even the complainant for the charges?

Monroe bolted from his chair. Grabbing the printout, he headed to the last known address for Chase Deerfield, who was listed as the initial filer of the complaint, to find out what happened.

"Marilyn hasn't made her way around here yet," Honor said as she continued to talk on her cell phone with Jay and stretch her muscles from her run. "I'm giving her five more minutes, and then I'm leaving," she said flustered.

"You know how Marilyn is, easily distracted," Jay said on the other end of the line.

Honor scanned the distance and saw porch lights beginning to turn on, but she still saw no one rounding the corner, and with the hilly park, parts of their trek had Marilyn out of her view. A slight chill began to rise up her back as the wind blew, cooling her off.

"She still isn't back. What do you think I should do?"

"You know I have tickets tonight. If you want to blow me off for your friend, what can I say about that?"

Honor bit her lip, as she looked left and right for some sign of her friend. "I'll make a quick lap to see if I can meet her halfway and then head to the apartment. It won't take me long to get ready."

"And if she's off doing her own thing? Remember last time you were waiting on her and she disappeared, only to have met up with her ex, who was playing tennis and they decided to go have coffee? Marilyn is flaky."

"I'll see you soon," Honor said and ended the call. Retying her shoes, she raced after Marilyn hoping to find her friend.

Patricia Abernathy was waiting for Xandy at her desk. With her dynamic and southern sass, coffee complexion, and laughter-filled eyes, she had a way of making even rain appear as sunshine.

"How are you doing this glorious morning?" Patricia asked in her raspy voice.

"Let's just say I've had a couple of hard days. It's been hell," Xandy said. She eased out of her long coat and hurried to get everything just right for the work day.

"Oh, well, if your outfit reflects that, then you need to have a hellacious day or two more often," Patricia said with a soft chuckle. "Did you hear about Marigold?"

Xandy turned on her computer, and heard its familiar hum. After typing in her passwords, she opened her Outlook and assessed the G-drive for new client files. "What's the latest office gossip now?"

Patricia turned her head to make sure no one was near. "Marigold was fired."

Xandy scanned her messages. There were several emails to read informing her of what was expected of her today. "Marigold was fired? For what?"

Leaning closer to Xandy, she said, "Griffin came in on Thursday evening after everyone was gone. He caught Marigold and Roger going at it in the conference room. I'm not sure if he was more aroused or amused by the situation. But I think this was the loan that broke the bank. We both know she was inept as an assistant."

"Isn't Roger married? I'm not even sure Marigold can spell the word *inept*, but it will be a shame to see her go. She did always provide some entertainment. Maybe they wouldn't let him join in." Xandy snickered.

"Married men have needs too, but that's beside the point. I can't believe they'd do it on the conference room table. It hasn't been wiped down since I started working here."

"That's what happens when you make the senior paralegal the director of human resources. They always get to make the call," Xandy said.

"I've been meaning to ask you, and don't think I'm being rude, but why are you still here?"

"Are you kicking me out of my office?"

"No, but why are you still here hidden in the file

room? I know this company has a high turnover rate and that Tom tried to give you an office up front."

"I'm addicted to receiving a paycheck, and let's be honest, Patricia, my history is not an asset to the company. Tom helped me out a lot. I'm not going to take advantage of it."

"Think about getting out of this dungeon. No one here thinks you're less, besides you."

"It would appear my schedule has changed, Xandy," Griffin's voice boomed out of the intercom. "I need you to bring me the Hanson, Metzger, and the Gordon files. I need them on my desk, pronto."

"Sir, I also need to speak with you about –" Xandy said.

"It will have to wait until later."

With a groan, Xandy gathered the files and headed toward Griffin's office.

Griffin Brooks considered himself to be the gateway to the attorneys. His beady eyes and hawk-like perception kept everyone in line and under his thumb. All he needed was a whip to bully the crowd. If the office were a ship, the crew would have threatened mutiny.

Xandy silently stepped into Griffin's office. He ignored her presence, ignored her attempt to speak, and ignored her very existence. She was a ghost to him – invisible.

Back at her desk, she took stock of her situation. Work could only distract so much from the reality that awaited her outside its doors. Her very life depended on solving her own mystery of who was after her and why.

Monroe knocked on the front door of Chase Deerfield's house door. When the door opened, he was greeted by an older man with salt and pepper hair and a clerical collar.

Monroe identified himself. "Mr. Deerfield?"

"Yes, I'm Father Deerfield. How may I help you, son?" Father Deerfield asked in his soothing voice.

"I have a couple of questions about Sister Hannah Salem," Monroe said.

Father Deerfield's brow furrowed with skepticism. "Please come in. I was just about to head out to the local parish to help with giving out food." Father Deerfield led Monroe to his sparsely decorated living room with its polished hardwood floors and dark green walls. "I'm surprised it took you this long to come see me."

"I was hoping and taking a long shot that you might be able to help," Monroe said, taking a seat on the vintage leather sofa.

"When I dealt with Sister Hannah and her ministry, it was based on finances. Basically, we would contact her, and after much effort, emails and the like, almost begging at times, she would then show up." Father Deerfield retrieved a small address book from his desk and flipped through it.

"Did you speak with her directly?"

"Most of the time she was too busy. Instead, I dealt with her associate. I believe his name was Hans. Here is the contact information that I always used." Father Deerfield passed the address book to Monroe, who jotted down the information.

"He was the one who set everything up usually," he continued, "but then again, I do remember a conversation that we had prior to my taking out the charges against her. She was looking for silent partners, or beneficiaries. I am not sure if she ever succeeded, but I might still have some of the information of how the silent partners or supporters would work."

Father Deerfield walked back over to his large desk and started to pull out drawers, one after the other. "My mother used to be a pack rat, so I hardly ever throw anything away. You never know when it might be needed." After finding a manila file and flipping through its contents, he pulled out the routing information for Sister Hannah and gave it to Monroe. "This is what she gave me last, before I was convinced of her treachery."

"If I may ask, Father, how is it that you are now in charge of a parish?" Monroe asked.

"I came back to my calling, you might say. I tried to protect my flock, but the ones in charge at the former church didn't want to listen. But then again, maybe they too were skimming from the top. It's taken a lot of prayer to forgive Sister Hannah. Marriages, families, and friendships were broken because of her lies. I know I shouldn't feel this way, but I sometimes wish I could have been stronger or at least smarter to have had the common sense to act sooner."

"Do you know anyone who wished her harm?"

"Too many people to name. When she was arrested, I remember my congregation rejoicing."

"Rejoicing?"

"Yes, she took from these humble people what they valued the most: their faith."

"A crime worthy of murder?"

"She was an apostate and deserving of the punishment so divinely ordained. What the legal system failed to do, He made sure to correct."

"Where were you on the night of the 11th?"

Opening another drawer, Rev. Deerfield pulled out another sheet of paper and handed them to Monroe.

"As you can see, I was out of town in Atlanta, speaking at a Believers' Fellowship Church. You can check their website."

Monroe scribbled down the pastor's alibi, promising to check it out.

"I hate to be rude, but I am running a little behind schedule. If you have any additional questions, please give me a call."

In what seemed like a swoop of the pastor's hat, Monroe found himself shown to the front door and was back standing on the stoop.

With his credentials, Lazarus found himself sitting across from the manager of the James Center Bank & Trust without having to jump through too many hoops. Xandy's bank envelope was stuffed into the front pocket of his leather jacket. If a safe deposit box was going to be anywhere, it would make sense to be at the bank she already used.

"Thank you for meeting with me. We spoke earlier regarding a safe deposit box," Lazarus said.

"You're going to have to remind me. What is the name on the account?" the bank teller asked. She pushed her red hair behind her ear and giggled.

Lazarus could feel her gaze perusing every inch of his toned body. Since the only thing he had was his charming smile and a copied key, he could only hope it would be enough to get what he needed.

She waved her hands over the keyboard, as if performing magic. The bank teller tilted her head and stared. "We've had a lot of interest regarding Mr. Gage. However, I am unable to provide you with any information since Mr. Gage assigned a deputy for the box."

Lazarus winked slightly and leaned forward. "I understand, Missus–"

"Miss, but you can call me Sara."

"The thing is this. I have the key for the box -"

"The keys? Mr. Gage's box requires two keys and the signature of his assigned deputy. Without a court subpoena, I am unable to provide you with any additional information."

"Can you tell me who I need to speak with about Mr. Gage's accounts and assets since he is deceased? Is there a next of kin listed or someone to contact in case of an emergency perhaps?"

"Yes. You will need to speak with Alexandria Caras."

"Monroe," Victor called him over into his office.

Monroe sighed. Hobbes wasn't around for another unscheduled meeting, which meant he'd have to bring the Captain up to speed on how things were progressing. Taking a seat, Monroe noticed Victor's square face was absent all emotion.

"Detective," Victor said. His voice was grave. Sitting across from Victor, Monroe could see the dark circles under his eye.

"These murders..." Victor pinched the bridge of his nose. "What have you got for me?"

"Well, I'm running information through the software, and–"

"That's not good enough. I need more than that. How are we supposed to investigate, if we don't know who we're looking for?"

"Everything I have is preliminary, but this individual has a lot of time to find out someone's weakness."

"The longer we wait, the colder the trail gets. I have to catch whoever is doing this–" The telephone interrupted Victor with its blaring ring.

"The killer is murdering women regardless of age, but they are all linked. Their lives overlap at the jail. I spoke with the jail's records' department. All three women were incarcerated during the same six week period. Salem couldn't make bail that fast, the Berkley family put pressure on the CA to make sure Kernbach wouldn't get released, and although only in jail over the weekend, from a Friday to Monday, Gentry still fits into the time scheme.

"Although it would appear that the killer's focus is their criminal charges, and especially those charges which have previously been dismissed, I think it could be more. These are not random women, but connected. The person we need to find is religious, but has his own god-complex, as he has equated himself with the Biblical God and the Greek gods. This is based on the fact that their charges seem to align with the Ten Commandments, or at least his understanding of them."

"We're looking for a preacher?" Victor shouted.

"I don't think so. This guy is highly organized, meticulous, but filled with rage, which seems to make him a little more careless. Because of how he is killing, I think he must have done this before without getting caught. I'm cross-checking the databases now to see if there are any crimes that have been committed that fit our victim profile. It seems to be godly retribution for their deeds, especially since two of the three victims were found after doing something similar to what their criminal charges were dismissed for. A feeling of justice being served."

"Do you think it's someone connected to these cases? An attorney, judge, or officer?"

"I can't rule that out because of his knowing the victim's past charges, since this is the one link we've been able to make between the three women. He will have either medical experience or a rudimentary understanding of the human body, or be involved with or have an understanding of animal slaughtering. As far as we are aware, he has not killed any men, which could mean that he regards women as the source of his psychological problems and stress. Due to the lack of physical evidence left at the scenes and on the bodies, I do believe that the individual has some knowledge of police protocol and may consider himself to be an honorary officer, if not a real one."

"One of our men?" Victor asked. "You think one of *us* is doing this?"

"Whoever he is, he is able to have contact with this part of society. He has contact with his victims, which is substantiated through Salem's phone records and Kernbach's date book, where he used the name Johannes Mensch, which is an equivalent of John Doe. Because of the intricate details and planning, I surmise that he has an above-average I.Q., and prides himself on thinking of every feasible hindrance. This signifies that his crimes are premeditated, scoped out in advance. In each case where video surveillance should have existed, he has slipped in like a ghost.

"He also takes mementos of his kill by taking the watches of the victims and leaving another behind. These watches are neither at the crime scenes nor at the victim's lodgings or dwellings. Additionally, he has left behind items relating to Greek mythology referencing Nemesis, which could be equated to retribution; Cephalus and Procris is thought to refer to an illusion of some sort; and, the *Tragedy of Phaedra* is based on forbidden love. He is connecting mythology to their crimes.

"Since I believe he's been contacting them, I've started checking the records for the telephone numbers dialed and calls received by the victims, including the cell tower reports. Because he is not hiding the bodies or leaving the city, I believe he is interested in only getting the attention of the city's police."

"Why us?" Victor asked. "We could call in the Feds at any moment. Do you believe he thinks we've done something wrong?"

"Not something wrong, but someone. Maybe it is also a personal vendetta, I just don't know."

"What are we looking for then?"

"A man with the agility and physique to kill like a barbarian, but also the cognitive ability to think it through and not be seen as a threat. He is the ultimate chameleon, regarded as a soft soul. He gets their attention, gains their trust and then takes advantage of it. It could be that it takes days, weeks, even months for him to get enough information to do what he needs to do, to ensure that his 'righteous justice' is needed. These women's crimes are over twelve months old. That being the case, he had at least that much time to not only concoct his plans, but to ensure their success. And so far, hasn't failed."

"That could be anyone," Victor said.

Monroe turned and looked at the men and women in the bullpen. He knew they were capable of doing great good. But from what his gut and research told him, one of them had a capacity for not just harm, but pure evil.

Who was the monster in their midst?

With the day's task completed, the killer sat back and focused on the woman's gold wrist watch, which gleamed in the light. The circular dial adorned with diamond accents and small droplets of blood reminded him of why he slaughtered them.

She'd want him to remember.

The killer tossed the newspaper into the green recycling bin. He didn't need another article or a "brag" book for his trophies. Removing a panel from his wooden sideboard, he placed his newest addition into his ever-growing collection.

Time was of the essence.

Now that they knew it was a cop, he had to make sure they knew which one.

Chapter 10

October 15

The day had been long, fading from one task to the next, until it was late evening. By eleven o'clock, with a new batch of rain-sleet mix lightly falling, Xandy finally closed the last file cabinet drawer and filed away the last expandable folder.

Xandy turned and made sure everything was in its place. She grabbed her coat and purse, picked up her office phone and dialed security.

"Good evening, Nick. This is Xandy. I'm going to be heading out."

"I'll meet you downstairs."

Nick met Xandy dressed in his black and white security uniform. He looked the part, but he was qualified for so much more, she knew.

"Ms. Caras, if you're ready, I can take you to your car," Nick said.

"Why so formal tonight?" Xandy asked.

"My supervisor is up my ass about being overly friendly instead of being professional. It's just his way of telling me to 'know my place' when dealing with people," he said, making air quotes and offering Xandy a sideways smile. "It's really smart of you to use my service, especially with the weird killings happening all over town."

Her heart thudded at his words. "What killings?" Xandy asked.

"It's been everywhere! Don't you read the paper? Watch the news? I don't know much, but from what I've been hearing, there has been a string of gruesome murders. One was yesterday or the day before at Morris Stuart Community College; some professor was murdered, and the other day, there was another murder at the museum."

"I guess I've been caught up a little bit in myself. When did this happen exactly?"

"I heard about it today, but I'm not sure when it occurred. Some white shirt was talking about it."

Xandy didn't want to think about more death. She thought he'd continue, but she then realized she was already at her car.

"Take care, Ms. Caras, and be safe out here. The roads are a little slick, but maybe it'll help to get rid of the rest of this white mess." With a tip of his hat, Nick headed back toward the building.

"I will. Thanks again, Nick," Xandy called after him. The last thing she wanted to think about was another threat. Even in a city this big, she still had the chance of hitting the lotto in a game she wasn't playing.

Brennan enjoyed being close to the heavens during twilight, or so he always told others when they asked. In all truth, he loved being on the roof because it put everything into perspective.

He leaned against the merlon of the crenellated wall of the roof and watched his warm breath materialize. The moonlight reflected off of the river.

Still he couldn't figure out why Aden had betrayed him. It nagged him. As his thoughts roamed, he heard footsteps before seeing his brother's pissed-off face.

"So let me guess. Trouble in paradise?" Brennan

asked.

"I came up here to ask you for a favor," Aden said.

Straightening, Brennan stared at Aden with an austere expression and said, "While you are seeking something from me, please be so kind in turn as to inform my ex-wife, your lover, that her presence is not welcome in my house."

Aden paused at the mention of his relationship with Jocelyn. "Brennan, I do want to talk to you about Jocelyn ...."

Hearing Aden even mention his relationship with Jocelyn riled Brennan. "Save your words. You could have given me a little foreplay before you fucked me! What you did to me was worse than what she could ever do!"

Brennan took a step toward him. His fist clenched. He wanted to beat the shit out of his brother, in spite of the fact that he'd sworn to protect him, even at his own pain.

He couldn't do it, though. Aden and Emily were the only family he had. He couldn't hurt him, even if Aden did the same to him.

"One day, you are going to have to hear what I have to say about Jocelyn, if you want to or not."

"Get the fuck out," Brennan said through clenched teeth. He turned back to his view and ignored Aden's sullen retreat.

Xandy had suppressed any thought of him all day until she returned home and saw her still disheveled bed. Victor had left without a word sometime during the night. Maybe it had been a mistake. Sure, she'd been a little wasted, and taking the Valium with the alcohol did nothing to curb her inhibitions. Instead, she'd thrown herself at him as soon as he walked through her door. Usually her judgment was better, but dealing with Victor wasn't a part of her normal routine.

If they continued like that, she knew soon she'd be

hooked. The idea of loving someone again almost hurt.

Xandy grabbed her bottle of Valium. She stared at the orange plastic container. It had been her constant companion. She reached for the glass of water, and with the pill in her hand, she caught her reflection in the bathroom mirror. Was she even ready to love again? For a moment, she was taken back to then.

She looked into Thornton's pale face. The silence was deafening. For that one moment, she could feel his angst, his tangible fear. The sweat on his brow and on top of his lip. He stared into her soul. His palms tightened on her arms.

Xandy dropped the pill in the sink and followed it with running water. The water caught hold of the pill, lifted it up like rushing waves carrying debris. Around and around it went, until it escaped into the dark hole. Staring at the bottle that contained her safety net, she grabbed it and tossed its contents into the sink. One by one, she watched the pills disappear until all that was left was clear, cool water.

It was late. He'd been the cat playing with his mouse for hours. She was a tortured soul like he knew she'd be. Now, it went from exciting to mundane. And even worse: risky.

He'd taken her to his kingdom, where he could still hear the river's water flowing and in the distance, a train.

The longer he let her live, the higher the chance someone would hear something.

And he wasn't ready to finish his overall game. No, not yet when he still had so many peas in the pod to smash one by one.

Her sobs had lessened, and in the almost too quiet darkness, he wondered what they'd say when they saw his latest gesture. It would be almost as dramatic as sticking his middle finger up.

Rising from his resting place, with his knees bent, he leaned toward her. She sat in an old wooden chair, hands and feet tied to it.

Her movement was limited.

And escape impossible.

Chapter 11

October 16

Another day was over; twenty-four hours had passed since her last pill. The metallic taste in Xandy's mouth was strong, her heart continued to race and everything whirled about her. She was caught up in her own cyclone of withdrawal.

Xandy stood in her bathroom, wrapped in a towel, scouring her tongue and teeth of the awful taste. The lights flickered.

Tapping sounds came from the living room. As she walked on the carpeted floors, water still trickling down her body from her shower, the sound of the front doorknob's rattle caught her attention.

Her already galloping heart shifted into overdrive, almost bursting through her chest. She inched forward as the doorknob continued to twist and turn. Her body quaked with each breath.

Closer, she heard a louder thump and then a thud against the door.

The lights flickered again.

Then all was quiet.

Xandy cracked the door open. Flooded with fear, she peeked into the dark hallway, seeing no one.

She slammed the door shut, bolting it once again behind her. Her hands shook.

Feeling someone watching her, she rushed over to the living room windows to draw the curtains. She glanced out into the night. The streetlights illuminated the parking lot, where, she saw a lone figure sitting in a car staring back at her.

Cars came and went in the luxurious apartment complex. In spite of the weather, people still moved around, bundled in thick coats. Instead of rushing on the assumed slickness of the ground, some almost stood still in their walk from their cars to the building.

Lazarus watched Xandy's apartment from the safety of his rental car. He had a clear view of the front of her building, which housed several units. There were two entrances: one in the front and one in the back. Both entrances required a pass code or key for access.

With the night-vision binoculars focused on her living room window, Lazarus saw Xandy's face for a millisecond before she turned off the light and yanked the curtains closed.

"Damn," Lazarus muttered and placed the binoculars back on the car seat. His hands were already half-frozen. He rubbed them together and continued to stare at the window where he couldn't see anything. Was his cover already blown?

The Captain had put the pressure on him to prove his allegations. It wouldn't bode well if he couldn't do surveillance.

Pulling his hat down to cover his face a little, he started the ignition.

He had other ways to waste time, and watching curtains was not one of them.

Upon his arrival, Brennan saw the police officer get into his cruiser. Brennan had heard of house calls, but this was ridiculous. He had tried for days to get out of having to see her again, to have to speak to her again, but with Victor, there was no way around it, not with blowing off his prior request. Victor was unable to leave the office to see to Xandy personally. Damn that serial killer, Brennan thought.

To rush out in the dead of night as a favor to a friend to drive over to the apartment of a woman he barely knew — all to chase after the boogeyman — was asking too much.

Exiting his car, he headed to the address given to him by Victor. He climbed to the second floor apartment and knocked.

"Who is it?" Not waiting for a response, Xandy threw open the door.

"You really should wait for an answer before you open the door," Brennan said. He looked at Xandy's pale face, and fingered-through hair. She looked past frightened, wearing baggy jogging pants and a shirt large enough to fit a linebacker.

"What are you doing here? Where's Victor?" Xandy asked. Confusion marred her features.

"He asked me to stop by and check in on you."

"For what? If I wanted a baby-sitter, I would have hired one," Xandy retorted.

"Do you really want to have this conversation with me in the hallway?" Brennan asked. He cocked his eyebrow and stared at her.

Xandy hesitantly moved away from the door, allowing him to enter.

"I can go if you want." He could almost hear her unsaid words telling him to take his bravado and leave. But then that would entail more minutes, and hours of being alone. And more of a chance that whoever had watched her would return. Instead she walked over toward the open kitchen.

"No ... no, please stay," Xandy said.

The apartment didn't match her outward appearance. It was warm, inviting, and bold with its dark maroon and cream walls. Everything had its place, or so it seemed. She didn't seem to be like that, at least any more. "How long have you been living here?" Brennan's gaze never faltered.

"That is what you think of? Asking me such a question at a time like this ... I've been here for the last four years. I just never got around to redecorating the place."

"Hmmm," Brennan said. "And why did you choose to live out here? It seems sort of out of the way from the life of the Fan and what people your age like to do."

"I'm guessing I've sort of outgrown that lifestyle. I felt...feel safe here... Thornton thought it would be better if we lived together. This used to be our place... until, you know."

"Why don't you sit down?" Brennan ushered her to the couch and walked into her kitchen. He opened cabinet door after cabinet door, slamming one shut only to open the next one.

"Is there something I can help you find?" Xandy asked.

"I'm trying to get to know you, understand you. I've read that the best place to come to know someone is through his or her kitchen. Just testing my theory."

"You're patronizing me, I can tell."

"No, I'm not. I'm really curious about how a girl like you could be afraid and live in a place like this."

"A *girl* like me? A lot of things go bump in the night."

"You're holding up okay."

"If I were, I don't think you'd be here," Xandy snapped. She pulled her feet under her and her hands into the cuffs of her shirt. "But I do think you're way too comfortable in my kitchen."

Within minutes, Brennan appeared with a hot cup of chamomile tea. "This should help calm you down some," he said, passing the cup to her.

"You didn't put anything in it, did you, like a sedative?"

"Let's get to the topic at hand," he said. He took a seat in her armchair and ignored her question.

"I'm glad you're here." For that moment, her words rang true between them.

"From what you've told me previously and with the events of tonight, I believe you have a stalker." Glancing away, Brennan leaned back in her comfortable armchair. "There are usually three reasons for stalking, and I hope by going over this list, we can try to narrow down who the stalker is. The stalker uses his or her techniques in order to try to control the victim, physically and emotionally. His goal is to get to you, and he is going to try anything and everything. Fear tactics. Is there anyone you suspect?"

"Yes ... no. I know you don't believe me when I say that things are out of synch. I feel like I am being watched, and whoever it is, is coming closer."

Brennan kept his poker face. Since she'd reappeared at the station and spoken with Victor, he'd heard a lot of murmuring and musing about her. She was considered a cold-blooded killer, but the woman across from him resembled more of a scared child than a woman who could probably shoot a playing card six times before it reached the ground.

"I ... I should really go." Brennan stood to leave.

"Don't. Please stay...just a little longer." He could see in her brown eyes the waking nightmare clawing at her soul. "Detective Tal–"

"Please call me Brennan, just Brennan," he said. He reluctantly took his seat again.

"I'd like that," Xandy said with tight-lipped smile.

Xandy chattered away about anything and everything. The tightness in her face lessened with each tidbit of conversation. He noticed her posture begin to slouch, and the fear relinquishing its grip. Yet, he knew in the silence, it was only a whisper away. During a pause, her idle talk finally turned into a slight snore. Something wasn't right, he knew. It was easy for him to act nonchalant about the situation, but in all honesty, he was disturbed.

Brennan was tempted to stay the night. Instead, he dodged the couch, choosing the stand-alone armchair. The urge to protect her from harm was almost physical and overwhelming, but he was ordered to check on her, not spend the night and not worry about the possibility of someone coming back. He was there for information only, any growing attraction be damned.

He reached into his pocket and retrieved his cell phone, dialing Victor's number. "We need to talk. I have an update on the situation here."

"Meet me at the station," Victor said.

"I hope you know what you're doing. There appears to be a connection, more than at first assumed." Empathy would be his undoing. He knew Lazarus wasn't capable of hurting her; he was just overzealous. "I can't get involved with this." Brennan said. "It's a conflict of interest."

"Just do me this favor. I promised myself I'd look out for her and her well-being. You're a cop and you have the smarts to access what is going on behind the scenes. I need her to be protected and nothing is better than one of us looking out for her. Think about Lazarus out there after her. You and I both know that her biggest threat is that cop; one that you've analyzed that's still on the streets. You're indebted to her for this, too."

Brennan didn't like the idea. His gut churned. His mouth dried at the thought of someone hurting her.

Victor didn't like smudging the line between right and wrong, but not everything had to be either black or white. Could he trust Brennan to do anything for him? IIe felt like a burr was stinging his backside, but then again, maybe it was just the threat looming over his head like a guillotine's blade about to come falling down.

Victor stared out at the officers under his command. They had no idea of the shakeup about to come. There were enough titles thrown around to make anyone fear. It could have been like the military, he imagined, with all the majors, lieutenants and his own title of captain. They were his men, though. He knew them all well, and the memo on his desk was proving that he was going to have to bet on them taking down the killer before he murdered not only his career but also the woman he was starting to love.

Chapter 12

October 17

She was suffocating; the air was almost nonexistent in her lungs. Maureen Hyatt kneeled down in the storage room, hyperventilating. She pushed the paper bag to her face and breathed in and out. Tears of panic ran down her makeup-covered face.

Any other place would have been better than returning to Richmond. Any other city would have been a success; but here, the feeling of failure clawed her spine like a cat climbing a tree. Its nails spiked into her flesh.

It was Richmond, the place of her shame, of her near downfall – what she could never forget.

The hairs on the back of her neck stood on end. She turned and saw the polished shoes next to her. Turning slightly, she noticed the silhouette of the man before her.

"May I help you?" she croaked.

She had no reason to fear, but something in the air made her want to flee. The storage compartment was empty. Everyone had left hours ago, and she'd stayed behind to have a moment with her statue and to compose herself. She was to meet with the governor, who she didn't vote for, to honor a history that she disavowed.

"Yes, we spoke on the phone. I'm here to see the statue," he said.

"Yes, I'm sorry. Nerves always have a way of getting to

me."

"I called out when I came in," he said with a slight nod.

"You followed the sounds to find me." She saw him scan the area. He'd called, asking to arrange a time to see her and view the marble statue for an exclusive with the newspaper. She needed the publicity, and pushed the ill feeling down.

"Well, let's get started. If you'll follow me." Maureen rose and walked toward her glorious piece. "I had the men open it for me before they left. As you will see, this is Ode to Hephaestus. I am very inspired by the classics."

The statue depicted the gallant and nude Hephaestus with a raised hammer in one hand and his other hand outstretched forward, as if reaching for something.

"What is he reaching for?"

"His lost love, Andromeda."

She felt him close the space between them. He was too quiet.

"I must say, you sound different from when we spoke on the phone. Do you have any questions so that we can start the interview?"

"Yes. I'd like to start with your charges that were dismissed," he said.

"I'm not here to talk about that." The nervousness she'd suppressed sprang back up. With a downcast glance, she went white with fear.

"I understand that you were jailed with Alexandria Caras?"

Maureen heard the slight sneer in his voice. "If you have no questions about my statue, I think we should conclude this. It has been a long evening, Mister—" She turned back toward him.

He caught her as she turned.

"Yes, too long."

Monroe dialed Marilyn's telephone number again. A sketch drawing was great, but they needed her to look at a lineup. Gentry's teaching assistant sat behind bars at the moment. They'd been able to pick him up after he tried to hock one of Gentry's rings.

Like the last few times he called, he only got voice mail. He hadn't heard from her since she'd been down at the station helping sketch out a profile, but he also knew witnesses suddenly went underground after coming forward on something as serious as murder.

Hearing the beep, he said, "Ms. Feife, this is Detective Monroe again. Please give me a call at your earliest. Thank you."

"Still no luck?" Hobbes asked. Today, he was almost friendly, Monroe thought cocking up an eyebrow. It was another tiring round of Jekyll versus Hyde.

"No, still only voice mail."

"Captain isn't going to be happy to hear that, though."

"Since we all are now suspects in this whole FUBAR situation, no one is going to be happy about our only lead disappearing."

Taking her favorite seat in the window, Xandy stared out over the busy street, watching people meander by. Dr. Edwards had asked another question she couldn't answer. He just wanted to keep probing her wounds.

"I shot him! I know this, and I've explained my regret. If I could take it back…. How does reliving my nightmare over and over help me? I know what happened and so should you. Is it your goal to make me fall to pieces each and every time? Is that what your success rate is based on? I don't want to talk about it, not today."

Dr. Edwards blanched at her remark. After a longer pause, he asked, "Then what's bothering you today?"

"I'm fine. Better than fine. I don't need this anymore. I don't need any of this crap anymore. I'm not a criminal!

With one overzealous cop following me, watching my every move and now a stalker, I'm starting to think that I'm a magnet for psychos, weirdos and the mentally deranged." Xandy took a breath. That was more than she'd said in months of counseling, and with more gusto. "I'm sorry, that's why I don't want to talk about it. I'm trying to take steps to get better, and looking back is not helping. It will be my undoing."

"What about the stalker?"

"It's getting out of control. The other night he was so close."

"The other night?"

"Whoever it is, is getting closer... dangerously close." Xandy then continued to tell him about what had transpired and what she'd found.

"Do you know who it is?"

"No." She wasn't going to tell him about Lazarus, the devil that wanted her own soul, or Lauren, the woman who wanted nothing more than to be her personal affliction.

"Why do you think you are being stalked? As you are aware, paranoia can also induce hallucinations."

"I know someone wants me dead!"

"Have you told the police this?"

"Of course, just like I'm telling you. But instead of getting real help, I get a pencil pusher as a chaperone. To them, I'm just a nut."

"When was the last time you took your medication?"

She crossed her arms. "I stopped taking it," she said.

"You should have conferred with me before you made such a decision."

"I'm telling you now, aren't I?"

"I'll reduce the dosage for you instead," he said. "By choosing to get off of it, and go 'cold turkey,' you've placed yourself in a precarious predicament. You could experience several withdrawal symptoms, ranging from anxiety, fatigue, insomnia, nausea, agitation, irritability, crying spells, and visual hallucinations, just to name a few." Dr. Edwards scribbled down a new prescription and thrust the piece of paper toward her.

Eyeing the outstretched piece of paper, Xandy jumped up from her seat. "I have to go."

Dr. Edwards also stood up and called after her. "Before you go, please see Anika and get a copy of the pamphlet. I'll buzz her to let her know which one."

Over the months, Xandy had never ended a session with him, but there was always a first. With her shoulders squared and her strut determined, she strode out of Dr. Edwards's office.

Xandy trudged into the well-adorned church. Her head ached and the pain itself was almost blinding, but her sense of duty kept her there. It was his annual memorial.

The sanctuary was filled with people who loved Thornton, but there was one person Xandy didn't want to see, not now. Still Lauren stomped forward, her face pinched and set.

Another confrontation.

Lauren did it every chance she got. Xandy knew the only reason Lauren had refrained from making a scene at the house and the club the other night was because Jonathan was there. She wouldn't want to appear surly in front of her new beau because she was still hot about her old one breaking things off to be with Xandy so many years ago.

"You could have had the decency to take a pill or two and *not* show up," Lauren taunted. The barbed words attempted to slice deep.

Xandy wasn't going to make a scene. Not now. Not with her.

"If he'd stayed with me, he'd still be alive, you selfish

bitch. You didn't deserve him, and you're the reason he's dead. If he would have just caught that flight .... I hope you rot for what you did to him." In a huff, Lauren pushed past Xandy.

How did she know Thornton was flying? Shoving the irrelevant question to the side, she focused on why she was there. She owed Thornton so much, she realized. She walked over to his parents and took their hands, kissing Thornton's mother, Anne, on her plump cheek.

"Thanks for coming," Anne said. "I hope you will be sharing tonight, as well. You know it's always good to see you, and everyone would love to hear a memory of Thornton."

"Thanks, Ms. Gage, but I don't think I can do it."

"I know this has been as hard for you as it has been for us. It just isn't the same without him," said Ted Gage, Thornton's father. With his eyes hollow, his cheeks sunken in, and his shoulders sagging, he seemed to have aged on fast forward.

"I understand. This time of year only brings back bad memories," Xandy said.

"You look as if you are doing better, though. You look nice. Very nice," Anne said with a tight smile.

Xandy was unsure if there was supposed to be a message in that statement. Did she look too nice, too "un-mourning?" She wanted to respond but found herself speechless. What could she say to the mother and father of her dead fiancé? Nothing she could say would make it better. Instead, like a scolded dog, Xandy ambled away to one of the hard pews.

Xandy fidgeted in the uncomfortable pew and listened as the sad sonata played in celebration of a magnificent life. She watched Thornton's friends and associates speak one by one. They told of how much they missed him, how they adored him and wished he were there.

For her the service was too long. Too much was said, and Xandy found herself regretting she had come. Her thoughts wandered from her shopping list to the weather to the what-ifs. Her heart was no longer in this. Thornton had not lost his relevance, but although she still loved him, like a good book closing, this story of her life seemed to be over.

Anne finally took the podium, wiping tears from her freckled face. "It's been so hard these past few months. The first couple of months, people understand grief, but not the time afterwards. I still find myself dialing his number to hear his voice. The sound of his voice soothes the pain some.

"He was my only son, a brave, intelligent and wonderful man. He volunteered at the *Daily Planet*, tutored high school students after work and was the most loving child anyone could have had. God blessed me when He gave me him. Even growing up, he'd take extra food from the house to make sure the other kids had snacks. And into adulthood, he continued to care, continued to give.

"I know I am not alone in missing him. This turnout is proof enough of his impact on our lives. Together we loved him; together we grieve; together we remember." Anne turned in Xandy's direction. "Xandy, please come and share."

Xandy shook her head, but Anne waved her forward again. Xandy stood and walked forward. At the pulpit, Anne leaned over and whispered, "Just say something to make us smile."

Xandy stood there, looking ahead and hoping for inspiration. This was the worst time to have nothing to say.

"Thornton was the man of every woman's dreams, but he was also so much more. I had the pleasure of knowing him, loving him. And through those moments, he taught me about truth, honesty, veracity. He taught me not to be afraid. It was as if he saw past all those bad things in this world. He was an optimist. A true gift. I am and will forever be grateful for having shared so much with him. He changed me. And in a matter of mere seconds, he gave me life." Xandy paused, gulping in a large amount of air. "Today we honor him. Although he is gone, he will forever live in my memory, thoughts, and heart."

Xandy left the podium, allowing the calmness to wash over her. This was the first time she was not filled with despair. Instead, she somehow felt relieved. She'd submitted to her duty and gained perspective: Thornton had died so she wouldn't have to. If she stayed closed away, she dishonored his memory. Sullying it by failing to take advantage of the new day's offerings.

The service ended on those rousing words. Before Xandy could leave, Anne called her name.

"Xandy, thank you so much. I think I may have been a little rude with you earlier, but it was not meant as it came across."

"It's okay," Xandy said. "I understand that this is difficult for all of us."

"No, it is not. It's just … you look so happy, and we … we can barely make it through the day. I know Thornton would want you to go on with your life. He wouldn't want you to continue to mourn him, not moving forward. Not my Thornton. He'd want you to be happy, too." Anne paused, reached into her purse and retrieved an envelope. "I'm to give this to you. I guess he wanted you to have this." Anne placed the envelope in Xandy's hand.

It must have been hard for Anne to utter those words, especially since she considered Xandy still to be the link to Thornton. However, Anne was releasing her to live, and Xandy no longer had the feeling she needed to be imprisoned in her own imaginary cell.

Xandy closed her hand around the envelope. It felt heavy. "Thank you for giving that to me."

"Are you going to open it?" Anne asked.

Unable to deny her request, Xandy slowly opened the envelope. Inside all she found was a bronze key.

"I guess that means something to you then? We've had it for a while, but he wanted us to give it to you after one year had passed."

"You had instructions from him about this?"

"Yes, the night before he died, he stopped by our house and gave me this, along with some other things. He said if anything happened, then I needed to make sure you received this envelope, but only after one year had passed."

"Why one year?"

"I don't know, Xandy. I wish I didn't have to give it to you at all. I'd rather just have my son back," she said with tears streaming down her face.

"I wish things were different too," Xandy said. She then wrapped her arms around Anne's frame, and held her until her weeping passed.

Upon exiting the sanctuary, Lauren intercepted Xandy again in the hallway. "You may be able to fool them with your words and fake tears, but I know the truth."

"Let it go," Xandy said with a sigh.

"How can I *let it go* when you took what should have been mine?" she asked through clenched teeth. A tear fell down her face. "You're responsible for his death and yet you stand here acting righteous. I know what you are. I know who you are, and if it takes me until my last breath, I'll prove it."

"Are you threatening me?"

"That's beneath me. Every action has consequences – even yours."

With a quick swiping away of the tear, Lauren disappeared back into the crowd.

With the words, "thou shall not" whispered in the victim's ear, the killer lifted the dull hatchet. With one sharp cry, the blunt blade sliced through the air with brute force.

Then again.

Severing.

Blood splattered and dripped on the statue's white marble base and the yellow straw.

He then grabbed the severed head of the once-beautiful woman and tossed it up into the statue's outstretched hand. With a simple knot, he secured it in place with her long hair.

Murder was easy.

Living was difficult.

<u>Chapter 13</u>

October 18

A light rain tapped against the tarp that covered the workers and the cold cement like an impatient lover.

Where is Maureen? Pearl wondered. It had taken her months to get the gig together, and Maureen not being present was not part of the deal.

She sighed and yelled to the gathered men, "Let's get the statue in place. I want to get it completely set up for the dedication. We're behind schedule, people!"

Pearl paced. She glanced constantly at her watch. Maureen was past late, she was overdue.

Suddenly, she heard swearing and Maureen's name.

"Charles! I'm not paying you to do a lot of nothing!"

"You need to get over here," Charles yelled.

Pearl's heart sank. The sound punched her in the stomach. She ran. The crate now lay open, and the packing straw was stained a dark red. Her gaze fell upon her friend's dangling head.

Pearl screamed.

Luck was not on Monroe's side. Each night brought with it the chance of a new body being discovered, and tonight was no different. Being a cop was an ongoing battle, but unlike others, he didn't enjoy the prospect of finding a bloody scene, or a body in rigor mortis. No, the red mist was not his forte, but solving crimes was.

Monroe parked his black sedan with its blue lights flashing on Tredegar Street. He wrapped his trench coat around him as the wind and rain picked up. It was still called Tredegar Iron Works for the locals, but the historic site now carried another name: The American Civil War Center at Historic Tredegar Ironworks. That didn't matter to him. The old building had a history and if the walls could talk, Monroe wondered what they'd say about the Civil War, and Richmond's burning.

The American Civil War Center stood on over four acres of land with the James River only feet away from its doorsteps and the view of the city's skyscrapers as its backdrop. The Bluestone Courtyard was covered with officers from the Crime Scene Unit searching for clues.

Monroe flashed his badge and crossed the yellow crime tape. "Who called it in?" Monroe asked the first officer he encountered.

"Over there," squeaked the pimple-faced patrol officer in a high pitched voice. He tugged at his peaked cap and stood across from Monroe. Monroe gleaned what was happening to him. Monroe could see his body's slight quake; his face glistened with sweat in spite of the cold. This was his first big call. "She's talking to the detective," the officer continued, pointing at a woman who was talking to Hobbes.

With the youngster dismissed, and Hobbes already taking notes, Monroe was able to see the scene for himself. Sheltered to preserve what evidence remained, it was the most inhuman thing Monroe had ever seen. Skin flaps, a severed head and a large puddle of blood on yellow straw. At least the sick son of a bitch had closed her eyes. He'd have a hard time getting that scene, the lifeless face, the tangled hair wrapped tightly around the priceless marble-white sculpture, out of his head tonight. Not even a double-shot of strong Russian vodka was going to help him suppress what he'd seen.

It took a desensitized person, or at least a psychopath to do what had been done. The nude marble statue of Hephaestus, sitting on an anvil with a raised hammer, and his once empty hand outstretched, now held the severed head. The edges at the neck's base were fragmented, torn. Whatever had been used had required a lot of force and repeated chopping. They needed to find the weapon, but looking at the wound, Monroe guessed it could be anything from a butcher knife to a small hatchet.

They were dealing with a through and through nut job.

"Thought you might want to know what I found out, partner," Hobbes said, standing next to Monroe. "The body was found about two hours ago by workers, who were setting up the exhibit for the unveiling. The area is on high alert."

"There was to be an art show here?"

"Yeah, the victim, Maureen Hyatt, had rented the place, since her family had ties to it."

"Any insight into her last twenty-four hours from the witness?"

"Not really. She was last seen at the storage facility checking on the statue. According to the witness, Maureen was considered to be an introvert and spent most of her time with her art and its pieces. So far, the Crime Scene Unit has found blood in the shipping crate. There isn't any word on if it was there when the crate was moved to this site, but my best guess is that it was."

"She was from out-of-town, I gather. When did the crate arrive and was it delivered promptly here?"

"Yeah, it arrived yesterday," Hobbes flipped through his notes." It was stored at The Storage Place on Lombardy, unit 210."

It was better to work as a partnership. With Hobbes

already procuring information at the scene, Monroe knew it made more sense to use his time tracking down the actual scene of the murder, or at least potential abduction.

"This means we have another potential place to investigate."

Xandy arrived at the internal affairs reception desk, flustered. She took a deep breath to calm her nerves. She could feel her hands begin to dampen, her mouth was dry and she had the suspicion that she'd squirted her perfume one too many times. "Good morning. I'm here to see Detective Tal," Xandy said.

"I'm sorry," said the receptionist, "but Detective Tal is not available. He is in a meeting. I will be happy to schedule you for an appointment, though."

The receptionist gave Xandy a look of pity, as she noticed the two cups of coffee and the newspaper. Xandy took the extra Arabian grande and thrust it at the receptionist. "Since he's not available, maybe you might want to have this?"

The receptionist looked at Xandy as though she had offered her a dead rat. "I'm sorry, but we're not allowed to accept gifts. You know, with the IRS and all."

"Well, can you at least tell Brennan—Detective Tal I stopped by?"

The receptionist lifted her forefinger and said, "Hold on a moment; let me see how long this will take."

Brennan sat behind his desk, his brow furrowed as he looked over the documents. The complaint against Detective Lazarus appeared legit– so far– he'd admitted to that according to Victor's and Dr. James' statements. Additionally, his file already reflected Lazarus's prior offenses– all recent– and almost all of his reprimands had to do with Ms. Caras– Xandy– who was now in danger.

Brennan grabbed his pen and attempted again to concentrate on the words before him. As his mind started to comprehend what he was reading, he was interrupted by a soft tap on his office door. He looked up to see the one woman he now detested.

"Knock-knock, I thought I'd stop by and, you know, maybe put that desk to good use," Jocelyn said. She sauntered over to him with an exaggerated sway of her hips.

"Hmmm, interesting thought, but you've got the wrong brother. He might take you up on the idea."

"Why don't you just put that to rest, Brennan? I didn't come down here to argue with you, but I was hoping we could have lunch and discuss a thing or two."

"Do me a favor and leave. At least then I don't need to remove you from my office. I can get a restraining order to keep you fifty feet or more away if I need to."

"I have strings I can pull, too," she said.

"I have something I need to do, if you'd go." Brennan pointed toward his office door to make his intentions clear.

"I'd be happy to pull a favor for you. We're not finished with each other yet," Jocelyn cooed and leaned over on his desk.

"I'm no longer inclined for cast-off goods. Leave!" Brennan's gaze never faltered.

His intercom buzzed interrupting her failed moment.

"Excuse me, Detective Tal; I have a Xandy Caras here, and she wishes to see you. She will not take no for an answer."

"I'll be right there," Brennan replied. He glanced over at Jocelyn. "I have someone waiting. Have your attorney call mine. And don't come back here."

As the receptionist told Xandy that Brennan would

see her now, Jocelyn stepped around the office corner. Her model flair and an air of superiority proved stifling. She needed to make sure that the other woman waiting for her ex got the message: He was still hers.

Their eyes clashed.

Jocelyn scrutinized the woman who stood waiting. She was everything Jocelyn wasn't. In comparison, she was frumpy, classless, and even less feminine. There was no way Brennan would take notice of this woman when he was used to someone like her. In comparison, Xandy was like cheap beer, while she was a smooth and expensive champagne.

A sense of triumph overwhelmed her, and she could not help but look at Xandy with a mixture of scorn and pity.

To put the final nail in place, Jocelyn said, "It's okay. I'm sure Brennan won't have a problem seeing Amy now."

"Xandy," Xandy corrected.

"Whatever," Jocelyn said, leaving in a cloud of expensive fabrics and perfume.

"I'm sorry to drop by without calling first," Xandy said, still holding the cooling cups of coffee. "I can see you were quite busy and, um, I'm … I'm sorry. I never should have come."

Brennan mentally shook his head, unclenching his teeth. He had business to do. "What do you mean?" He crossed the room to stand beside her.

"I'm not too sure why I came. I mean, Victor …I came here at the wrong time and …"

Brennan took her hands in his. Her eyes darted to the floor. "Listen to me. You came at the perfect time." He forced a smile, wanting her to see his *joy* at her presence.

"After the last night, I thought, maybe we could do lunch or something, as my way of saying thank you." She thrust a cup at him.

Instead of taking the offered drink, Brennan checked the time. "I have a lunch engagement shortly, and we have a few things to discuss...what about dinner instead?"

After a moment's pause, Xandy grinned. "Sounds like a great idea."

"I'll pick you up around eight," he huffed with an impatient sigh.

Monroe pulled into the parking lot of The Storage Place. The brown bricks with their hazard orange sign reminded him of the bright colors of jack-o-lanterns. It would be his kids' first Halloween in Virginia, and no turning back to the past of Texas. They needed to heal and there was nothing like a holiday filled with candy to help the process along.

Pulling open the glass door, Monroe walked to the counter. Flashing his badge, he leaned in toward the sales clerk, a young man with a washed out complexion. He could smell the scent of pot radiating from him. Could he scare the kid enough to make him go straight? He wondered.

Probably not.

"Good...good... how may I help you," the sales clerk stuttered. His evasive, glassy stare darted around the room, avoiding Monroe's direct glare.

"I need to speak with someone about Unit 210."

"Are you the renter?"

"No."

"Sorry, without some sort of authorization, I can't give you any information. Don't you need a warrant or something?"

The clerk's drug haze must have induced in him a bit of cockiness, Monroe thought. "Look kid, I know and if I had time to search you, I'm sure I'd find the weed you've been smoking, and maybe even something else. What I need is to know if anyone was in unit 210 and if there is any video for that floor or around the unit."

The clerk gulped, "I've seen those crime shows. Without a warrant you can't see shit!"

Monroe huffed, pulled out his phone and called Hobbes, "We need to get a search warrant. They are not going to release the information without it."

"Alright, I'm on it. Wait there."

Somewhere between yesterday and today, Hobbes had gotten a grip and grasp of what it meant to have a new partner, Monroe assumed. What else could be his reasons for going out of his way to help?

Fifteen minutes later and with blue lights flashing and a siren blaring, Hobbes walked into The Storage Place's lobby.

"As promised," Hobbes said handing the warrant over to Monroe.

"Okay kid, here it is, now let me see the video tapes," Monroe said. He was past waiting and playing games with someone who was barely old enough to proficiently wipe when there was some maniac out there hacking people up to put them on crude display.

"Alright, alright, hold on a minute."

"Look, you have exactly five seconds to do as I told you or I will take you down to the station, and charge you with obstruction and of course anything else I can come up with, like your possession of an illegal substance," Monroe sneered.

Hobbes placed his hand on Monroe's shoulder. "Let me talk to him," Hobbes whispered.

Hobbes moved forward, letting Monroe go cool his head.

"I don't know what your partner's problem is. He is almost as bad as the other guy that was here. I don't know why you cops are so interested in that unit. I just work here. They don't pay me enough to do what I do!"

"What do you mean about another cop?" Hobbes asked.

"Some guy drove up in a gray SUV, and he just seemed like an undercover cop or what not. I'm thinking its narcotics. You know when I was younger, before I got in trouble awhile back, I wanted to be a cop too. You know, do all that CSI shit."

"So, you really watched him then?"

"Yeah. He was a Vice sort of cop though. He was wearing a suit and carrying some sort of carrying case."

"What made you think he was worth watching?"

"People who want to store stuff here don't come wearing fine suits, and he had that cop walk."

"Can you describe him?"

"Yeah, white guy about five foot ten, longer black hair, but not the metal type, with a porn-stache, and huge dark shades and of course a fedora."

"A fedora? And his build?"

"He seemed pretty fit to me. I mean, I didn't see any spare tire wrapped around his waist."

"Can you come down to the station and meet with a sketch artist? It could help us a lot."

"I got my own problems here. I don't– "

"We'll make it short and sweet. Help us. Did the other cop talk to you?"

"Yeah, he asked for the sign-in book and the surveillance tapes. My manager was pissed when I told him I had to give it to the 5-0."

"Do you have him on tape?" Hobbes asked.

"Nah, he took it all with him."

Chapter 14

October 18

Finally back at the station, waiting for the sales clerk from The Storage Place and the sketch artist to finish, Monroe and Hobbes sat at their desk, each flipping through the details of the murders.

"What happened back there," Hobbes asked Monroe.

Monroe knew sooner or later Hobbes would inquire as to why he dealt with the sales clerk the way he did. The murders of Houston flashed before him; butchered bodies, blood smeared across walls and the face of finding his own dead son in the midst of horror. "I had my reasons. Let's just leave it at that. You're attempt at playing nice with me isn't going to cut it."

"Alright you got me," Hobbes said with a chuckle. "I've put you through the wringer since you've been here, but you've been a good cop."

"Is that a compliment or something?"

"I think we can work well together as partners. The Captain gave you this case to get your feet wet, and because back in Houston you had the reputation of being a killer catcher."

"You did some research on me?"

"Yeah. I had to see who I was really working with. You were too nice to be working Major Crimes, especially Homicide."

"Then I guess you also know why I left?"

"I sort of wish I didn't. It had to be hard losing a kid like that."

"Every day," Monroe gruffly whispered.

"I know I didn't say this when you first arrived, but welcome to Homicide," Hobbes reached out his hand and patted Monroe on the back.

"Gentlemen, I have your drawing," said Pamela, the sketch artist. She was one of several the City used. Monroe thought of her more as a Pixie for some reason. Maybe it was her petite frame, and strawberry-blonde chopped hair. But he could imagine her with wings and flying.

"Where's the kid?" Hobbes asked.

"Oh, he said he had to get somewhere," Pamela said. "Since he was only helping us out, I let him leave."

Monroe placed the old sketch next to the new one. The new sketch showed a man with an oblong face, long dark hair that covered the top of his forehead, along with a fedora; large dark sun glasses blacked out his eyes and rested on his long pointed nose; a thick mustache covered his thin lips. The first sketch looked nothing like the newer one, except the face shape, but in this sketch it was more oral. In the first sketch, the hair was curly and described as blond; he had long thick sideburns that extended from the hair down to the jaw line.

"I don't know if you two want my artistic opinion or not, but it could still be the same person," Pamela said.

"How do you mean?" Monroe asked.

"I think he may be using a disguise to hide his true identity. The *Today Show* did a feature on how criminals are using them now, and how they can be ordered online. It's thought that some are taken from the back lots of Hollywood's greatest special effects makeup artists."

"Special effects makeup?" Hobbes asked.

"Yeah, look it up and you'll find video after video on how to do the stuff at home. Maybe that's what your suspect is doing– taking his features and building upon them to create a cover of sorts or masking them all together."

"That would explain a lot," Monroe muttered. "It would explain why our perp is able to disappear so easily, like a ghost."

"Are you saying that both of our witnesses could be correct on what they saw?" Hobbes asked.

"I can't guarantee it, but it could make sense," Pamela said. "You might want to have the victim's checked for any type of silicone residue to confirm my hunch though."

Xandy checked her voicemail. She still hadn't heard anything from Victor– either he was too busy or … she didn't what to think of the other possibility: the one man she trusted turning her out and then away.

Instead, she flung open her closet door. Everything was muted in color– blacks, browns and grays– and lacked style. She hadn't dressed up on her own volition in so long, wanting only to shield herself from further unwanted scrutiny. An unwelcomed sigh escaped before she could catch it.

Why was she going out tonight? There was no one pushing her to do it. Yet the idea of being stuck in the house, by the phone, waiting for Victor to call– a call that wouldn't come wasn't appealing either. If she stayed alone, she risked not only pining away for a man who obviously wanted nothing to do with her, but also the chance of becoming the next victim on the newspaper's front page.

There was safety in numbers. She quickly dialed Rebecca's number. She needed a wardrobe warrior, stat!

"You've reached Rebecca. I'm unavailable right now,

but if you lea—"

Xandy would just have to try to pull out all of the stops on her own. As she tore through her closet, tossing clothes on the floor, her phone rang. Relief flooded her at hearing Rebecca's voice.

"I need your help! Get over here as soon as possible!" Xandy said, flustered.

"I'm out of town, but what's going on?"

"I'm going out tonight, and I have no idea what to wear." Xandy couldn't stop the nervous giggle from erupting.

"You're doing what?"

"I know, those words disappeared from my vocabulary a long time ago, but I haven't done this alone in what feels like forever ...."

"Where are you going?"

"I don't know. He said he'd pick me up at eight."

"He? Not Victor?"

"No, but he is just a friend. Someone I met through Victor."

"Well, it is a respectable time ... hmm. I take it you've already ransacked your closet. I have this nice outfit back at my place. It's not too couture, too indie or anything. You can wear it if you want. I just picked it up from the cleaners with some of my costumes. I think it's still wrapped in plastic."

Xandy peeked at her watch and saw she still had time to drive to Rebecca's house, grab the package and make it back to put on the final touches. "Thanks."

Richmond traffic was horrible at all the wrong times. Xandy couldn't rush fast enough to Rebecca's. The highway was backed up because of an accident and she lost too much time waiting for the rubberneckers in front of her. She hurried inside Rebecca's house, grabbed the first thing she saw and dashed back to her car. She could only hope it was the correct outfit and that she wouldn't get a ticket with her lead-foot driving.

Upon making it back to her place, she noticed she had twenty minutes at the most to finish getting ready. Where did the time go? All of her preparations were thrown out of the window as her body perspired through her haste and nervousness.

She sprang under the shower for a thirty-second refresher, dried her dampened skin, and dabbed her favorite perfume on her wrists, between her breast and behind her ears. Bolting to her room, she ripped off the plastic wrap only to find the most hideous of outfits. Xandy tossed it on her bed. She scrambled for something else to wear. Saddened by her prospects, she took out what she thought would work: black skirt, white blouse with sheer sleeves, a violet scarf, and wide violet belt for color. It would have to do, but she didn't think she'd win any prizes for it.

She applied a minimum amount of make-up and some silver earrings.

"I can do this; I can do this," she repeated." Just as she put on matching pumps, she heard a knock on her door. It was exactly eight o'clock.

Monroe pulled up to his Victorian home. Turning off the car's engine, he listened to the city's rhythm. Besides a calm, soft breeze, and a few cars driving by, the night was calm, but knowing someone was out there, playing a twisted game of catch, made him pause. His conversation with Dr. Reynolds gave him nothing to go on. He hadn't been able to find anything on any of the victims that could confirm Pamela's speculation. It would make sense that the killer was wearing a sort of disguise so as not to not risk detection, but without a clue to go on, it was just a well-conceived hunch.

Now home, Monroe had to focus on his family. He schlepped his tired frame up the short path to his front door. Light was still burning behind the dark curtains. Paula Sue would be waiting up, while his toddler son, Andrew, and his teenage daughter, Lena, lay tucked away safely in their beds. He didn't want to talk to her about this. She'd ask; he'd hedge, and in the end, the night would be over.

He needed to keep this to himself to protect her. She couldn't go through it again– another serial killer and another case that he was working on. He couldn't let her fear more than what she did in Houston. Their marriage couldn't take another strain like that. That would mean that he'd failed again. He had to protect his family at all costs and that included making sure that sometimes they stayed in the dark.

His mind still focused on the decapitated head. Besides pure evil, what would possess someone to do something so heinous?

Tonight he'd brought his work home. He would have to catch that sick bastard before he couldn't stomach being a cop anymore.

Seated at a window table at the Le Baroque restaurant in the Jefferson Hotel, with linen napkins placed on their laps and white wine in their glasses, Xandy, seated across from Brennan, glanced around the restaurant's dining room. Candles and soft overhead lighting illuminated the room; fine china, silver and crystal covered the linen table cloths; and, men and women ate in their designer best. Self-conscious, Xandy stared down at her un-manicured nails and unfashionable clothes. In such a restaurant, even the waitress's frock put her to shame.

The wait staff donned formal black-tie wear, only substituting the black blazer for a black vest. They moved almost silently through the room, speaking in whispers while light music played in the background. For a moment, Xandy stared at a couple hidden in the corner, almost out of sight of spectators. She heard them clinking their champagne glasses and the woman squeal in delight. Xandy flushed with envy. That should have been her.

"Xandy? Xandy?" Brennan said. He waved his hand before her face. "Everything okay?"

"Just peachy. I'm sorry. I must have zoned out for a moment."

"I noticed you hadn't heard a thing I said." Brennan turned and looked in the direction of the canoodling pair. "Do you know them? Seems like they have your attention tonight."

"No, don't think that. When life give you lemons–"

"You make lemonade." Brennan interjected.

"No, you squeeze them until you can use the peels," Xandy said with a snicker. "I apologize for my inattentiveness. What did you ask me?"

"No problem. I was just wondering if you were originally from here."

"No. I'm a transplant from New Jersey. My dad and I moved here when I was in second grade. You?"

"Born and raised southerner. My family's lived in this area for generations now. Do you miss it?"

"I barely remember Jersey, to be honest. Thinking about it is like trying to recall a dream after getting up. I often wonder how my life would be different if..." Xandy caught herself. She felt stiff. She didn't want to play twenty questions all night and began to wonder why she'd agreed to come to dinner with him after all.

"I was talking to Victor and–"

"Victor?"

"Yeah, we had lunch today and I told him about us heading out for dinner tonight."

Xandy sat up a little straighter, itching to hear anything to confirm Victor's true feelings for her. "What did he say about that," Xandy asked.

"Not much. He wanted to make sure you were okay from the other night."

"I haven't seen Detective Lazarus, so I expect so."

"I can't talk with you about that, but I am glad you are at least feeling a little safer."

"And I have you to thank for that." Xandy grinned; it was her first genuine smile of the evening.

"Let's order though, I'm starved."

Distraction. He was to be a good distraction for her, and yet each sentence they shared, each laugh she echoed, felt hollow. There was nothing he could give her and nothing she wanted from him.

He couldn't make her scarlet sins as white as freshly fallen snow.

No one could.

She kept glancing at her watch, hoping he wouldn't notice her stiff posture or how he was doing most of the talking. Each minute felt like a minute served in purgatory. When the maître d' finally appeared with more wine, it was as if angels on high had heard her cry. With graceless hands, she swiped the glass off the table and took an unladylike guzzle.

"Damn it," Lazarus shouted as he followed Brennan's Audi sedan down Franklin Street. Somehow or another, Xandy had gotten to his Internal Affairs investigator. How was he going to have an impartial investigation with her emotional tie to the guy?

Finding a parking spot on the street, he exited his car and entered the hotel in search of them. Seeing them seated together in front of a large window chilled him. She had the power to ruin everything he'd been working for since he was eighteen. If he went in and approached them, it could cause him even more harm. Maybe he could play it off as just following up. With his cell phone in hand, he pressed the video record button and zoomed in until he had them both laughing in the frame.

"Then, he took out the Scope bottle and threw it on her!" Brennan said.

Xandy's boisterous laugh sounded throughout the restaurant. It started off as a snort, crested at an unruly cackle.

As their plates were taken away, Brennan realized he didn't want the evening to end. "This was fun!"

"It's too bad we already had dessert."

"Would you like to drink some coffee or have another drink?" They'd had too many as it were.

"Coffee at this hour might not be too great of an idea."

"What about another glass of ... water?"

"Did you just ask me if I wanted more water? Why do I have the impression you are not ready to end the evening?" Xandy said with a laugh. She took another swig of her wine. The alcohol was doing all the talking.

"If it gets you to spend a few more minutes with me, then no, I am not ready to part. I'm sure if I keep trying, I'll come up with a great idea ... I just have to think of it." Brennan had been smiling the entire night; his cheeks ached as if he'd been blowing up balloons for hours. Somehow or another the night was turning into some fun after all.

"If we don't call it quits, one of us is going to be tired tomorrow."

"True, but we can make it worth it. Let's go dancing."

"Are you serious? I am not dressed for that."

"You look lovely though," Brennan said and signaled the maître d' for the check.

Jocelyn placed the house key back into her purse. She didn't know how long she'd have until Brennan returned, and surprise would be her best weapon. She hurried through the house, barely seeing the fall décor, as the scent of fresh pine assaulted her senses. It made her think of Christmas – a family holiday that she no longer had a family for. With gusto, she opened Brennan's bedroom door. The large solid bed they used to share had been replaced by a sleeker and more modern edition.

Jocelyn quickly slipped off her clothes and tossed them on the plush reading chair. Striking a pose, she waited.

If she couldn't get him to talk to her one way, maybe this would work.

October 18

What was the price of life and its value if it's lost? What bonds were stronger than one's soul? Nothing was more sacred.

The killer sat in the midst of the guffawing group. Smoke filled the quaint room at Crack 'em Up Comedy Club in Shockoe Slip as comedian after comedian titillated the crowd with vulgarity. He waited for his opportunity, as he'd waited for days. It was the final show of the evening.

As the last comedian was announced, the killer took notice of her. She used her femininity as a prop for her set. Her act was as crude as any male's. Her perfidiousness was hidden well. Almost. Profanity poured from her pout.

The killer lightly caressed the small metal dagger hidden beneath his coat. Just as Philomela's tongue was cut out so her shame would be kept a secret, so would the comedian's. The act of betrayal required compensation.

As the show ended, and the crowd dispersed, the killer lingered. Blood would flow. She'd beg. Scream for mercy. But in the end, it wouldn't matter. He had something to leave behind in her esophagus.

A sinister smile crossed his face. Let the morgue have a little fun fishing it out.

<u>Chapter 15</u>

October 18

Metro News

The body of renowned artist Maureen Hyatt, the creator of the famous Ode to Hephaestus statue scheduled for exhibition at Tredegar Iron Works, was found this morning. No other details are being released at this time.

Ms. Hyatt was in Richmond for the inaugural viewing of her statue, Ode to Hephaestus, which was scheduled to take place tonight and has been postponed until further notice.

This marks the fourth murder of a prominent victim left at a public location. The murder comes on the heels of Greater Richmond Police Chief Sidney Zimmerman's press conference. The force's inability to protect the public has caused many taxpayers to question what the Police Department is doing to keep the city safe.

Brennan broke into a sweat. He had never understood a woman's signals, but what her body language was saying to him, even the blind could read. Xandy leaned in too close, rested her hands too long on him. He had to try to keep himself under control. When she turned and her rump rubbed against him during the rumba, he knew he wouldn't last the entire night with her tortuous foreplay.

"Come on, let's get out of here," Brennan said.

Sitting next to him in the car, his hand brushed against her warm thigh, as he reached for the gear shift.

Brennan looked at Xandy, seeing only her inviting full lips. He leaned toward her. Pushing her hair behind her ear, and taking her neck in his large hand, he closed the space between them. Their lips brushed. The pressure swelled, as he tried to pull her closer. He tried to remember to slow down to make the first kiss last, but pulled away.

"My place isn't too far away, if you're interested."

"I can't..." Xandy pulled on the car door handle and opened it. "I should really be heading home."

"Did I misunderstand something here?"

"Let's just say that it would be a mistake for us to do something. I may be tipsy, but I know this is not something I want to do."

"I'll give you a ride home then."

"To be honest, I think we both should take taxis. Thanks for a nice evening though."

Xandy stepped back into the nightclub, leaving Brennan wondering what he'd do with all the sexual energy he'd worked up.

Victor cracked his knuckles, flexing his fingers, and glared at the radio's clock. Sitting outside Xandy's apartment in his car, he wanted to make sure she got home safe. *Who was he kidding?* Thoughts of her and Brennan going at it irritated him. He felt physically sick thinking about it.

It was his fault though. He'd pushed her into Brennan's waiting arms, and seemingly gave them both the okay. No, he wasn't happy about their rendezvous any more than any man would be happy about his woman stepping out with someone else. *She was his.*

Victor flinched at the thought. *His?*

An oncoming car's lights distracted him from delving

deeper into that thought. Seeing the taxi cab pull up, and Xandy almost stumble out of it, he sighed in relief. He yanked open his door and practically flew to her side.

"Hey Xandy," Victor said. He tried to act casual, but the school boy smile on his face did nothing to hide his excitement at seeing her without her *date*.

"What are you doing here?" Xandy asked. She removed her key and walked toward her apartment building's entrance.

"I wanted to make sure you made it home safe. That's all."

"That's all?" Xandy paused. He saw her squint up at him. "What is this really about? Oh, I see, my date."

"Did you have a good time?"

"You don't want to know that. What you want to know is if we connected and if so, if it was consciously or physically."

"I want you to be happy," Victor whispered.

"Come on up. We need to talk."

"I can't stay long...I have... some things to handle down at the station."

"It's up to you if you want something with me or not. I'm almost getting to the point of wondering why I'd throw away the blatant interest of another man for one that I seem to only be pining for."

Victor closed the space between them. "You turned him down?"

"I kissed him, but it didn't feel right. All I could think about was you and wishing I were out with you and not him." Xandy placed her palm on his chest. "You know I love you, but I don't know how you feel about me."

His radio's crackling and squawking broke the moment.

"I really have to go Xandy. We'll talk another time, okay?" He leaned in and planted a chaste kiss on her lips.

Chapter 16

October 19

Xandy awoke to Amarillo's kitty kisses on her cheek. Cats were better than alarm clocks. Light pierced her skull and even the thought of words was too loud. With cotton mouth and an unquenchable thirst, she rose from the warmth of her bed and flipped on the news.

"...Can't understand what is taking the police so long to find a suspect," said the male news anchor. *"These women were butchered and placed on display. It's an atrocity!"* The pictures of four women popped up on the screen. *"If you have any information in the murders of* Sister Hannah Salem, Ilene Kernbach, Walker Gentry and Maureen Hyatt, *please contact crime solvers. You can even leave an anonymous tip."*

Xandy stared at the screen. This was worse than she'd first assumed! She had to tell someone that the women were all connected.

Connected to her.

That they were all housed together at the local jail. But would that place her under even more scrutiny? Would they look at her as being a suspect since she knows them all? More importantly, did this mean that she was also in danger? More than just from a mere stalker, but someone who also wanted to possibly flay her?

Xandy reached for her phone and dialed the Crime Solvers line. Hearing the feminine voice on the other end, she tried to disguise her voice, and said, "I was just watching the news about those women. They are all connected to each other. They were housed together at the Jail."

"How do you know that ma'am?" said the officer on the other end, boredom laced her monotone voice

"I'd rather not say, but you all might want to check them out."

"Do you have any more information?"

"Yes, there were several other women in their clique, I guess you might say. They might also be in danger since–"

"Thank you for calling. Your anonymous tip number is 78531. Thank you."

Before Xandy could continue her sentence, the officer hung up, leaving Xandy staring at her cell phone screen.

"If I can't get them to listen to me, then I'll have to tell Victor or maybe Brennan might listen," she said aloud. Someone would have to do something before another one of the *family* showed up in the city's morgue.

Brennan strolled along his land beside the James River in the early morning dew. The sun was rising in the distance. In the light of the dawn, he contemplated his next move. All he wanted to do was fix the problems circling him like buzzards over road kill. Jocelyn, financial repercussions, and Aden's betrayal– it all surrounded him.

Jocelyn would have let him do anything he liked last night. Her touch was at first gentle, then demanding. It all was and had to be to her liking. She unwound him, and now after tasting her again, he couldn't wait to repeat it, but not at the expense of losing everything he'd worked for, not for another dip of his quill in her ink. He ached to have her scream his name. To feel her hands on him. He'd never had anything as hot, wet, and willing.

He needed to think about something other than the woman who had been haunting his every waking moment since leaving his side. Emily was always a good distraction. He saw his sister exiting the house. Unlike the other members of the family, Emily was pure sunshine, guileless. At the age of eighteen, she'd towered over most of the other girls her age.

"I can tell you're determined early this morning. What do you have planned today?" Brennan asked.

Emily smiled her shy smile at her eldest brother. "I'm heading to the city to meet Jocelyn to talk about the silent auction."

Brennan frowned.

"Don't scowl at me," Emily protested. "Maybe I'll even find out some new information for you."

Brennan responded with a grimace. "I am not going to have my little sister spying on my ex for me."

"You need someone to help you."

"To help me do what?"

"You're always there to help me and the family, but who's there to help you?" Emily asked.

Brennan glanced away. He'd never admit it. How was he to tell her of his greatest fear coming true, to fail at everything he held dear? With Jocelyn's infidelity, she took not only his pride, but also his confidence. With one selfish act, she destroyed what he thought he was, along with the bonds of a family. All he had was his desire for affirmation. Someone to tell him that he was okay, able to do all those things that he once did. Now, emasculated, he only had himself.

"I'd like to help, even if it's not wanted," Emily murmured. She placed her small hand on his shoulder. For a moment he thought of his mother and felt her absence.

Emily was sometimes wiser than others were, but Brennan still couldn't understand why she chose to spend time with the woman who'd pitted brother against brother. He only wished he'd had the sense to tell his mother that she was right about his being too young to get married.

The time was near, the killer knew. He ran his blade over the gray sharpening stone. Grinding the steel against the hard surface soothed him. It allowed him to rework each aspect of his plan. To make sure there were no kinks. Nothing that would stop him from achieving his success. Tomorrow he'd strike and there'd be one less bane.

He continued to sharpen his knife with the strop.

Only a couple more hours until she died, he thought, and then he could have some semblance of peace.

Chapter 17

October 19

Brennan sat in his leather easy chair, glass of Scotch in hand, with furrowed brow and set jaw. He stared at the telephone. He hadn't spoken to her since last night. He'd awakened alone. Maybe it was supposed to be only about the sex, the beast that needed to come out and play, and then coldly disappear. She'd known what she wanted.

Hard, rough, animal sex.

Jocelyn always knew how to stroke him. She was fuel to his flame.

In his aroused and drunken haze, he was honest about his desire – he wanted to do it again. To smolder under her passion, tantalize her senses with his hands, mouth and tongue, and make her toes curl without interruption.

With a quick swig, he turned toward his picturesque view and stared out into the beginning of twilight.

"Sorry, I'm late," Tom called out. "Robert let me in."

Brennan turned his grimace at the sound of Tom's voice. "You seemed to have taken one up the ass, if you don't mind me saying." A joker-like grin attempted to ease the tension. "You all right?" He took a seat across from Brennan in one of the leather armchairs.

Brennan ignored the question. "I hope you have some

good news for me."

"Okay, right to business then," Tom said. Opening his briefcase, he removed a file folder and flipped it open. "I received another email from Jocelyn's attorney. They want to set the hearing to request temporary spousal support. She's going to ask the court to order pendente lite relief, or basically a temporary order to create a smooth adjustment. It will order how everything is to be handled between the two of you."

"I guess back to normal now," Brennan murmured. "Is this because I wouldn't give her the frequent flyer miles?" He massaged his neck. "I know she is just being Jocelyn, but I thought we were past this."

"What do you mean?"

Brennan sighed. "I slept with her last night."

"That's one way of negotiating," Tom smirked.

"I came home, she was naked in my bed – what else could I do?"

"Not that. You may have just forgiven your wife!"

"What?" Brennan asked smacking the recliner's armrest.

"It would seem that Jocelyn didn't like the negotiations at all. This morning they filed an order stopping you from transferring marital assets until the divorce is finalized. Even though the prenuptial agreement is decisive on what was yours and what was hers before the marriage, the courts will try to have an equitable distribution of the marital property, including that commingled property, which also includes the value of your stocks."

"That was from my effort."

"I'm aware of that, but since the value increased by thirty-five percent during the course of your marriage, we have to look at that percentage, which is marital property and could be subjected to equitable distribution."

"I'm happy that it at least lists what was mine in the beginning and what she has no right to. At least I was smart enough to create some sort of agreement before I made this mistake," Brennan said.

"If my memory serves right, you thought you didn't need it because ... oh, I remember. You stated she was 'the one' and loved you for you. She did not even know your true worth and would always be faithful to you and the idea of marriage."

Brennan's face contorted as he reflected on the bitter argument he'd had with his mother. She had truly known this would happen all along, he suspected.

"Okay," Brennan said. "So I was naive, but at least I let my mother and you persuade me to the path of cautiousness."

"You really mean to say of callousness. If I remember correctly, she told you to get a prenup or get another family." Tom snickered.

"Damn your memory." Brennan recalled his mother's face, red with anger and Tom's determination to keep him and Jocelyn from saying 'I do.' That's what friends were for, Brennan knew. If only he had listened.

"The problem is we now have to show that your drunken night of pleasure had nothing to do with reconciliation, but more of her trying to manipulate the court."

"How do we prove that?"

"One: don't sleep with her again; and, two, find a hobby."

Brennan watched Robert, his stepfather, come into the room and take a seat. Like clockwork, every Friday since his mom's passing, Robert had made it a point to come over.

"I have an inkling that her demands are going to get worse," Tom continued. "She is after what's in your pocket."

"What do you suggest then? I give in to everything she wants and just write her a blank check? I think not. I am no one's fool. I've built up what I have. She did nothing except spread her legs, and not even for me, until last night. She either does it my way or I'll see her ass roast in court!"

Robert broke in, "I understand this is hard to bear, Brennan, but–"

"My decision is my decision. I am not backing down from it. She is to receive only what that document says and not a cent more!"

"Give Tom a little more time," Robert said.

"We still have motions to file for interrogatories," Tom said, "and they will have to produce documentation, just like we will. There is one other thing that concerns me though, Brennan. I would not put it past her to try to offset her wrongs by showing some infidelity on your side."

"I've never cheated on my wife."

"I'm only saying that you need to make sure that in all appearances it stays that way."

"But I'm single, Tom."

"No, Brennan, you're not. You're separated and in the process of getting a divorce, and a nasty one at that."

"What? Are you saying that I am unable to have any type of social life as long as this is in court?"

"If she gets proof that you are with someone else, and are sexually involved, it is possible that she will attempt to use it as proof to offset her own deeds."

Listening to Tom, the image of Xandy from last night gyrating across the floor flashed before Brennan. "She is the one who broke the sanctity of the vows, not me. I think there should be some sort of repercussions regarding her actions. The truth of the matter is she's a loose woman. I think we are to proceed as planned. Once you provide me with any additional documentation or whatnot, I will be sure to sign and submit it. I want this taken care of ASAP."

"Friends, but no sex Brennan!"

"Listen to me," Robert interjected. "The other problem, Brennan, is that by this going to court, the document becomes a part of public record, and has the potential of shaming not only Jocelyn but her entire family, and a part of yours."

"And?" Brennan asked.

"Simple," Robert continued, "it also airs out your dirt. Remember, Old Richmond doesn't take kindly to their business being turned out on the streets."

"You know the rule: keep it in the family and behind closed doors." Tom said.

"Okay, okay. I get it," Brennan said. He had the nagging feeling it was already too late for that. She'd use anything against him to get what she wanted.

Xandy arrived home after her fifteen-hour shift from work exhausted. Work was better than meditating. She was too tired to think about anything or anyone. She hated trials, and being in the courtroom for a civil jury trial didn't do anything for her nerves either. After a day-long trial and then hours of deliberations, she was happy to have made it back to her apartment before midnight.

Throughout the day, she'd checked her call log for missed calls. She still had not heard anything from Victor, but then she also didn't call him. Her mind replayed the details of their last conversation. Now, staring at her phone, she didn't know what she'd say if he did call.

Piling her mail high on the countertop, she placed her cell phone down, tired of constantly looking at the screen. Instead, she kicked off her shoes, and thought to distract herself with what her body needed – sleep.

Walking barefoot to her bedroom to change into

something more comfortable than business attire and unpinning her coiffure, she turned on her bedroom light. Bold strokes in the shape of an oak tree stared back at her from her once bare wall. From four of the painting's ten branches hung the postcard she'd received from the Mosque Theatre, along with one from The Arts Museum, one from Morris Stuart Community College, and a picture she'd never seen before of the Greek God Hephaestus. The other tree limbs were left open for more to be tacked on, she thought.

Panic swelled like a balloon. Cold sweat ran down her back. She couldn't breathe. All she could see before her were their faces. She fell to her knees, banging them against the hardwood floor. Tears ran down her face. She panted for air, as stabbing pain coursed through her torso. She tried to suck air in. Her lungs burned. She attempted to rise, to crawl further away from the danger.

As Xandy trudged forward, she heard the sound of running water and the soft voice of the man she'd never forget. "Xandy, it's me, Thornton. Just checking on you, firefly. I love you ... I love you ... I love you." The words looped, interrupted only by a small click.

Unable to move, she placed her hands over her ears and screamed; her glass-shattering screams reverberated throughout her apartment.

She screamed as loud and long as possible.

She screamed until her throat was raw.

She screamed until she no longer could.

Lazarus waited outside Xandy's apartment. Could this be the push he needed to get what he wanted? He could only hope so. He tried to shake the feeling that he was crossing the line, and going after her at every cost, but if he could catch her, the murderer that got away with it because of a wink and sheepish grin, then he'd do what needed to be done.

Once he'd followed her home, he started recording. Hearing Xandy's screams, he reached for his phone and dialed his employer's number. "It's working."

Xandy sat in Victor's office. Shame covered her like a dirty blanket. She itched under his scrutiny. Her face reddened and then paled as she remembered the last time she saw him. Her once-lively eyes were red-rimmed, and puffy with dark shadows. The memory of Thornton's voice looped in her head, but the wall mural and the faces of the dead shadowed her. They'd been a group of women seeking solace, comfort and protection in numbers, a family born out of necessity. She'd promised not to forget them, but she had, as they had forgotten her, until only two remained behind the iron bars.

She sat in Victor's office, barely lucid. A new day had dawned while another team checked out her apartment.

Dropping the phone into the cradle, Victor said, "We checked your apartment. I don't think you should go back there unless it's with someone to get your stuff."

"What did you find?" Xandy asked. Her body shook from the shock.

"Your apartment is bugged," Victor said. He placed a blanket around her shoulders.

"What? I don't have anywhere else to go," Xandy said. She pulled the blanket tighter around her. She could feel herself unraveling, losing control. The anxiety beat against her like a tidal wave, the fear clenched her in its vise grip.

"Everything is going to be fine. You're safe."

"Safe?" She wasn't even sure if she knew what that meant anymore. Xandy took a deep breath. "The women. I know those women!"

"What do you mean? Enlighten me."

"We were in jail together, in the same pod. We looked

out for each other."

"When was the last time you had any contact with them?"

"By the time I left, only one still remained there. I was one of the last two."

"And the mail?"

"For the last few days, I've been receiving mail, like I did right after my charges were dismissed. It started with a kind word or two. Something flattering." Her sweaty hands clenched and unclenched with each word.

"From our preliminary tests, the writing appears to be human blood."

"This is no longer about a message, postcards, or a threat at the door. This maniac was in my apartment, Victor! If he killed them, he is going to try to kill me next. I don't know what to do. Oh, my God, I'm going to be next. He's going to kill me," Xandy rambled.

"Who, Xandy, who?" Victor pleaded.

"The man outside my window. I can feel it." Xandy leaned forward, rocking. "He's coming for me and all he's done until now has been foreplay." She fell back in her chair and placed her head into her hands.

"Can you describe him?"

Xandy could only look at her hands and shake her head. "It was too dark."

"I can't let you go back there. You are going to be under police protection, and that means with someone from here or with whom I feel you'll be safe." Victor said.

"Not with you?" She asked in a whisper.

"I'm sorry, but..."Victor hurried out of his office and pulled out his cell phone. He punched in Brennan's number. "Brennan, we have a serious problem, and I hope you might be able to help."

Lazarus sat under the street light watching the forensic team walking in and out of Xandy's apartment building. Something wasn't right, he thought. He'd bugged the place, sure, but what were they referring to about fresh human blood? From listening in on the radio, he didn't get any clarity. They'd found the recording, sure, but with it wiped clean, it wouldn't come back to him. At the most, they'd cast it off as a sick prank. He reflected on his conversation with Lauren from earlier today.

"Don't put it past her to make it seem like she's the victim in this. She's done it before and she'll do it again," Lauren said.

Lazarus didn't know how he was supposed to understand this. He was there to catch a criminal, nothing more, but here he was sitting outside in the cold watching his former colleagues do his job. As he sat staring straight ahead, he noticed Monroe and Hobbes walk in. Someone must think this was now linked to the serial killer. Only Victor would order them to be there. Lauren kept mentioning Blackwell and that an officer was also on the take. Could the Blackwell link be what got Xandy police protection?

Not wanting to be noticed, and with the thought of speaking with Constance again, he placed his car in gear and headed away from the scene unseen.

"What are you talking about? I know this can't be about the case," Brennan said as he listened to Victor on the other end of the phone.

"It's about something a hell of a lot more important to me than that. I need you to take care of someone. I need you to provide protection for Xandy. Something went down last night, and the threat is too earnest not to take as being genuine. You're a cop."

"Victor, I've gone out with her. I can't get involved. And this could overly complicate–"

"The only thing you're doing is giving her police

protection."

"This makes absolutely no sense," Brennan muttered.

"Right now, my thought is about the woman sitting in my office, too scared to close her eyes."

After an awkward silence, Brennan said, "I'm guessing you're going to fill me in on this."

"I'll do even more than that. Get over here as soon as possible."

Brennan arrived at the station, still feeling a chill from the cold wind. Each step brought him closer to dealing with the question he didn't want to ask: How the hell was he supposed to keep Xandy safe?

Once seated in Victor's office, Brennan glanced at the certificates, awards, and plaques mounted on the wall. Victor had done his job well throughout the years. But looking at him, Brennan noticed the concern as it wrinkled Victor's brow. Victor was hiding something, but what? Xandy was out of earshot in the break room, so Brennan had the chance to find out what was going on.

"Victor, you're getting way too involved in this with her, and I need to know why." Brennan had never demanded an answer from Victor about anything, but his friend's behavior was out of character. The image of Victor and Xandy going at it made Brennan ask, but maybe it was more of Brennan's need to not be humiliated by someone so close to him again.

"I don't know if you remember or not, but there was a massacre at one of the law firms on Franklin Street. Before the at-work massacre took place, Xandy came down here to make a report about her co-worker's behavior … and how she thought he was planning something. She didn't have any concrete information, and every officer she spoke to pushed her off to the next one. She came across as an exaggerating woman and had nothing to substantiate what she thought was going to happen. She finally got to talk to me about it, after waiting for hours and speaking to anyone and everyone who would listen.

"She told me she'd overheard this guy talking about shooting up the office. She didn't have anything credible to say. It seemed at the time just a woman trying to get back at a co-worker for some ill will. I cast her assumptions aside and told her to go home and leave it in our hands. Something more important came up and the report got conveniently lost. A couple of days later it was too late." Victor stared at Brennan. "Then she was charged with murder since she was the only one to walk out alive, and conveniently the one that shot the shooter and her boyfriend. Even I dismissed her assertions, when she came in.

"When the massacre happened, I promised myself I'd do what I could to save her from having to go through that again. Because of me and my failure to act she's in the position she's in. I have to help her, Brennan. I hope you understand."

"And the murder charge?"

"It was all circumstantial. Besides the fact that she's a great shot, the prosecution found an insurance policy of which she was the beneficiary, and they needed someone to be charged for what happened. Since she was the only one that survived, and with the potential to benefit from it, the Commonwealth assumed she was behind it. Additionally, there was a lot of money moved around that pointed to her being the one behind it all."

"It was the money trail. What was her connection to the shooter?" Brennan asked.

"According to her, none. I did do some digging and found a list of accounts, some offshore and some local. There was a paper trail in her name. If I hadn't dug a little more on my own time, she'd be on death row.

Everything was set up in her name, with her personal information. The only loophole I found was that her signature didn't match the signature on the accounts, and coming from a poorer family, there was no way the prosecution could prove that the monies transferred between her account and the shooter came from her. Her attorney was able to find a partial fingerprint on the account creation documents that didn't match anyone in the bank or Xandy, which left the theory open that someone wanted to make it appear that Xandy was behind it all, but in reality, she was just a scapegoat."

The image of Xandy's apartment flashed in Brennan's mind. It was neat, well decorated and didn't look like anything in it was a hand-me-down. "That's a stretch. Someone would have had to gain access to her information to create something so detailed in her identity."

"Exactly."

"And this Thornton guy?"

"From what I've heard from some," Victor whispered, "he was as dirty as they come, but that has nothing to do with Xandy, and I don't think she knows this part of his reputation. She is my concern, not her dead boyfriend."

For Brennan red flags rose and waved. Something was worse than wrong with this request, and he was getting no answers from the man making it. He'd have to find them another way.

"But this is going to be one hell of a task to accomplish," Victor said.

Even to Brennan's ears, this entire situation didn't make sense. How in God's name was he supposed to protect someone from a potential killer when he was only on desk duty? With this new information, Brennan couldn't help but wonder who was telling him the truth, or if no one was telling it at all.

Lazarus's gut lurched. He needed to find out what was happening. He opened the bottle of antacids and popped two into his mouth. Everything nowadays was rushed. Between heartburn, headaches and lack of sleep, trying to nail Xandy to the wall was taking a toll on him. He needed just one more piece of the puzzle.

Heading to the clerk's office, he caught Constance in-between calls.

"Good to see you again so soon." Constance said, as she puckered up her lips and leaned in toward him.

Lazarus skipped the familiarity, the flirting that she so enjoyed. He glared at her as he would a suspect during an interrogation. He didn't have time for games, lustful ones or otherwise. "Have you heard anything?"

Constance straightened at his abruptness. After an uncomfortable swallow, and a quick glance around the clerk's office to see if anyone was actively paying them any attention, she grabbed a manila folder off her desk.

"I was thinking about our last conversation and did some digging," Constance said. "The contact information for Marcella Henderson is in there."

"Marcella Henderson?" Lazarus asked.

"She is the wife of the alleged rampage shooter." Constance took a deep breath. "What you won't find in there, though, is my contact with her."

Lazarus paused.

"Don't go thinking anything crazy, now. I ran into her, unknowingly, about two years ago. She was coming out of the CA's office, while I was delivering something to the receptionist. I was about to head out for lunch, when she asked me about restaurants or whatnot in the area. To make a long story short, we had lunch together. I've never seen someone grieve like that. She cried in every breath."

"And?"

"She told me that Alphonso was a loving husband

that had gotten fired by Thornton Gage shortly before all of this happened, and that the reason for his firing was based on his work performance."

"His work performance? That is sound," Lazarus said. "Why would she tell you that?"

"I don't know. All I know is that she needed someone to talk to and sometimes the lowly court employee is better than no one. Maybe she even thought I could help. All I did was listen. I didn't even know who she was until after everything was over. She might be able to give you more details."

Lazarus opened the file and found Marcella's name and telephone number scrawled across a white sheet of paper.

"And Lazarus, next time I do you a favor, don't act like I'm the enemy." Constance called behind him from her cubicle.

"Thanks, Conni," Lazarus said. He now had at least one more person to talk to and hopefully get the answers he needed to connect a few more dots.

Hearing Victor's explanation for Brennan's presence did nothing to stop the war raging within Xandy.

"I don't know what you two are up to," Xandy said, "but I am in no way going to shack up with him! Since when can the police not take care of the civilians in its jurisdiction? I came here for help, nothing more. And Victor, you're going to cast me off on him." She rose from her comfortable spot on the old couch and started to pace the length of the small room.

"It's just for a couple of days," Victor said. "Look on the bright side; you'll have someone around to talk to while you hide."

She turned and looked at Brennan. "Is this all right with you?" She glared at him as if throwing icy daggers.

Brennan had been avoiding looking at her since she'd

entered the room. Everything about her was disheveled: her hair unkempt, her face red and pain filled, her clothes wrinkled and slightly stained. How could anyone not want to help her? He felt callous for having taken so long. "Yes," was all he could say, although his gut screamed no.

"Good," Victor said, patting him on the back, "I think it's a great idea. No one is to know about where you're staying. No one! Not even your best friend."

"You're trying to cut me off from everyone and everything I know to be with someone who I am merely acquainted with?" she asked. Her voice rose an octave.

Brennan ignored her horrified outburst. She needed someone to step up and help her out. Why not him? "We are going to be taking shifts, right, Victor?"

"Actually, Brennan, about that...I can't take anyone off of their cases for this," Victor said, looking around the room.

"This is childish," Xandy said. "I'm sure..."

"I'll let you two figure out the details, but Xandy, you are in Brennan's care for the next few days, and I need you to be diligent in making sure that no one knows where you are."

"But I am still alive–" Xandy said.

"And we are trying to keep it that way," Victor said.

"I understand that, but surely you will be sending me to a shelter or safe house or let me stay with you?"

"No," Victor said clipped. "You are to stay under his care and with him."

Brennan sucked his teeth and tried to quash his irritation as the conversation continued almost around him. His head bounced back and forth between them like a volleying tennis ball. Something was going on that he wasn't seeing.

"If I'm staying with him, there has to be some leeway on my side," Xandy said to Victor. "You want me to give up all that I know to stay with a man who I met only a couple of days ago. How do I know that I'll be safe with him?"

Brennan arched an eyebrow. After their date, he thought she'd have trusted him more. "I can still protect you," he said.

Xandy glowered at Victor and Brennan.

After a moment's silence, she whispered, "I need to head home to get some clothes and clean up if I'm going to go through with *this*."

"We'll have to discuss the changes necessary to keep you safe, but I know Brennan will do everything in his power to make you comfortable in your new surroundings," Victor said with a broad grin.

"Get me out of here. I have to get my things from my apartment, get Amarillo, and then ..." Xandy's shoulders sagged with defeat.

"I'll take care of it, okay," Brennan interjected, noticing her back losing its ramrod straightness. "My sister can watch your cat for a couple of days until you get settled. She loves animals, and it will give you peace of mind to know it's taken care of."

"Not 'it,' but she," Xandy whispered. "Now what?" She leaned back into the worn cushions.

"Let's head back to my place to get things set up. When we leave, though, I need you to duck down in the backseat, just in case someone is waiting outside to try to find out where you are."

"Why is this happening to me?" Xandy cried.

"I don't know, Xandy," Victor said. "But that's what we're going to try to find out,"

Chapter 18

October 19

Brennan pulled his car up close to the fire exit, where Xandy cowered. Cracking the door open, she eased into his car, lowering herself on the back seat. He moved into traffic.

Dejected, Xandy watched the clouds drift above her. She tried to appear asleep when she noticed larger vehicles alongside, but was distracted by her thoughts. Her armor was cracked.

There was so much she'd wanted to yell at Victor, wanted to fling in his face, but she couldn't. Not there in the station, before another cop, when Victor was trying to be all *professional*. A scene wouldn't make him love her, she knew, instead it would push him indefinitely away. Knowing the truth didn't abate her anger. Not only had he cast her off on someone else, he refused to acknowledge anything between them. Her world spun on its axis, ready to tip topsy-turvy.

For that moment when they were together, when he could just be himself – and not the Captain, and she could be Xandy – not the alleged boyfriend killer, she knew they had something. But in this reality they were on two opposite sides of the field. It didn't matter if she'd given herself to him. All she got in return was a cold knife thrust into her now hemorrhaging heart. She refused to shed one tear though. It wouldn't help her heal.

Arriving at her apartment, Xandy haphazardly packed some clothes and items she thought she'd need for her short stay with Brennan. With him watching her every move, she attempted to hurry, throwing clothes and everything else into the two suitcases. With the car trunk finally closed and her cat in tow, they then hurried to Brennan's home. She felt his constant gaze. She had the sneaking suspicion he wasn't too pleased about her being there either, at least not this way.

His estate at first glance was more of a museum than a home. There were crypts that had more life in them than his four walls, she thought. It was all sleek and shiny, or dark, depressing wood and colors.

Brennan slipped an extra key off his key ring and thrust it to her. "Follow me." They were the first words he'd spoken to her since leaving the police station. This was not how she had imagined she'd spend time with him, especially not after their dinner date.

He carried Xandy's bags and she followed him to the guest room. She saw his muscles tense. After dropping her bags, he bustled wordlessly away from her.

Xandy scanned the bedroom. It was decorated in light blue, airy and comfortable, but lacking feeling. She wandered from her room around the elaborate corridor, with all of its doorways. She felt sure that it provided more sanctuary for someone to hide than her small apartment had ever done. She opened the different doors to orient herself. For only one person, it was large enough to house a family of at least fifteen. Walking along the marble floor, along the tapestried corridors, she discovered the large picture window overlooking the breathtaking James River. How could a cop afford this place?

With the exploration, she realized that Brennan had

set her up in the room farthest away from him. She couldn't think about that now. Instead, her thoughts drifted to Rebecca. How was she going to explain all of this to her? How was she going to figure out a way to say she was staying with him without giving away the danger she was in? Xandy could never lie well, especially to her best friend. But was failing to tell the entire story the same as lying? It was only withholding tidbits, right?

Having satisfied her curiosity, Xandy closed her bedroom door and fell on the bed. She laid upon the feather comforter, exhausted, but her mind sought answers to her dire predicament.

Weary, she started to drift off. Tomorrow was soon enough to figure out the answers for her new life. She gave in to the much-needed sleep.

Holly Wilkerson's husband, Jim Wilkerson, sat across from Victor, with his shoulders slumped, his chin covered in stubble, and bug-eyed. All the while his little girl clutched her white teddy bear and sucked her thumb.

"What don't you understand? Holly's missing and you're doing nothing to find her. I've spoken to the management at *Crack 'em Up Comedy Club*. They told me Holly performed her last set on October 18th. I hoped she just needed some time to get some fresh material. You know, scouting new information, research," Wilkerson said. He gripped the sides of the chair until his knuckles whitened.

"Sir, we are doing what we can to locate her," Victor said.

"I know my wife … she is a kind soul. She was working to help us have a better life, and now … now she's missing. Something has happened. This is all the information that I have." Wilkerson leaned forward, giving Victor a folder filled with pictures and papers.

"That's a picture of her, along with her physical description, date of birth, Social Security Number, name of employer and friends. I gave a copy of this to the officer at the desk there." He pointed to the information desk. "But I want you to have it, too."

Victor tapped his pen against the stacked-up paperwork. He was losing his patience. He'd been sitting there letting Mr. Wilkerson ramble, when all of what he was saying could have been handled by Bob at the front desk. It was time to interrupt.

"How do you know?" Victor asked. "You just said Holly was working to help make a better life for you. You're not really sure who she knows or what she does when you're not around." Victor was almost as shocked by what he said as Mr. Wilkerson. First dealing with Xandy and now this? He forced all thoughts of her from his mind. He had to concentrate on the man across from him and his plea for help, and not how he was going to deal with the woman he'd just spurned.

"Don't criticize me or my wife!" Wilkerson yelled, bristling. "She's an angel … a godsend and something has happened to her."

Victor leaned over and pressed his intercom, buzzing one of his officers for assistance. "Mr. Wilkerson, if you will follow this officer here, he will take your statement and of course keep you posted on anything that we hear."

The hunched-over man had aged under Victor's scrutinizing gaze. As he stood, he leaned over and forcefully grabbed Victor's lapel. "Don't you get it? My Holly is missing!" he sobbed.

Bob pulled Jim from Victor and out the door, and the little girl then followed. With a quick look back at Victor, her face was filled with unspoken pleas. She continued onward after her father.

Victor understood what the little girl wanted him to

do. He wanted to do it, too. How was he supposed to help bring her mommy home, if he wasn't sure she was missing or even if she wanted to be found?

Monroe stared at the deceased women's pictures hanging on the white boards on the wall; he pinned the newest pictures of the drawings from Xandy's apartment, including cards connecting them and her to the murderer. They were ex-cons and all in jail at the same time that Xandy was incarcerated.

With over 1,500 women in jail at any one time, and the daily turnover rate changing dramatically, it would be difficult to say who was in contact with whom, he knew. Removing his pad, he drew a circle. If Xandy was the nucleus, he needed to find out who communicated with her, and for that, he'd have to see her jail records. Who did she come in contact with who had it in for the Department? Something tickled the back of his mind. If she were the "star" of the tragedy, what was the reasoning behind it– the MO? And what was the triggering event? By knowing Xandy was the target, maybe it was the piece of the plot they needed.

Barricaded in his room, Brennan received a call from Tom. "I'm holding in my hands a cross-complaint from Jocelyn's attorney. They're saying that you are seeing my file clerk, Alexandria Caras. Is this true?"

Brennan could hear the suspicion and something else in Tom's voice. Anger? "Well, we did go out the other night and ... and ..."

"Did you sleep with her?" Tom asked. "Hell, does she even know about your situation? I can't believe this!"

"Get control of yourself. We had a great time like two responsible adults. I couldn't know that she was connected to you, but–"

"That's not the point, Brennan. Now our entire strategy has to change. This also means that Jocelyn has a private investigator on your tail. You're taking the risk of losing your fortune for a piece of ass!"

"Wait. What do you mean?"

"Her attorney was so kind as to send me pictures from your rendezvous."

"Well, things are about to look worse. She's staying with me for a couple of days. Victor asked, and … and I said yes. It's work related."

"The pictures say something different. You're giving them more and more ammo. This complicates things. I'm saying this as your friend and not your attorney. Is she worth it? Really worth it? Plainly put, you could be seen as being just as guilty of adultery as Jocelyn. Sooner or later you are going to have to decide what you want, even with Jocelyn's threats. My advice: don't shit where you eat. Do as your job requires, but not more. You need to make it clear that you two are not together."

"Tom, you haven't been single in a while. How do you expect me to do that?"

"Get her out of your house. You're not a freaking babysitter and make it clear to her, Jocelyn and anyone else who asks that she is part of a case and nothing more."

"Is there a loophole?" Brennan asked, wondering how he'd gotten himself into such a predicament. "I can't just throw her out on the street. This is only for work."

"We don't kiss women we work with. My advice is to get Jocelyn's blessing, but then again, I don't think it's snowing in hell now, is it?"

Lazarus pulled up to the Gas and Go. The convenience store's green, white and orange sign flickered, as a car's loud stereo blared. Looking at his notepad, Lazarus double-checked the address to make sure he was at the correct location. Marcella Henderson should be there tonight, at least from what her supervisor told him earlier today.

Entering through the glass and metal doors, he saw a tall woman with long dreadlocks and smooth ebony skin in her late forties who fit Marcella's description behind the cash register. With assured steps he walked over to her, cutting in front of a waiting customer.

"Ms. Henderson," he said. "If you have a moment, I need to speak with you."

"I can't right now, Mister. I'm at work." Turning to the customer, she said, "That will be three dollars and forty-nine cents." Taking the money, she pushed a couple of keys; the cash register rung, and the drawer popped out.

"I'm here about your husband, Alfonso," Lazarus said.

Marcella blanched. He could see her gulping for breath, as her hands started to shake. "Don't you even mention his name! I've done everything you people told me to do. He's gone and I'm still here, having to take care of a family he left behind."

Lazarus had no idea what she was talking about. What people?

"I don't understand. I'm trying to find out about his relationship with Thornton Gage."

Marcella scoffed. Her eyes darted around the store. "Aren't you under Hawthorne? I remember seeing you at the Caras trial."

"Yes, I was there on that case."

"Then you should know the answers to all you're trying to find out. If you want my advice, stop snooping around. Alfonso is dead, and nothing that you do is going to bring him back. Now, if you don't mind, I need to do what I'm paid to do here. Work."

Lazarus ambled away, wondering how much more

convoluted this private investigation was going to get. She'd just thrown in a name with a connection that he'd assumed had been there for a while, Victor Hawthorne. What was his connection to Alphonso and Thornton, and ultimately Xandy?

<u>Chapter 19</u>

October 19

Standing at a crime scene for hours on end was not what Monroe had planned on doing, as one evening melted into the next day. First the processing of the scene; the searching for any small clue that might lead somewhere and then the talking to the witnesses, it all proved draining. Until he found the spark: Jason Fink. He'd called in the body's discovery. Long hair, barely shaven, and one from the hipster crowd, who desired to live in the lofts downtown, Jason didn't appear to be easily shaken by the discovery, Monroe noticed.

"Let's go over this one last time. You saw the body while you were running?" Monroe looked at how far the body was away from the path. With the high grasses, now trampled by the multitude of officers and emergency staff present, he knew Jason could not have seen too much – unless he was looking for something.

"Yeah. I went to go take a leak and saw her there."

"And the phone?"

"It was next to the body. I didn't have one on me, and it looked like it might still work – I called it in."

The cell phone, already placed in a plastic bag, looked as though it had been wiped off.

"Did you wipe it off?"

"I don't know, man. I mean, I saw the phone and

called. I was doing, what do you call it... my civic duty."

"We are going to need your prints to eliminate you, then."

"I'll give you my DNA, if that means I can get out of here."

Monroe walked back over to Hobbes. "Did the kid give you anything?" Hobbes asked.

"Only that he had to take a piss. We need to get the telephone analyzed. Maybe our perp left something on it."

"Since he actually covered the body instead of posing it, maybe he wasn't ready for it to be found," Hobbes said.

"At least not yet. Makes me wonder why he's changing his pattern."

"That's what the million-dollar question is tonight."

Xandy awoke disoriented in the unfamiliar bed, surrounded by unfamiliar things. It took her a moment to remember she was at Brennan's.

It had been three hours of being locked up in his place. Three hours of quiet, boredom, and thumb twiddling. Three hours of her mind warring for peace. Three hours of clawing the walls.

She stood, paced her room like a caged lion at the zoo, and then stopped, only to pace again. Even though she wasn't in a jail cell, no matter how comfortable it may have appeared, she felt trapped. She had to head out of there, get back to her life, instead of staying in her new cell– a nicely decorated guest room. She had mixed feelings.

Xandy looked at the clock. It was shortly after eight in the morning. She wanted out before she started to claw at the wallpaper and mark off her days in hash marks. She rushed into the adjoining guest bathroom. Taking a cat's bath, she quickly dried off and hurried to her closet to find something to wear. It was her least favorite task of any day, made even more difficult by the lack of time. Digging into the last piece of luggage, she found a pair of slacks and a snug-fitting polka-dot blouse. Seeing her reflection, she took a cleansing breath and hurried from her room.

She found Brennan in the kitchen, barefoot and dressed in a t-shirt and pajama pants, reading the newspaper and having a solitary breakfast.

"Good morning, Brennan," Xandy said, clipped.

Hearing her voice made Brennan even more tired. He didn't sleep well after getting her settled in her room earlier this morning. He yawned wanting only to crawl back under the sheets.

"I have to head out to work. I guess I'll see you tonight," Xandy said. She then grabbed an apple from the table's fruit basket and bustled over toward the door, pulling her jacket on.

"Not a good idea considering the situation." Brennan didn't even put down his paper to look at her. He'd be distracted and want to give in.

"I still have to make a living."

"If you're not alive, it won't matter."

"Okay, point taken." Xandy brushed back a strand of hair from her face. "I guess I didn't know how difficult it would be with me staying here."

"It's only been a couple of hours. Plus, it's not about you being here with me, but someone out there being after you," Brennan said. "I'm here to protect you, but if you don't want it, there are a million other things that I could be doing with my time instead of watching out for someone who believes they can handle the situation. You asked the police for help. Now you have it."

"Ugh! Did you wake up on the wrong side this morning? I am not the enemy, but I also don't need a guard or babysitter."

"Is that how you see me? Alright. Your blood will not be on my hands. I'll give Victor a call and drive you to work myself." Brennan stood, dropped his newspaper on the counter and headed toward his bedroom.

"Wait!" Xandy called out. "Maybe I am being irrational. This person or these persons have taken so much from me. I just want to be in control of something. To have something normal in my life. At my job, I'm able to do just that. I work my predictable hours, and everything is fine."

Brennan stared at her. At first he didn't notice how she wasn't so put together this morning. Distracted by her fashion fumble, he didn't see that her clothes were wrinkled, her shaking hands, or the stray hairs that wouldn't stay pulled back.

Silence. He could see her biting her lower lip, deciding what to say next. "There are a lot of things going on now, if you haven't noticed, and I'm placing you in danger by staying here."

"I can take care of myself. I can also take care of you."

Xandy turned away. "I understand you want to help me, but I can't remain imprisoned in your house."

Something flickered across her features. "Is there something you know that you're not telling me?" Brennan eyed her, hoping to pry her secret loose. "Forget it … I'll drive you in."

Xandy paused. She stared at him, almost as if weighing the pros and cons of divulging something or staying quiet. "This isn't your fault, but my own."

"I don't think you could ever do anything wrong," he whispered, closing the space between them.

"Of course I can, but I just don't want to stay here when I know that something could happen." A lump was forming in her throat. As he neared, she would have loved to throw herself into the friendly comfort he might provide, and then he stopped and pulled away. Shutters fell back in place and the moment they'd almost shared disappeared.

"Let me hurry and finish up. You can call and let them know you're going to be a few minutes late."

Instead, the shadows she'd been outrunning continued to give chase.

Thanks to Hobbes, Lazarus stared at a photocopied chart. White boards were nice, but he needed his own overview, especially since he wasn't to be involved. The victims had all been in jail within the last two years. The names seemed familiar, but that didn't mean anything when the force made so many arrests and through the notoriety of the cases. Their names became even more prominent, unless they came up with other tags for them i.e. "Super Man" for the jumper, "Tony" for the latest wannabe drug kingpin, and of course, "June" for the latest prostitute who claimed to be a loving housewife.

Each woman had a charge that was dismissed and each had continued to do what they were given a clean slate to not do again.

The art of the murder was the same, although the places that the bodies were dumped were different. Could the locations have significance? Or were they only out of convenience? Lazarus flipped open the copied files again.

There wasn't much in Xandy's file. She'd been earning good time or jail credit for obeying the rules. There were no reports to document any problems in the jail. That piqued his interest, considering that most that entered the jail were tried by one person or another. He'd have thought someone would have wanted to test her, but her file didn't give him any clue of it until he reached the last page of her record. She was not to share a cell with Elaine Trite. She'd be the person to talk to then, he knew.

With her docile attitude, Lazarus couldn't help but wonder what Ms. Trite would have to say about the Alexandria Caras who had been behind bars with her.

The camera lights flashed as Flower tossed the red large scarf over her shoulder and around her body. Her fiery hair flowed down her back against the black background. Her porcelain complexion and crimson lips contrasted with the stark darkness behind her, yet her eyes were solemn, like a child looking out the window on a rainy day. Silver toy handcuffs chained her to the low-hanging pipe above.

Harlan Jacobs leaned his lanky frame forward to capture another shot. "Remember, I need you to be a victim. Look the part, feel the part."

The lighting accentuated her contours, bold, embellished by the handcuffs.

"Are we done yet, Harlan? I really need to get to work," Flower said. She pouted, allowing her high cheekbones to protrude even more.

"A couple of more shots, and then we're finished. This could be my big break, you know?" Harlan said. His twenty-seven years showed. "Vamp is in, and we're going to catch the wave."

"I'm not a professional model. I thought we were going to do something else when you called me over." She puckered her lips.

"Like what? I told you I needed your muse-like qualities," he said clicking the camera, taking another set of pictures, while Flower swiveled with the handcuffs.

"Most guys would think I was hot," Flower said. She stuck out her breast even more, allowing the scarf to fall to the floor. "With my looks, nudity helps that even more."

"You know I can't, Flower. Claude is my best friend. He wouldn't be happy about me tasting your fruit."

"But Claude's not here," she said. Undoing the handcuffs, she strutted over to him. Taking the camera from his hands, she placed it on the small table. His hand reached out and touched her naked body. After a few minutes, the sound of his phone interrupted them. "Your cell phone is ringing," Flower said, as she leaned in to his suckling and touch.

"I must be doing something wrong if you're thinking about that," he mumbled with his mouth full.

"Didn't you say that someone was supposed to be calling you about some of your photos on the internet?"

Harlan reluctantly removed his mouth from her breast and grabbed his cell phone. "Can you give me a minute? I have to take this."

"Then, if that's the case, I'm going to head on out. I have something else I need to do. Maybe you'll score a hand-job next time Harlan," Flower said with a chuckle. She scooted out of his grasp and hurried to dress.

"This is Harlan."

Flower watched Harlan pace in front of his photo spread. "Yeah, they'll be ready when you drop by," he said

She slowed her movements to hear more. "I'll be here for a while. I just finished a new shoot, but they won't be ready for viewing yet." Harlan paused and their gazes met. He shrugged his shoulders and said, "No, she was just leaving."

"You should really be careful about something like that. People are not always good," Flower said when Harlan disconnected the call. She slung her bag over her shoulder and walked toward the loft's door.

"I'm a deputy. I deal with criminals all the time. ."

"You're a *suspended* deputy."

"Potato potahto. This guy sounds legit."

"Do you want me to leave?" Flower asked. "I'll stay until this is taken care of." Worry lined her words as her brows crinkled.

"I'm a man. I'll be fine," Harlan said as he fiddled with his camera.

"All right then," Flower leaned over and kissed him on the cheek.

"You know what? You really are my favorite flower," Harlan said, stealing a kiss.

"I'm sure you say that to all the girls."

"But only with you am I telling the truth." He grinned, releasing her from his light embrace. "Don't forget to lock the door on your way out. I'm going to look at these on the computer. Same time tomorrow?"

"I'll see you then," Flower called behind her, leaving Harlan to continue with his first love: photography.

Elaine Trite watched her reflection in the large dance studio mirror. Her next aerobics class was to begin in an hour and her routine for the *Pole Dancing Championship* still needed to be perfected. She gripped the silver pole and spun. She then pulled herself horizontal, like a human flag. The sound of street shoes broke her concentration. Staring, she saw the cop who'd locked her up months ago.

"Ms. Trite, I hate to disturb you but I have a few questions for you regarding–"

"Officer Lazarus. It is always nice to see you," Elaine said in her hearty voice.

"I wanted to speak with you about Alexandria Caras."

"Oh my, what did that girl do now?"

"Now?"

"What do you want? I don't have a lot of time to waste on unformulated questions?"

"We're looking into a string of murders and during the course of our investigation, your name popped up. I understand that while you and Ms. Caras were incarcerated at the jail that you were not to be housed together. Could you tell me why?"

"I've cleaned up my act since then. I don't know anything and haven't done anything."

"I'm not accusing you. Please, it could be a big help."

"Xandy and I used to be cellmates. We were down together waiting for bond to be posted, and she talked a lot."

"What did she talk about?"

"Mostly about how she was innocent; how she'd tried to save all of their lives and how the real culprit was some Blackwell guy, and how she had something on him to keep herself safe."

"Did she ever say what is?"

"No, but Blackwell did send her a couple of messages saying he'd take care of her. Once word got around that she was Blackwell's girl, for lack of better words, and protected by the Blackwell brand, she became untouchable almost overnight. Everyone tried to join her family."

"Family?"

"Yeah, she was the matriarch. She looked out for those in her pod. Best pod in the whole jail to be housed in. Once she left though, it reverted to how it was before."

"Why were you taken out of the pod?"

"Word got back to Blackwell about me being there. Since I was to testify against one of his runners, I was suddenly ousted. I didn't have a problem with Xandy though. She was a really nice person, and I believed her when she told me she tried to save those people because while we were in there, she tried to save us all too."

The needle moved in and out of the taut skin. The thread maneuvered like a tamed snake as the killer sewed the folds of Harlan Jacobs's right eyelid shut. Pleasure smothered him until he could barely breathe in his own frenzy. The sight of the blood of the wicked on his hands soothed him for a moment. As his heart palpitated, his victim's heartbeat weakened.

It was good doing what the rules never let him do. He now could bend them, do as he liked, and no one could do a thing to stop him. It was his spark before dying.

His last chance to make justice still have a sting and a brutal bite.

No more of that legalese bull that they wanted the public to swallow. Now there was a hand throwing out the punishments.

He loved his job.

A wolf stalked its prey. It had taken time to find them, but now he knew their schedules, their favorite pastimes and even their facades. Every aspect of their lives was his for the taking.

Removing a metal rod, the killer leaned over Jacobs' body and plunged it into Jacobs's left eye socket. With the flick of his wrist, he turned and walked away, ignoring the gurgling of his victim's slow demise.

With the torturous distraction gone, his thoughts settled again on Xandy. She'd made a promise— but instead played Absalom to his David.

Money was the root of all evil, after all.

Chapter 20

October 20

> *Metro News*
>
> *Yesterday afternoon, a jogger discovered the mutilated body of twenty-eight-year-old Holly Wilkerson on Belle Isle. Ms. Wilkerson's body, according to the eyewitness, was nude and found in the thicket along the James River. An autopsy has been scheduled to determine the cause of death.*
>
> *Wilkerson leaves behind a loving husband and a young daughter. She is best known for her recent string of five criminal charges for obscene and threatening phone calls. Wilkerson was scheduled to stand trial for another such charge in the Richmond General District Court, where each previous charge brought against her was dismissed. These dismissals prompted an investigation into the practices of the Commonwealth's Attorney's Office, and a demonstration outside of the John Marshall Courts Building.*
>
> *It is speculated that this could be the latest victim of the Thou Shall Not Killer. Many are questioning the Mayor's and Chief's roles and asking why the FBI has not been called in to help. Questions to the police have gone unanswered.*

Victor watched Mr. Wilkerson and his child walk heavy-heartedly away. Helplessness washed over him. There was not too much he could say. The Chief Medical Examiner had only provided him with a preliminary report of his findings, and since the autopsy still needed to be concluded, he could only work with what he was told. His guess was that she'd died of asphyxiation, since her tongue was literally lodged in her throat. It had been severed and shoved in.

This was one of the most uncommon things Victor had seen, but that, in addition to the tree of death painted on Xandy's wall, had convinced him of the need to keep Xandy safe. The detectives were still trying to find out where things overlapped, and Brennan was spending time protecting Xandy, which was most important.

Forensics had come back with little information from the items found at Xandy's apartment. The mail was touched by so many people. Whoever was doing this wanted them to know that Xandy was the target.

Victor felt the sweat dripping from his temples. The one person he had to protect was the one at the center of the killing spree. She had the anti-Midas touch, turning everything she touched into manure instead of gold.

Lazarus pulled up to Xandy's apartment building. Seeing no officers outside, he slipped up the stairway and stood before her door. Bypassing the yellow tape, jimmying the lock, Lazarus entered without problems and located the item Lauren had told him about: Xandy's journal. Peaking inside, he found a passage.

Thornton came home tonight smelling of someone else's perfume. I've smelled it before, and I know it's not mine. Maybe I am being overly suspicious, but he's changed in the last few months. I've noticed more strange calls, evasiveness and something doesn't feel right.

Lazarus continued to flip through the pages until he read the name Alphonso.

While in the office today, I heard the unthinkable. Alphonso asked Thornton for his share of the Blackwell account; an account that he was personally responsible for. I know the numbers are not adding up from the time logs of hours worked. Could Thornton be forging his hours, invoicing the client for nonexistent hours and attaining unearned monies?

Lazarus quickly closed the journal and placed it in his bag.

The killer sat at his favorite spot in the city overlooking the James River at Hollywood Cemetery. The quiet and serenity of the cemetery's gardens calmed him. It was juxtaposed against the city, with its blaring horns, begging homeless and endless activity. Cool air whisked by and life continued.

Except for his.

The bouquet of pink roses with goldenrods and lavender-blue asters lay heavy in his gloved hand. The pink blossoms were fragrant; the vibrant lavender and yellow coloring were too bright. But she'd loved them. More than that, she'd loved him.

She had been as warm and bright as a Virginian summer, boisterous and full of life. After years of protecting her, the time she needed him the most he wasn't there. Instead, he'd been caught up in the whims and words of another. The false promises of a woman she'd introduced him to in passing as a friend, one that would look out for her when he couldn't.

She'd been no angel, he knew. For that reason, she had been in jail. But she'd not deserved such a death. Only wanting to teach her a lesson, he'd refused to bail her out – hoping to cleanse her. Yet it hadn't been that simple. Now she was forever gone. She'd been dead for six months. He'd had time to plan for six months. For six months, he lived in bedlam, like a Bedouin caught between what was then and what is now. Now, just as the game of chess was played, he moved his pieces, anticipating his opponent's move.

The loud beeping of his watch dragged him unwillingly back to the present, to the immense loneliness and, the fire-hot anger.

It was time to prepare for tonight. The next victim's demise was waiting.

Wiping away the leaves on the tombstone to reveal the deceased's name, he placed the large bouquet on the marble headstone. He could almost hear her hearty laugh at his gesture and see her sweet smile.

With one last glance at the grave of his beloved baby sister, Pia, he walked away.

"Think of it this way, either you do what you're fucking told, or I will make sure there is more than one corpse," Lionel yelled over the phone. "I've given you enough time to locate what I need. I'm not paying you to dick me around."

"Let's get this straight. I'm doing you a favor," Tom said.

"And a well-paid one! I own you and that high-priced chair you're sitting in! Get my money. I don't give a rat's ass about anything else."

Lionel slammed down the phone. His contact had told him what he needed to know. Crime sprees provide opportunities for people such as him to get rid of unwanted burdens. Things were now about to get interesting.

He'd given her time, sent her messages, and never heard a peep back from her.

Lionel rubbed his manicured hands together and wondered how she felt about dead bodies. A wicked grin formed, while his plan took shape. Yes, there were consequences for stealing his money, and Xandy was about to experience them personally. And with so many people wanting a piece of her hide, there would be volunteers lining up to settle the score.

No one stole from Blackwell!

No one!

Monroe and Hobbes stared at the schematic. "From what I can see," Hobbes said, "The one thing that these murders have in common, is that their prior arresting officer was Peter Lazarus."

"You think he'd do this?" Monroe hadn't interacted with Lazarus. He only knew what was being said about him, and now, since he was suspended, his reputation was taking a hit.

"Well, we've seen how obsessed he is about the Caras matter. What's to stop him from doing something similar, just taking it to another level?"

"He was your former partner, right?"

"Let's just say the Caras matter contaminated the partnership. I think we need to tell the Captain. Maybe we can bring him in."

"We need more than just that as a lead. There is nothing at the scenes to even suggest that he was there."

"A good cop wouldn't leave evidence behind." Hobbes said. "I'm just playing devil's advocate."

"A good cop wouldn't even do this. You think he morphed into a serial killer because of the Caras' matter? I know we need a viable suspect; the key word is viable."

"Look, the killings are connected to the Caras case and he's the only officer obsessed enough with it and her to go even half as far."

Monroe dragged his hand over his face. That was the difference between them; one was looking for the real answer to the city's problem and the other only wanted what *appeared* to be the correct suspect. "I think you're looking at the wrong guy," Monroe said, "and if he was your former partner, what makes you think he'd be able to butcher all these people? You should know him better than anyone else here."

"You want the truth? Alright. The guy Caras was accused of killing was one of Lazarus's friends. He was the type of guy you either loved or hated, but in my opinion, he was a real sleaze ball. I think Lazarus is really out for revenge because his friend is gone and the woman who did it got off. It's his way of grieving or something. Plus, we don't have anyone else. It won't hurt to look at him a little more closely."

Monroe shook his head, but with the Captain's pressure on them, on top of the media's scrutiny, he knew they needed someone to bring him in– even if every atom of his instinct told him they were about to go after the wrong guy. "Alright, let's fill the Captain in on this then."

Lazarus had been following Xandy's every move. He knew she was guilty; he'd bet the life of his first unborn child on his instinct. However, Xandy's and Thornton's journals were proving the opposite. Sitting in his car again, he pulled up the recent email from his contact at the Virginia State Bar.

At the time of his death, Thornton Gage was being investigated by the Internal Revenue Service, Criminal Investigation Division for his role in the use of fraudulent powers of attorney to steal over $2,000,000 from four different clients.

With corroborating documents– appointments with an Al. W. Beck aligned with large deposits into a mystery account that were then transferred to several other accounts– Lazarus's hunch had taken form. Al. W. Beck was Blackwell, he knew, not only from prior investigation work, but the want-to-be-smart bastard had used an anagram or at least his skewed version of one. He tried to hide in plain sight.

Thornton was indeed involved in money laundering for Blackwell – the drug kingpin who had a grip on the heroin traveling up and down Interstate 95. Thornton had been depositing into his trust account the money from Blackwell's illegal activity, by taking the money from one account, issuing a check for it and depositing the check into one of his own private accounts, of which he had several. He'd been able to keep Blackwell in business for years. He must have gotten greedy, Lazarus thought.

Opening up the journal again, he read Thornton's last entry, dated the day of his death:

Tomorrow, everything is going to be simple. Alphonso has already agreed to his part. Now, I just have to do everything else that is needed.

Did he know about the impending massacre? When the journals were located, they'd been bound together, still sealed in the plastic evidence bags, which meant Xandy still had no idea that the man whom she loved had created her nightmare and wasn't even supposed to be at the office at the time of the massacre.

Lazarus stared out of his car window, his mind working like an intricate clock. The person protecting Xandy from the beginning was the logical place to start. Captain Victor Hawthorne. How was he really tied to Xandy then? Is that why he testified on her behalf? To make sure that if she said anything, he could then take out his boss's threat?

Who could he to talk to about this? Who would believe him? With all the evidence they had about the massacre, the journals in the victim's handwriting indicated his own role. Why'd the criminal charges go so far, and who decided to dismiss them? Lazarus figured it out like puzzle pieces fitting together.

Victor placed the pressure on the Commonwealth to pursue the charges against Xandy. They'd hoped to find out what she knew by making her wait behind bars. When that didn't work, the charges were dismissed.

The real person who had something to do with it all was the one he worked for: Captain Hawthorne. With a true threat out to get Xandy, why was Hawthorne still so involved and on whose orders? Was he just waiting for a chance to get rid of her under the guise of the serial killer? Lazarus had heard of people trying to cover up one crime with another. It wasn't about sex as he'd first assumed. Instead, if Hawthorne was really on the take, and if the massacre and Xandy's being charged had to so with the missing money, then it was still the money they all were after – Blackwell, Hawthorne and Lauren.

Maybe Lauren could provide some insight on what was really happening.

Lazarus trudged into the precinct. Bob sat at the front desk taking another complaint, while Monroe and Hobbes stooped over a file or two. Lazarus tried not to miss that feeling of inclusion. They had a lead, he guessed, or something to make them huddle together.

He too had a lead, his first step in getting the goods on his number-one suspect.

"Hey Pete! Come here for a minute," Bob called out. He looked around and nodded his head in Hobbes and Monroe's direction. "Did they tell you about the latest victim?"

"What you talking about?"

"The serial killer? Man, it's been crazy around here since we heard about it. It was Holly Wilkerson. You know, the comedian. She's done several gigs around town before, and I think even for Drew Jones's retirement party back in April."

"Yeah, I remember arresting her, too. But I think that was before she cleaned herself up. Her case was thrown out, though," Lazarus said.

"Like all the rest. It's some sort of scheme he's following. Weren't you the arresting officer on some of these other ones, too?"

"What are you saying?"

"I'm not saying anything, but sitting at the g'dam

desk all day with a cup of coffee got the wheels turning and I checked into it. Your name popped up a lot."

"Anyone else's name?"

"Not as much as yours. I think you might want to check into it. Sounds like someone might have it out for you." Bob grabbed his cup of coffee and reached for an envelope under his newspaper. "I thought I'd give this to you. It's a printout from the recent victims. It points to your involvement, but hey, I'm just a desk cop. You might see something that can save your hide from more trouble. If I've seen it, I'm sure the others have, too."

"Have you said anything to Hobbes or Monroe? Or even the Captain?"

"Nope. That is not my job. This conversation here never even happened." With a quick glance behind Lazarus, Bob raised his hand and gestured for the next person in line to come up to his desk.

With the new information, and a quick glance over his shoulder at Monroe and Hobbes' retreating figures, Lazarus quickly left the station. If they wanted to suspect him, that was fine, but they'd have to bring him in then. He wasn't going to do it for them.

Back in his car, Lazarus stared at his notes. If Xandy had attracted the attention of a killer, could it all be a bluff? He'd heard about Victor being on someone's payroll, but until now, he couldn't find out who the criminal mind was with the police in his pocket. First, Xandy's charges were dismissed, even though the prosecutor had the information to charge her for murder– and now, someone was after her. Crazy fans always came with a highly publicized case. The letter that he'd caught a glimpse of at the station showed something else, though. This wasn't a fan per se, but someone who knew more and wanted to get rid of his personal plague.

His cell phone rang.

"Couldn't stay away from this place, huh?" Hobbes asked Lazarus in a hushed tone.

Lazarus carefully looked over his shoulder. "Trying to put some things together, that's all. Paperwork."

"Nice way of saying continual review."

"You remember that Gage murder we worked on?"

"The big one in Lawyer Alley? Yeah, why?"

"I think there ... I can't stay away from the truth. We both know ...."

"Whoa ... whoa ... I don't know a damn thing, and you'd be better off leaving that case closed, where it belongs! Have you spoken with the Captain?"

"No, I'm to meet with him later on. Why? "

"Just curious is all. Like I said, leave those things alone, Pete. There's too much here that might make it seem like you are trying to stay on top of what's going on with this case and..."

"I don't know what you mean."

Hobbes paused, "This is me giving you a heads-up. Captain is going to want to talk to you about the murders. Your name is connected."

"You know that those cases weren't even worth the effort of trying to get an arrest!"

"That is what you say now, but the Captain believes that you may be his only suspect, and he needs to make an arrest."

"He's really looking at me?"

"Right now, he's telling us that we all should be looking at you. I think whatever you did, you pissed off the wrong cop on the wrong day."

Lazarus didn't try to come up with an answer. Ending the call, he pulled into traffic. The conversation had confirmed what he already knew. Victor was trying to rid himself of his threat to Xandy. But he also couldn't understand, how did the murders connected to her and why. It could only be about the money or about his boss's money. He'd have to try to contact Xandy without anyone finding out. Now, with the Captain on the payroll and him being coined the scapegoat, her hours were ticking by, and the threat of her really ending up on the front page as the next victim was almost imminent.

Chapter 21

October 20

"I want to report someone missing," Flower Burton said as she stood in the harsh overhead light talking to the officer unlucky enough to be on desk duty.

"How do you know he or she's missing?" Bob droned.

"Because, he never stands me up. I'm his ...."Her voice cracked.

"You're his what?"

"I'm his muse," Flower whispered as her thoughts drifted to the last time she saw her beloved Harlan.

"I'll kindly take a report, ma'am," Bob said. "When did you last see him?"

"On the 19th, but you don't understand! He's not the type to just leave. I went to his apartment. Newspapers were piling up in front of his door. Something has happened!"

"You can file a missing person's report, "Bob said, monotone, "and I'll circulate it. I'm going to need some information from you though. Please fill this out for me." He passed Flower the clipboard.

"Next in line," Bob then yelled.

Shuffling through paperwork in the conference room was taking up a lot of Monroe's and Hobbes' time, as they looked for another viable lead.

"Looking over Cara's record," Monroe said. "I got a hit from Crimtech when comparing the names of the inmates newly restrained and missing with the roster of those who either worked at the jail or were incarcerated there– and I got a new hit."'

"Any info?" Hobbes asked.

"Missing person's received new information about a Harlan Jacobs. He's thought to be missing by his friend, Flower Burton."

"And"

"Officer Samuel didn't find anything out of place or any evidence of foul play. Right now we don't even know if a crime has taken place. According to the report, the landlord informed Samuel that Jacobs often left for days on end with only his camera. We can't just jump on the first plausible conclusion." Monroe said to Hobbes.

"Tell me about the man missing, Harlan Jacobs? He doesn't have a record, but you believe the MO from his disappearance is the same as the first victim, Hannah Salem. What do we know about him?"

Monroe flipped through his notes. "He was a hobby photographer, and last seen talking on the phone at his place arranging a meeting with an unknown individual."

"Did we place a trace on his cell phone?"

"Yes, but we haven't had any luck getting a ping since his disappearance. We're waiting to hear back from the telephone company regarding his last calls. Should be here in the next hour," Monroe said.

"What was his day job?"

"He was on administrative leave from the Sheriff's Office."

Hobbes crinkled his brow. "What did he do?"

"Let's find out." Monroe grabbed his jacket and shrugged into it. Since Jacobs worked at the jail, and was on paid leave, it could confirm his initial thought and the connection between the victims.

Fitzgerald was on the list, too. From his position, the killer watched and observed to ensure the potential sacrifice indeed needed purifying. The killer was never one to act quickly, having taken his time to hunt. Time was not important; he could wait for an opportunity. Each person was a piece in the game of life. Some were worthier than others.

He sat in a booth at Apollo's Greek Restaurant. His head turned to follow the sounds of the keyboard keys being punched. With a raised voice that bespoke her arrogance, demanding the absolute servitude of the waiter, Petra Fitzgerald caught the killer's attention.

It appeared to be a family outing, but the woman in question continued to tap away, moving from one gadget to the next. She paid little to no attention to those present, choosing to heed the call of her compulsion. Instead of answering any question, she remained unresponsive to her husband's and child's continual prodding. The answers seemed to be the same throughout the entire meal: silence or "uh-huh."

Attorney Fitzgerald was a plea-deal lawyer, worse than court-appointed. She lived off her ill advice, seeking only to expand her coffers. He could blame himself for letting his whimsical sister try to be the adult, but no. Ms. Fitzgerald had taken advantage of her innocence, ignored her inmate calls and letters, and did nothing until they stood in front of the judge's bench to plead out to charges of which she was innocent.

They'd be better without her, just like the rest of the world would.

Chapter 22

October 21

> *Metro News*
>
> *Reports are surfacing that the body of Harlan Jacobs, a deputy at the Sheriff's Office, was discovered late last night in the parking lot adjacent to Lumpkin's Jail also known as the Devil's Half-Acre. The historical archeological site is currently undergoing excavation.*
>
> *Site workers made the gruesome discovery, but no further details have been released regarding the cause of death or if this relates to the recent serial killings.*
>
> *These recent murders have caused vigilance in police investigation with an overextension of hours and manpower. Community leaders are stumped as to how the city will be able to afford the ever-increasing price for capturing a killer who remains free.*

Monroe studied the work file of Harlan Jacobs. He'd gotten off easy by being placed on administrative leave. According to the file, he'd been assigned to work at the jail. His supervisor, Deputy Cabot, noted his "liking" of working in the women's section, but that was for all the wrong reasons.

"*Come on. You do me a favor, and I'll do you one,*" Harlan Jacobs breathed. He reached out to stroke Inmate Spencer's cheek.

Pia Spencer flinched at his touch. Her petite figure disappeared in the hazard orange jumpsuit with large black letters on its back; long bangs hung over her forehead emphasizing her youthful face. She stepped away from him, backing into the eggshell painted concrete wall.

Looking right and then left, he reached his arms out, blocking her retreat. He licked his lips. "Not here, doll. You see, it has to be at the right time. What I propose is simple: you take care of me, and I'll take care of you."

Pia shook her head no and cowered before him.

"You don't have a choice. You see there are several here who'd love to be the first to break you in. And I can give you a good recommendation for court on those charges."

"You ... you don't have any power in here," she whispered.

"More power than you."

"Jacobs!" snarled Deputy Cabot.

Deputy Jacobs backed up, allowing the inmate to pass. "What was that?" Deputy Cabot asked, watching the retreating figure.

"She wasn't listening to what I had to say, and maybe I got too close, but she wasn't following my orders."

"Which were?"

"To walk the line. I'm going to go write her up." Jacobs then turned and walked back toward the command desk.

"And I will have to do the same to you," she said to him. He continued to strut down the corridor.

"Do what you want, but I'm only doing my job," he yelled back at her.

Officers like Jacobs gave good ones a bad reputation, Monroe thought. The worse part of it was the SOB had not only gotten away with it but had later assaulted the same woman. He shouldn't have gotten paid administrative leave. He was a predator in a deputy's uniform, using his position to manipulate women into doing what he wanted. Monroe tossed the papers, letting them fly over his desk.

He wasn't sure if they needed to bring the serial killer in or shake his hand. At least no one else would fall victim to Jacobs. It was karma for those whom the system couldn't or wouldn't touch.

Monroe clenched his jaw and ground his back teeth. Jacobs had defiled his badge and the sheriff's office. Even if he only speculated, his instinct screamed that the reason Jacobs was dead was because he'd hunted under the guise of helping.

Victor eyed his cell phone flashing her number. It had been two days since he'd seen Xandy; two days and nights of trying not to remember what it felt like to be near her; two days of struggling not to get more deeply involved with her, and only mere seconds since she'd crossed his mind yet again. What could he say to her? There were no words to make this wrong right.

"Captain, you have a call on line 1 from Ms. Caras," Bob said through the intercom.

"Take a message," Victor shouted.

"She said it's important."

Victor saw the blinking red light on his black office phone. Inhaling deeply, he picked up, "Captain Hawthorne."

"Victor, I need to see you," Xandy stammered.

"I'm a little tied up here."

"I know, but this has to do with your case. I've been following it through the papers."

"You have some information for me?"

"Yes, maybe. Can you meet up with me soon? I want to discuss it with you in person, not over the phone."

"I don't know when I can stop by, but what info do you have?"

"It's just a hunch, but check out Pia Spencer; I'm scared she might be next."

"Why her?"

"Because almost all of the victims have been a part of my *family*."

"Your what?"

"I'll explain it in more detail when I see you."

What could he say to that? A lead was always welcomed. "I'll try to see you tonight," Victor whispered.

He ended the call before she could say more. With the name Pia Spencer scribbled on a yellow sticky note, he pulled up the Crimtech software and typed in her name.

"Someone, call a doctor!" screamed Zoe Lewis. The smell almost stopped her from getting closer. The stench of rotting meat slapped her. Her ponytail bounced behind her as she scooted to Petra Fitzgerald's side.

Petra sat straight up behind her executive-style desk, with her head slumped forward. Her pale skin had a blue-greenish hue.

Zoe's stomach lurched. With a cough, she placed her hand over her mouth. Her other hand touched Fitzgerald's rigid back.

It didn't move.

EMTs rolled out the body on a covered gurney to the waiting ambulance. Red and white lights combined with the flashing blue lights of the responding police. Uniformed officers swarmed the office building, securing the scene. Upon Monroe's arrival, Detective Hobbes acknowledged his presence with a spit of brown goo into the Styrofoam cup he held.

"A new habit?" Monroe asked, pointing at the cup.

"Yeah. Some habits are hard to kick."

"Let me guess, another victim?" Monroe asked, standing next to Hobbes.

"The poor paralegal is still shaking from finding her boss's body."

"Have you spoken to her yet?" Monroe asked.

"No, I wanted to wait for you. And it stinks up there. I wonder how they've been able to hold out so long. The heat has only exacerbated the decomp."

"Did you see the body?"

"Yeah. It's being shipped to the ME now."

"Maybe we'll get word soon on the cause of death."

"From the large puddle of blood soaked into the carpet, I'm guessing blood loss."

Zoe sat at her desk, hearing the can of deodorizing spray *ppsstting* again. Whoever it was, their finger was stuck pressing the nozzle down, in hopes of ridding the office of the rotting stench. She tapped her foot, checked her email and waited. Her body continued to shake in panic.

"Zoe," the firm's receptionist, tapped Zoe lightly on the shoulder as she gestured to two men standing silently behind her. "Some detectives are here to see you," she whispered.

Zoe turned and looked at the two men who had entered her office. She'd expected to see detectives in flowing trench coats, not men that looked so normal. One was tall, and the other a foot or so shorter. She wondered if she was considered a suspect already, even before she opened her mouth.

"My partner and I just want to ask you a few questions," Monroe said, taking the lead.

"You discovered the body?" Hobbes asked.

Of course I did, she wanted to scream, but such behavior would pinpoint her more than anything else. In a calm voice, Zoe said, "When I arrived this morning, I knocked on her door. I didn't think anything of it, since she had the do not disturb sign on her door, as well as DND on her phone. The only thing I heard was soft music playing. She liked to listen to it when she worked.

She said it helped her concentrate."

"How was your relationship with her?" Monroe asked.

"She was my boss and my friend." Zoe crossed her arms, tucking her cold hands under them.

"How was your relationship?" Hobbes asked.

"It had its good days and then some bad, but because of her recent case load, she seemed quite stressed. She was really emotional sometimes." She paused. "I was left a sticky not to disturb her, and I didn't." She couldn't keep the attitude from seeping into the conversation with each additional detail. Instead of investigating her, they should be looking for clues on who really did it.

"I've heard that you and the others have been using air freshener throughout the office," Hobbes interjected.

Zoe wondered why such a detail would be important. Was this detective Hobbes trying to say that she was covering up a murder with a can of *Oust*?

"That's saying it politely. I was using it, hoping to be rid of the wretched smell, but nothing helped. When we came in this morning, it was burning up in here. Since Petra was going through early stages of menopause, no one questioned it. But, it smelled worse than a bathroom. The stench coming from her office was overpowering. When we received a call from the Supreme Court about one of the cases she was working on, I used it as my excuse to disturb her. She always took calls from the Supreme Court. So I went in there, thinking it was bad food, I saw her...her sitting there. It was just like she was working. Her hands were on the keyboard, and she stared at the screen. At least I thought she did ..." Her voice trailed off.

"I've heard that you were passed over for a promotion and raise, and that you were very upset about it," Hobbes said.

"If you're looking for someone to blame, you might

want to view her file at the Virginia State Bar. There are enough complaints for anyone to have done it. From what I've heard, she had been making up fake deeds and stealing from clients. She had no scruples. It was always about a win. Nothing more. Put it this way, she had a lot of enemies." Zoe looked away at her clock hoping the interview would be over soon. She just wanted a moment to breathe and not think about this. She shook her head thinking of all the faces that had passed through the office over the years, clients and co-workers – innocent and guilty faces.

"You're saying someone had reason enough to kill her?"

"No, I'm saying many people had reasons to do it, and it's your job to find out who had opportunity."

The tactics room tables were stacked high with files. Monroe and Hobbes shuffled through the large amounts of paperwork. The number of serial killer victims was rising, with seven people having been killed since the first discovery. Pictures of the deceased hung on a white dry erase board with writing scrawled under each, along with the statement from each tag.

From all that they both read, Fitzgerald had shot through the ranks. Although starting out with next to nothing, she'd been endorsed repeatedly by delegates, senators, CEOs, and the like. She handled high-power Virginia divorces, usually for the cheating spouse and criminal cases.

Both Monroe and Hobbes dug through the boxes perusing each piece of paper for a clue.

"From looking at all this crap, it seems like this gal had a slew of criminal complaints filed against her. The most recent is still being investigated by the Virginia State Bar," Monroe said.

"I know her," Hobbes said. "After she lost the run for

city council, criminal complaints against her started to rise. We had someone come in here almost once a week for a while there, but then as the Commonwealth got involved things started to settle down."

"The Crimtech software is no help with this though, since the VSB documents are confidential," Monroe said. "However, the latest feed is showing a seventy-five percent connection to the Jail. I just checked, and it is still scanning the different databases to locate a connection."

"We'll have to do this the old-fashioned way and head to the VSB office. I'll call their hotline. Since this is a criminal investigation and she has been suspected of wrongdoing, they should share with us what we want to know. "

Dr. Reynolds took the last picture, orally documented his findings for later transcription and tried to concentrate on the procedure. He shook his head again, viewing the large strangulation marks around the Petra Fitzgerald's throat. He'd measured and photographed them several times. No one deserved to die like that.

Having finished the autopsy, he readied the needle to sew up the body. She'd not only been strangled but also repeatedly stabbed, leading to exsanguination.

He'd seen so much over the last thirty years, and man's cruelty only increased with each passing year. Tonight, he'd scientifically solved the question of how she'd died, but only the detectives could determine why.

Scanning over the file's contents, Hobbes pulled out the complaints. "Each complaint references a similar situation; that Fitzgerald represented the complainant's spouse in a divorce; that she pilfered the opposing party's bank accounts and falsified documentation to help her clients win. The problem for Fitzgerald came, of course, when her client went to the Bar and corroborated with the victim that the documents used to help her win the case were indeed fake. One document even claimed that the husband had land, which was supposed to be part of her retainer. She was trying to sell the land when the police stepped in."

"How much was the land going for?" Monroe asked.

"Somewhere around a quarter of a million dollars. The problem wasn't her plan. The problem was she got caught. After we received the initial complaint, we started to follow her. Every Sunday, like clockwork, she'd head into the office and then out to Apollo's for dinner."

"That means that if someone watched her and knew her habits, they'd be able to find her easily," Monroe surmised.

"Yeah."

"Who was the officer on tailing duty?"

Hobbes flipped through the reports until he found the officer's name. "Lazarus."

"That name keeps coming up."

Hobbes lowered his voice "If you ask me, the 'Thou Shall Not Killer' has some agenda against those who have gotten over on the system. He's going after the prominent ones that have escaped prosecution. He's like freaking Robin Hood. Except instead of giving money to the poor, he's saving the tax payer the cost of prosecuting all the people for the same crimes."

Monroe stared at him in disbelief. He'd thought about it, truly thought about it. There was some psychopath out there chopping people up, and he was supposed to agree with it because he was getting rid of those who'd escaped justice. No. That sick prick just wanted everyone to think he was a vigilante. Instead, he was nothing more than a criminal. "He's diabolical!"

"He's not diabolical, but very altruistic, Monroe. Why

can't you see that? He's just cleaning up this city the way it should be. No one wants it to go back to the way it was in the late 80s and early 90s," Hobbes said.

Monroe couldn't believe what Hobbes was saying. He wanted the monster to escape because he was making things easier for the police. There was no justice in that, but trying to tell a know-it-all-barely-busting-his-balls-cop that was like trying to swim without water. "He's not a vigilante, Hobbes. He's a psychopath looking to find another extravagant way to slice and dice. The question isn't why he's killing. I don't really care. I want to catch him before he does it again. Too much is riding on this."

"Why?"

It took Monroe a minute to gather his wits. "Simple. I have a family at home that depends on me taking care of them, of making sure they are safe. I have to do all that I possibly can to ensure that they are well. Maybe...maybe then, things can start to heal."

"You know, the arrest of a new criminal doesn't make amends with old crimes. I'm sorry for everything you and your family have been through. Is he still out there?"

Monroe didn't want to divulge anymore or think about the man he believed to still be on the loose, although someone else pled to the crimes. He had to concentrate on the rest of his family still alive and not the child ripped away from him.

"I want to solve this. I don't care about his motive. I want to stop him from doing this to this city."

Hobbes nodded his head. "Then let's keep digging until we find some answers."

"This is Channel 11 News at 11. The police need your help in locating Marilyn Feife. Feife disappeared during a routine jog in the Byrd Park area. If you have any information on this crime or any other crime, please call your local police station or crime solvers ...."

Chapter 23

October 22

Hobbes and Monroe were busy. Ever since the plea to the public, they'd received call after call about Marilyn Feife and what might have happened. On the white board, they'd been able to piece together that an unknown man ran up to her, and she'd tried to escape. After being reported missing at another precinct, the information didn't trickle down to the main station until a couple of days had passed. For now, she was only missing, and they hoped to find her alive.

"Detective, I've been on hold for the last twenty minutes. I would think that if what I had to say was important, I would not have had to hold for so long," said the woman on the other end of the line.

"How may I help you, ma'am?" Monroe asked, not wanting to be rude.

"I'm eighty-three years old. I don't have time to waste on such trivialness as waiting when I am only trying to do my duty."

"Ma'am, I apologize for the wait," Monroe conceded.

"Thank you, but ma'am was my mother. Please call me Samantha, Samantha King. Now we can get to the reason I called. Well, on that night, it was the night that I serve meatloaf, you know, that's how I remember, because I made it with the green catsup instead of the red one. Anyway, I heard this screeching scream coming from the street. I peeked out of my window ever so slightly. I mean, I can't take the risk of being seen with these hooligans everywhere doing only God knows what and listening to that satanic music. When I was younger, there was no way we'd get into a van with someone just because they may be handsome or whatnot. I am–"

"Ma'am–"

"A woman, too, but to think that woman just let herself go with him." She finally took a deep breath. "And then, dressed in such revealing clothes in such weather. I'm surprised she didn't catch a kidney infection or better yet catch the flu. Did you hear about that new flu that's going around?"

"And, where do you live, ma'am?"

"Didn't I tell you? You remind me of my son, Bernie, he's just as unobserving as you are. I live off of South Robinson Street dear, and you're looking for an attractive man."

"Was there anything noticeable about him?"

"He made me wish that I were a lot younger. I would have given that young girl a run for her money, but then again, I'm sure any man might be good, right about now. You know, detective, I'm looking for my fifth husband, but be warned. I do outlive them all."

"Thank you, ma'am, let me get your number just in case I need to follow up," Monroe said. He tapped his pen on the paper as he sought a way to end the call.

"Oh, you really are a charmer. In my day, such a man like you was hard to find. Maybe I lucked out," she purred.

"Thank you, ma'am, but I'm happily married," Monroe chuckled.

"The good ones always are, but here's my number anyway, honey."

Constance sat across from Lazarus on a wooden and red brick bench. She raised her ceramic mug to her lips, taking a sip of the rich cappuccino. "It seems to me that I'm doing more of your grunt work than anything else," she said, setting down the beige and brown mug. The ambling people, some wearing uniforms and others, plain clothes, were either leaving or heading to court. "With me doing this, I'm not calling you by your last name any more."

That got his attention. Everyone, besides his immediate family, called him Lazarus. He seemed to have a reputation for beating the odds– at least that is what he thought others understood by his name. He waited for the punch line.

"No, I am going to call you Peter."

Lazarus chuckled. His first girlfriend in Ohio had called him Peter, but then again, at that age, it could have had something with his mother dressing him up on Halloween as Peter Pan. Cindy had wanted to be his Tinker Bell.

"I have what you wanted. I was able to get copies of the docs from my friend at the bank." Constance laid the papers down between them. "Your girl has a safe deposit box there, set up by the deceased. Now, what I do know is that there were two people listed on it and it takes two keys to open. Each of them was provided with a key, I'm guessing."

"Who are we talking about?"

Constance looked around. "Alexandria Caras."

"Victor, if your men are unable to produce a viable lead, I'm going to suggest to the Chief that we bring in the FBI for help," Major Vernard said.

"I understand the frustration, but the investigation is producing leads–"

"Do you have any suspects?"

"Not as of yet, but–"

"Then let me make it easy for you. You have until 15:30 Friday, the 26th, to produce something for me. If not, we'll have to consider a different leadership approach. Until then, get me an update, as well so we will know what we need to do to potentially take this off your hands."

Victor slammed down the phone. Chief Zimmerman didn't have a clue about what was going on and the constant calls from Major Vernard to micromanage him and the investigation were infuriating.

Hearing the knock on his office door, Victor pushed his anger down.

"Come in," he called out.

"Got it!" Hobbes said. He jumped up and hurried toward Victor's office. Monroe followed. "You were right. He's killing according to their crimes, and citing biblical texts to rectify it, but we have several problems."

"He's killing out of order?" Monroe asked.

"Yes. I am not sure if this means he won't repeat the list when he finishes, but we have seven dead."

"We are missing the link in between the chains. We find out how they are connected and then we find the killer."

Hobbes knocked on Victor's door. "Captain, after speaking with you, I went ahead and cross-checked the location of the inmates, by their attorneys, courts and the deputies' schedules."

"You have my undivided attention."

"Salem, Kernbach, and Gentry were in the same pod. Harlan Jacobs was one of the deputies in charge of guarding them. The common key is Pia Spencer. The name you gave me. She was also in their pod, and her attorney was–"

"Petra Fitzgerald."

"Yep. She was Ms. Spencer's criminal attorney."

"How does Ms. Caras fit into this, then?" Victor asked. He knew the question was going to come up sooner than later.

"She was in the same pod with the women."

With the common thread between all of the victims, Victor knew he couldn't continue to put Xandy off. He had to speak with her and find out everything she might know about the women who died.

His time was running out.

Chapter 24

October 22

"Thank you for tuning in to the news at 11," the news anchor said. "Here is our top news tonight. Police have discovered the body of the Morris Stuart Community College student, Marilyn Feife, who went missing during a routine jog at Byrd Park. After pleas to the media for information..."

Every night there seemed to be more violence happening in the city, Lauren thought, as she clicked off the television and turned on her stereo. A night out would be a nice distraction while Jonathan was away in Washington. She pulled on her skin-tight dress, knowing that soon she would not be able to show up wearing something so flashy. As she slipped on the low-cut V-neck dress, she thought of how surprised Jonathan would be when she told him about the baby, their baby.

Lauren groomed and dressed with utmost care. Just because she was already with someone did not mean she could not spend the night having fun with someone else. She moved to the music playing on her stereo, putting on the final touches. With her bobbed haircut, she looked more like a high-priced call girl than anything respectable, but she didn't care. Tonight was about having fun and lots of it. She grabbed her six-inch pumps, car keys, cigarettes, and cell phone.

Checking her phone, Lauren saw the missed calls from Lazarus. She paused. What if he'd found out something? After minutes of the what-ifs lingering, she punched in his number.

"I'm heading out. If you want to talk, meet me and tell me in person." Lauren quickly gave him the address of where she was headed and disconnected the call. With her phone tossed into her purse, she stepped out under the wonderful night sky.

The harvest moon loomed in the distance.

When Lauren walked into Spike's, it was more than crowded. There was barely space to think, let alone breathe. It was almost as if the entire city had converged on the one spot. After searching, she found a partially free table. Making her way through the crowd, she took a seat. Once comfortable, her upper body moved to the music, like a snake hypnotized by the sounds of a flute.

Lauren watched the people, their outfits, their limited dance moves. Disregarding the no smoking sign, she smoked one cigarette after the other until she noticed her daily allotment was already gone. She'd smoked them so fast; she couldn't help but interpret it as a sign to give the habit up. Rummaging in her purse in hopes of finding a loose one, she heard the chair across from her creak.

"Hard to find parking," Lazarus said. He edged closer to her until she could smell the scent of musk cologne that wafted from his freshly shaven skin.

"Did you get all dressed up for me?" Lauren asked. She would have liked nothing more than to take their arrangement to another level, but with the news of her expecting, her desire to be more of a free spirit had to be placed on hold. There wasn't anyone who was going to give her a check each month to take care of the *mistake*, no one except Jonathan. She couldn't ruin that.

"So tell me what you got," she said. She leaned further away from him, crossing her legs and sitting up straight.

Lazarus looked around the packed place. "Maybe we should talk a little more in private about this. This is sensitive information."

"No one comes here to find out stuff like that. They're here to have a good time. Or don't you know what that is?"

Lazarus's right eyebrow shot up. "I'm here because you told me to meet you here."

"Then spit it out."

"Okay. You're right."

Lauren stared at the detective next to her. If anyone could find out something about Xandy and her deviousness, then it had to be him.

"Right about what?"

He moved in closer. "The money," he whispered. "Alphonso's wife gave me a little hint about bad things happening to those that ask questions. It's not concrete, but something. Plus, Xandy was and is an excellent shot."

"You're not telling me anything I don't already know. What I want to know is where it is?"

"That is the million-dollar question."

"No, it is a question worth several million."

"I've located a bank, but I need a warrant to access it." He paused and glanced around the room. "How do you know about the money?"

During the pregnant pause she could practically feel him questioning her motives for the money, so she wasn't surprised when he asked.

"Is this a cop or the P.I. I hired asking?" Lauren asked. "Look, it's simple. Thornton was my friend. We'll call him that. And when it all went down, he was to be joining me for us to start our future. She had to have found out, I can only assume. She never was a good loser."

"How long have you known her?"

"Since middle school, believe it or not. We used to be friends – best friends. But good looking men have a way of ruining that."

"What evidence do you have that she killed him besides out of self-defense?"

Lauren smirked. "She left me a message on my voice mail. The prosecutor said it didn't help his case, but I knew she'd do anything to keep him, and ultimately, his money." Retrieving a matchbook from her purse, she scribbled on it a website address, login and password. "I saved it there."

"I'll check it out and catch back up with you when I get some more information."

"Lazarus, no one knows her like I do. I know she did it because I would have done the same thing." The walls of people seemed to close in on her after that admission. Talking about Xandy whetted her appetite for another cigarette. Needing a breather, she rose from her seat. "I've got to get some fresh air," she said, "but I've given you motive, opportunity and now with the info of the money – it spells probable cause."

Making her way through the crowd, Lauren stepped out into the loud night, hearing the music from the surrounding clubs. The sidewalks were filled with people. Her neck tingled as if someone glared at her from behind. Texting Jonathan, she sauntered in the direction of her car. She could feel someone following her. But the throng on the street was too overwhelming. Just as the thought came, she pushed it aside. Who would follow her?

With each step the crowd began to ease until she thought she heard a second set of footsteps behind her. She walked on further down Main Street and found herself alone.

The Old Main Street Train Station stood upon the hill,

hovering over the open-air farmer's market and the unpaved lot where her car was parked. There was nothing there except gravel and pieces of broken glass.

As if suddenly by design, a hand shot out from behind her. It latched on her arm, yanking her into the darkness. All time stood still when the moonlight caught the flash of silver in a hand. Lauren's hands rose to protect her.

She could now only hear a mumbled whisper of "Thou shall not" before she felt the unbearable pain slash into her flesh. Numbing pain seized her. She ripped herself away from her assailant and staggered back into the light, toward a pub. She could feel the blood oozing through her fingers at her neck and her side.

Hobbling away, Lauren neared the lights. Her breathing labored with each movement. She tried to hear if footsteps followed, to see if someone was closing in to finish her off.

With her last strength, she stumbled through the weathered door. The smell of blood and its copper taste lay on her palate. Opening her mouth, she tried to speak. Only a mere gurgle came out.

She collapsed.

With heavy rings around his eyes, Monroe resembled more of a raccoon than a detective. He sifted through the papers looking for a bit of sustenance for the investigation, anything to keep them going in the right direction. The case was taking more than it's due on him. He felt his age. Even the heavily caffeinated coffee wasn't doing anything to keep him awake and alert.

Like a man trudging in quicksand, his muscles ached; he was weary and bone tired. Only the thought of his wife at home kept him moving in the deathtrap, hoping to rid the city of its greatest burden.

"So let's start from the beginning," Monroe said. This

was the third interview with the witnesses who'd come forward. The first one, the bartender from the club Lauren Donovan visited – as evidenced by the stamp on her hand, gave him nothing to go on. He wasn't even sure he'd served her anything; the patron from the train station told of having seen her walk down East Main Street.

"I'd finished up and was coming out of the station. It sits on an incline, and I saw this woman being attacked," said Calvin Jones.

"Did you get a look at the person?"

"It was dark, but he was shorter for sure."

"Which direction did he flee in?"

"He ran south, like he was headed toward Dock Street. After I saw him leave, I called 911 and rushed toward her as soon as I could. Is she going to be all right?"

"You saved her life by being there."

"Monroe, you got a sec?" Cynthia Chen asked.

"Sure." He walked over to where Cynthia was waiting.

"I just got off the phone with the hospital. They've placed Ms. Donovan in a medically induced coma."

"Thanks for letting me know."

"That's not the issue. Because of the EMTs, and all the blood, there might not be any useable DNA under her nails. I've received her nail clippings from Hobbes for testing and will get the results to you as soon as possible. Did you get the video I left on your desk?"

"Yeah. Thanks." Monroe rubbed his tired face. Even smiling was difficult.

"After you're done with him, go get some fresh coffee or something. You're about to fall on your feet."

"You sound like my wife."

"Good. She must be a wise woman then."

***

Dr. Reynolds finished the last of the notes on Marilyn Feife. It always struck a chord in him to see someone so young on his table. He'd carefully clipped her nails and collected all of the trace evidence available, including the duct tape that had covered her mouth and nose, and the plastic cable tie used to tie her hands behind her back.

He heard the door swing behind him. "So what do we have, doc?" asked Hobbes.

"Is Monroe not with you today?"

"He's following another lead."

"She'd been missing since the 15th is what the report stated. Is that correct?"

"According to the friend we tracked down, yes. Why?"

"She hadn't been out there that long."

"What do you mean?"

"The state of decomp is in the range of three days, evidenced by the cadaver's blisters on the skin and its filling with gas. However, I took a sample and found intracellular fluid leakage."

"You're losing me."

"In layman's terms, she was frozen. Unfortunately, I am unable to provide you with an exact time frame. Thawing doesn't restart decomposition at the same place it was before she died."

"Do you know the cause of death?"

"Yes. Asphyxiation. Another thing, detective. This individual did not have any sort of tagging or knife marks. I did however find trace evidence of something under her nails. I sent the sample to the lab for analysis."

"It doesn't fit with the other murders then."

"That I cannot say. I only know what the body is telling me. The contents of her stomach were sent to the lab as well. But, she seemed to have died without receiving the markings or the bruising of the others."

"Thanks, doc. I'll inform her family."

As Monroe approached his desk, he saw the nice package of surveillance reports, including copies of the videos he needed from the recent murder. He sat down and pulled up his email from Cynthia Chen. The victim, she wrote, had been followed from the nightclub.

Monroe grabbed his telephone. He needed to talk to Chen now! With a steady hand, he dialed the number and got voice mail. Having no time to play phone tag, he dashed to the third floor.

Cynthia Chen gasped at the results of her latest tests. The sound of approaching footsteps ripped her out of her shock. She looked up and waved when she saw Monroe walking toward her. "So, what did you find?"

Chen grabbed the coveted package off her desk. She opened the sealed envelope and took out the DVD. "This is the original. I burned a copy for you, which is on your desk."

Chen placed the DVD into her computer and clicked on play. She fast-forwarded to the time of the victim's entrance. "That's the victim there. Something about this caught my attention. Look at the woman to the far left, with the long curly black wig and sunglasses approximately seven people to the left. All night, in every shot on the tape in which you see the victim, the woman in the wig is also seen. The farthest the black-haired woman was away was seven people; she eventually moved up to three. But then, a face I know showed up."

"Could it be that the black-haired woman was interested in our victim? Wait...who?"

Chen fast-forwarded. "I was able to capture a good still for you. I've upped the quality of the still. But it gets even better. When the victim leaves, Detective Lazarus follows."

"And the black-haired woman?"

"She melts back into the crowd. I wasn't able to find her on another shot. She could have been out of range though since the camera is stationary, and they only have one camera in the bar."

"That is more than most."

With the click of a few buttons, the printer started to hum. Within seconds, Detective Monroe held the picture in his hands.

"I don't want to make any assumptions, but ... maybe the woman was interested one way or another in the victim, but there is never any direct contact between her and Detective Lazarus."

He didn't know Lazarus well, but to injure and kill one of his own people, that went beyond obsession with a case. It made him no different from the average killer on the street. Now the police have a lead to solve the case and get rid of his *rookie* status.

"I wish it weren't so, but ... considering all we know about his obsession with that case. It's even reached the lab's rumor mill."

"Thanks, Chen," Monroe said.

"Call me Cynthia."

"Thanks, Cynthia. I owe you one."

Chapter 25

October 22

Metro News
The body of Marilyn Feife has been located. The murder of
one so young and loved has touched this big city, but town-like
community. Marilyn was the guardian of Jose Hughes
Stewart, a pioneer and beloved community leader who rallied
for universal healthcare.

Mr. Stewart was diagnosed with early onset of Alzheimer's
in the early 2000s. He used his personal plight to bring the
spotlight to the undiagnosed in the city and throughout the
nation and lobbied for additional federal funding for
Alzheimer's research.

Mr. Stewart and his family are seeking any information
that may lead to the arrest and capture of the individual
responsible and are offering a $25,000 reward.

If you have any information, please contact Crime Solvers.

Xandy's drive to work wasn't remarkable by any
means. The city was full of traffic, the lights all alternated
between yellow and red, and the thought of her daily to-
do list drifted around in her head. Waiting at a light, she
saw something different from her daily commute. A man
in a designer suit with a cardboard sign stood on the
street corner. He wasn't the normal bum, if he were a
bum at all. He looked clean-shaven, dressed to work at

any of the office buildings not far away, yet he stood there on the street corner waving his sign at passersby. The sign's large, black marker lettering read: "Change your situation, change your paradigm."

Once at the office, the image of the well-dressed man haunted Xandy. She kept seeing his sign before her. She plopped down at her desk and looked around. She'd never been more than someone's eye candy or someone's assistant. She needed change. A paradigm shift.

Xandy stood up and walked toward Tom's office. The morning chitchat wafted throughout the halls. With a deep breath, she knocked on Tom's door and walked in. Tom sat at his overly massive desk, and soft rock music played while he lounged back in his large office chair.

"Good morning. If you have a minute, I'd like to speak with you. It's sort of private, though," Xandy said, her heart racing.

"Come on in and close the door," Tom said, turning toward her. "Today is going to be quite slow. I was thinking of letting everyone leave around two this afternoon. Where's your pad? You should be writing all of this down."

"That's what I'm here about. Today is going to be my last day."

Tom paused. "I'm sorry to hear that. I thought you were happy here."

"Happiness is relative," Xandy paused. "If I may be frank, you've helped me a lot, but it's time for me to live my life unburdened by my past."

"If this is about—"

"Please let me finish. My time here served as a good springboard of self-examination. I've been letting my criminal charges hold me back from living. I am a woman with character, worthy of admiration, love and self-forgiveness. It's just too bad that it took a man standing on a street corner for me to realize my worth."

"Xandy, we've been friends for a while now. I'd hate to see you walk away from this opportunity that I've given you. You have a future here at this firm."

"You were my paid attorney who worked on my criminal case. We are associates, Tom. The only thing you know about me is what I tell you and what you continue to update my file with. Thanks for the opportunity that you've provided, but please accept this as my notice."

Victor hunched over his desk with a magnifying glass. He peered at the pictures he'd received from Monroe of the most recent attack. This incident didn't fit the others. Everything was different – no tag, no sewing and no staging of the body.

So far, they'd determined that the savage murders had been premeditated, which could only be deduced from the use of the tags. From what he could figure out, the tags were used not only to tell of their crime, but also as a warning to those connected to the circle of victims. Crimtech had spurted out the probabilities. Not only were they all connected through their respective incarcerations in the jail and/or work at the jail, but also through a Pia Spencer.

Pia Spencer, a prior vet tech, had been charged with one count of grand larceny and one count of possession of an unauthorized controlled substance. Flipping through the pages, Victor discovered a report from Lazarus, the arresting officer:

At 23:00, officer arrived at Spencer Veterinarian Hospital, in response to a silent alarm. Upon securing the premises, suspect was located in the cat kennel area, passed out with a syringe and a vial of Ketamine beside her body. After checking her vitals, I requested an ambulance. EMTs arrived and the suspect was transported to 13th Street Hospital.

Victor flipped the page and perused the next report, as taken from Deputy Harlan Jacobs at the Jail.

Inmate Spencer was found this morning unresponsive in her cell. Taken to medical, she was declared dead at 14:42. Next of kin to be notified.

Next of kin, Victor wondered. Who was it? Finding the initial intake, a Robert Natas was listed as the only relative for Pia Spencer. Copying the telephone number and additional contact information listed, he forwarded it to Monroe.

But now, just when all the lights went on in his head, they started to dim. His head ached and his eyes burned. He needed a break. He'd been looking at the documentation for the better part of three hours. Whoever was committing the murders must have stalked each individual and known their secrets, calendars, and routines. There was no other way to guarantee access. And for this to have happened, it took time to plan and to carry out.

Xandy's hand rushed to her mouth. She stared at the bloody crime scene photos and recognized one too well. Lauren. Her mind clouded. Confusion coursed through her, and the only name that ran rampant in her mind was Blackwell. It was the truth she didn't want to verify or consider, but she knew it lurked just there in her subconscious.

Blackwell was capable of many things, and most of them beyond bad. He had to be responsible for this. He was the one who knew of Lauren and possibly her connection to Thornton. She could taste the bile rising and her tongue lay like a dead fish in her mouth. Was this how she would end up, too? The bitter taste of bile mixed with disgust lingered.

Now he'd forced her hand. She had to tell them what she knew. Or was this his way of warning her to remain quiet or face the same fate? The secret she was so desperately trying to hide was rocketing to the surface. If asked, she'd tell everything she knew about Blackwell, but she couldn't say a thing until the time was right. His hammer was strong; his grasp wide, and his disposition brutal. By all accounts, she was a tadpole in a too large pond, a pond that in all appearances belonged to him.

She noted the deep lacerations. She'd wished Lauren harm, but never a butchering, she thought, as the image churned around and around in her mind.

Victor watched Xandy's reaction as if watching a play. "Are you okay?"

Xandy looked at him, blurry-eyed. "I know her." She pointed at the picture. She stood and needed to move, to pace, to do something or she was going to pass out. Who'd want to kill Lauren? She was a bitch, which wasn't a secret. But murder was serious. What could she have done to warrant such a demise?

"What do you mean, you know her?"

"Although her hair is different from the last time I saw her, her name is Lauren. She is my ex-roommate's new girlfriend ... Oh, my.... Wh--what happened to her?" Xandy stammered.

"That's what I'm trying to figure out. I've been looking over these pictures for most of the day." Victor hesitated. "I need to know what you know, Xandy. I can tell you have something to get off your chest."

"I don't think I can do this."

"I'm sorry. Were you close?"

"No, but ... I can't."

Shuffling through his notes, he continued, "She was approached from behind and her throat was slashed, as well as her abdomen."

"It was a close contact encounter?"

"More than that. It was almost a brutal butchering. Miraculously, she's still alive and is in ICU in critical condition. Whoever did this did it with passion. There had to have been a lot of emotion involved. Maybe even too much."

Victor picked up the picture again. The knife had sliced twice and created a large gash. She didn't have anything sewn into the body. Maybe it was a copycat. This victim didn't exhibit the same modus operandi.

Xandy could only shake her head in response. "I think I need something to drink."

Victor handed her his bottled water.

"I need you to tell me everything you know," Victor said.

"Do you think I'm connected?" Xandy asked.

How could he tell her that he didn't believe in coincidences?

Xandy had bad luck before, but this beat it all. The tiny interrogation room smelled of fear and old coffee.

It was like bad déjà-vu. Detectives Hobbes and Monroe joined her in the cramped room. "We have a couple of questions regarding the deceased, Lauren Donovan," Monroe said.

"We understand that there was an exchange of words at your fiancé, Thornton Hawthorn's memorial between you and Ms. Donovan," said Hobbes.

"That is correct." Xandy brushed her hair behind her ear. "Lauren didn't particularly like me. Every chance she got, she'd blame me for Thornton's death."

"That must have been hard. Hard enough to even make you kill her," Hobbes said.

Xandy looked down at her fingers and took a deep breath. "There are many things that I'm capable of, but that is not one of them." She pressed her lips tightly together.

"We know the last few days have been stressful for you, with all the threats going on and such," Detective

Monroe said. "And we are not trying to waste your time. We only want to clear up what happened to Ms. Donovan. You two used to be close?"

"We used to be close? That could be a stretch of the imagination."

A loud knock on the door interrupted the interrogation. Xandy saw a manila folder handed to Detective Hobbes by an officer in blue. He opened it and looked at her. He then tossed it on the table in front of her.

"So, Ms. Caras, you say you were not there at the bar. Can you identify anyone present in this photograph?" Hobbes asked.

Xandy looked down at the picture. She saw a dressed-to-kill Lauren speaking with Detective Lazarus. But she gasped when she saw the crisp surveillance picture of a woman who resembled her, with curly black hair. She looked at the tight black dress the woman wore. It didn't hide anything. The closer she looked, the more she noticed it wasn't even a great replica of her by far.

"This is not me! Someone is going through a lot of trouble to make it seem like I had something to do with that."

"We've heard that story before," Hobbes said. "Just tell us the truth."

"But I can prove it's not me. Look here," she said, pointing to the woman's bare left arm. "She's wearing a short-sleeve dress and there is something important missing." Xandy pulled up her sleeve and revealed her long scar, a daily reminder of the office massacre she'd survived. "When the shooting happened two years ago, I was injured — shot, actually — and this is from the bullet entering my arm and the doctors having to create an incision to extract it."

"Is there anything else you notice?" Detective Monroe asked, frowning.

"Yes. Her face looks familiar, but the dark hair color is throwing me off, as well as the shades."

The detectives exchanged a look. Xandy could read it too well. She'd given them something they didn't have before.

"There is also someone there in the background I see. He's been following me a lot lately." Xandy pointed at the silhouette of a man not far away from Lauren and Lazarus.

"Any idea who he is?" Monroe asked.

"No." For once, Xandy's logic took control over her frail emotions. She looked at the two detectives sitting across the table from her and said, "Either charge me or let me go."

The polluted air never smelled so good. She did not want to concentrate on something as miniscule as friendship in such a situation. Instead her thoughts turned to the true killer. He or she was still out there, but why would the killer want to make sure to get her involved in the murder investigation? Whoever it was had gone through a lot of painstaking detail to ensure that they played the role, but just not well enough.

"Xandy!" Victor called after her. "We need to talk." If she could've started a fire with her mind, she would have set him ablaze. She grimaced, but stopped walking.

Victor jogged up to her. "Let's go talk, but not out here."

"Why? Do you want to interrogate me some more? Oh, I forgot. You'd rather hide behind your men for that."

"It's not like that. I'll explain everything."

"Right now, there is nothing you can say to make me want to talk to you or have anything to do with you. And here, I was naïve enough to think we could have something." She pointed her finger in his face. "Shame on me for trusting you, and opening my heart to you. Someone who doesn't give a damn if I'm dragged back into hell or not."

"That's not true." He placed his palm on her finger and lowered it, but refused to release her hand.

"We'll talk tonight after I get off."

'Don't bother! If you haven't been able to return any of my calls or have time to talk to me since, you know, that night, then I'm not going to hold my breath for it to happen now. I'm done!"

Yanking her hand out of his grasp, she stormed to her parked car, leaving him and unbeknownst to them – his officers– staring after her.

Xandy needed someone to talk to –an unbiased party. She found herself pulling up to Dr. Edwards' office. Maybe he'd be able to squeeze her in for an emergency session.

Crossing the foyer into the office building, she tried to calm down, but the hurt was too raw, almost physical. If he'd hit her, at least the sting would be over, but now, now her mind replayed the scene over and over. She'd given him the chance to say he cared, but he'd done nothing but try to throw her to the wolves.

Standing in front of the receptionist's desk, Xandy gawked at the woman in the chair, for she recognized her as the one from the picture the police had just shown her. Xandy's mouth hung open at that realization.

"Hello, Ms. Caras. Did you have an appointment today?" Anika asked, smiling.

"Uh...no, um, I would like to schedule an appointment with Dr. Edwards," Xandy said. Her mind raced. *Why would this woman impersonate her?*

As Anika droned off available dates, Xandy nodded her head and took the first available one. With the appointment card in her hand, with the appointment written in calligraphy-like-script, Xandy said goodbye and rushed to her car.

Although the last person she wanted to speak to was Victor, she quickly dialed his number.

He scrubbed away the food on the stainless steel pots and pans at the local soup kitchen. The crowd of hungry homeless slowly thinned out, leaving behind the lull of running water and the sound of scrubbing scouring pads. It pulled him back toward his goal, reawakening his quandary.

The news depicted him as some sociopathic beast, someone killing without purpose, but they didn't understand. We are not black or white in our actions, but shades of gray.

Like a monkey springing from one tree to the next, his mind pounced on the image of her face. Her face, like smoke, wafted before him. He missed her more with each passing day, and although the deaths of those responsible would not bring her back, they could never bully someone again – neither collectively nor individually. No more pushing someone towards suicide, unable to live with the hurt, embarrassment or pain they dished out.

He did it for her, for her memory, to ease her broken soul.

He did it to forgive but never to forget.

He did it for eternal peace.

<u>Chapter 26</u>

October 22

The fire roared in the fireplace. The smell of fresh cinnamon and apples permeated the air. Brennan couldn't help but keep glancing at Xandy, as they enjoyed the fresh hot cider she'd made. She'd been different today. With a book in front of her nose, and his flipping through the *Forbes Magazine*, he sighed in contentment. He'd been indirectly ogling her from the side of his eye. The tucking of hair behind her ear, the casual sweet smile.

She snorted with laughter.

"Whatever you're reading must be interesting," Brennan said, turning his head in her direction.

"I was just trying to distract myself." With a grin, she closed the book and looked at him. "You don't know how much I appreciates being able to stay here. You are truly a great friend. I don't know what I would have done if you weren't there these past few days."

"Yeah, I know you like me," he said nonchalantly, guzzling his drink and rising. She'd given him the best compliment in ages, she'd called him friend. Xandy grinned in response.

"I'm going to go do some work while I leave you chuckling," a hearty chuckle escaped. Even with her secrets, he wished it could stay like it was between them.

***

Anika grabbed her purse and her new marching orders. Before leaving her small apartment, she unzipped her leather bag and stared at the metal pill case, which contained her reprieve. Removing it from its confines, she placed the pill in her pants pocket. She was headed to the police station and might need it sooner than she wished.

With Halloween approaching, the city was alive. Haunted houses, hayrides and orange and black lights hung from banisters. Shopping mall parking lots overflowed, restaurants had waiting lines, and trying to find a table for a last-minute business luncheon was almost impossible. Sitting with his menu in hand, Brennan waited for Tom's less-than-punctual arrival. He knew that Xandy was hedging something.

He'd made his decision. He wasn't going to let anyone come in between him and his happiness, including the money he potentially could lose. Even though the arrangement with Xandy was only temporary, it made him realize how much he wanted someone like her in his life. With Jocelyn, he knew he'd never be able to get over her betrayal. What was money when he could re-earn it? But time and his own happiness, once gone, he could not so easily recoup them.

"Sorry I'm late. Had a brushfire to take care of," Tom said, sliding into the seat across from Brennan.

"No problem," Brennan said.

"Traffic is horrible out there, and trying to find a parking spot was worse than finding one for court. What did you want to meet about?"

"I made a decision. I think I'm going to try to take things to a new level with Xandy."

"Are you fucking kidding me? I knew that conniving

bitch quit yesterday for a reason."

"What?" Brennan asked, perplexed and irritated. "Why?"

"Xandy quit yesterday with this long speech about how I was too involved in her personal life, and now you call me here so I can draft the paperwork for you to hang yourself with a thirteen-million-dollar noose. She is just a girl. There is nothing special about her besides her criminal charges that were dismissed. Hell, if you are looking for that *type* of woman, I know more than enough them."

"Don't demean her in front of me."

"Sorry, a little frustrated is all." Brennan saw shadows pass over Tom's features, which he quickly quashed. "And you and Jocelyn?" Tom asked.

"I don't think I can ever have something with her again without seeing what she's done to me and my family."

"So, you want to press forward with the divorce, no matter what she throws up at you?"

"Correct. I'm not going to waste another minute of my life dealing with her *issues*. Instead, I think it's time for me to start living again,"

Anika sat in the interrogation room with her shoulders thrown back. The officer's psychobabble was to begin shortly. Her head hurt with her decisions.

Monroe and Hobbes walked in. "Ms. Mandisa, I'm sure you know why you're here," Monroe said.

"Actually, I don't have a clue. I was told to come down here to answer some questions. Am I under arrest?"

"Do you think you should be?" asked Hobbes.

"I have nothing to hide. I'll freely answer any of your questions, if you'll tell me what this is about."

"Alexandria Caras, do you know her?"

"There are several people I know through my job at Dr. Edwards's office. Why?"

"We know you are acquainted with Ms. Caras, and have been stalking her," Hobbes lied. "We've found your fingerprints on mail received by Ms. Caras." Detective Monroe pulled out the evidence bag that contained a poem they'd found at Xandy's.

The watches tick, time I have stopped.
Death reaches them all, except the immortal.
When we are conjoined into one
Then I will rest
Then I will be all you need
To live, to breathe, to die
Then I will forgive.

"Detective, excuse me for my rudeness, but I can see this is going to take a long time, and I stayed up quite late and still have somewhat of a headache. Would you mind if I had something to drink?" Anika asked.

"Not at all, ma'am," Monroe said, and exited the room.

When Monroe brought a bottle of cold water back to the interrogation room, Anika reached into her pocket and grabbed the needed tablet. "I suffer from intense headaches. I'm sorry. Just a moment, please." Placing the pill on her tongue, she swallowed it with water. "And I'll answer any question you may have."

"Tell me about Dr. Edwards," Hobbes said.

"He's a kind man, with an even kinder heart," she gushed.

"What is your relationship with him?"

"He's my boss."

"And how are you connected to Ms. Caras?" Monroe asked.

"She is just a patient."

"How did your fingerprints get on that poem?" he lied.

"That's preposterous detective." Anika arched an eyebrow. "I take capecitabine, which has the side effect of producing hand-mouth syndrome. Besides occasional pain, it has caused me to lose my fingerprints. Nonetheless, your suspicions are correct. I mailed the letters to her." Anika grinned like a cat that had swallowed the canary.

"Why would you do that?" Hobbes asked.

"We wanted to play a nice game with her, different from all the others, but then again, there were also different motives."

"What motives would that be?" Monroe asked.

"I'm not the killer," Anika said. "You would need to ask my associate."

"Who, Ms. Mandisa?" Hobbes asked.

"Now, officer, you know I can't tell you that. But what I can tell you is that I would like a lawyer now. I'm feeling quite tired of your questions and–" Before she could finish her sentence, she slumped over at the table. Hobbes checked her vitals and found her unresponsive.

As they tried to revive her, it quickly became clear that it was too late.

Chapter 27

October 22

Dusk was on the horizon. Brennan stared at the phone, remembering Emily's Halloween party tonight. It was high time he showed Xandy all of his life, including his family. The party would be a prime opportunity to introduce her to his circle. Bolting from his chair, he rushed to the kitchen to see if Xandy was still there.

"I'll be by," Brennan overheard Xandy say. "I have to check on my apartment first." Hanging up the phone, Xandy turned her attention toward Brennan. "What has you so excited?" Xandy asked.

"I wanted to find out if you would do me the honor of joining me for some festivities tonight."

"What do you want me to do?"

"Put on your nicest outfit and meet me in the living room in two hours."

"It is not going to take me two hours to get ready."

"But it will take that long for me to do what I need to do."

"Do you want me to head out then? I do need to go to my apartment and check on everything. My landlord has given me thirty days to move out. Something about the increased police presence not being good for the neighborhood's reputation. When this is over, I'll start looking for a new place. Sort of a new start, you know?"

"I don't know if that is the safest thing."

"Rebecca will meet me over there, if she can."

After a moment of thought, he said, "Okay, let me call the station and get Officer Jenkins over."

"Okay. I'll see you in a couple of hours, then," Xandy said. As she turned to leave, he caught her arm.

"We're going to have a great time tonight."

Confusion crossed her face.

"I'll explain everything tonight. Tell Officer Jenkins I said hello."

"I'll be fine, Brennan."

"If I don't hear from you, I'm coming after you."

A smile tugged at her lips. "I'm sure you will," she said with an uncomfortable chuckle. "A pain in the ass isn't hard to find."

"No, but friends are."

Officer Jenkins parked the patrol car in Xandy's parking space in front of her building.

"It shouldn't be long, but I just need to take a look around, grab my mail and all."

"Do you need me to come up?" Jenkins asked. His rosy-cheeks combined with his Santa Claus-like white hair and round belly, comforted her.

"I don't see any reason. I'll only be a minute or two."

"I'll be waiting when you get down here," Jenkins said.

He watched Xandy's retreat. Sitting in his patrol car, he saw a blue Chevy Impala pull up behind him. He was surprised it took Lazarus so long to walk over. No matter what the Captain said, they were brothers in blue. He'd trust him with more than his life.

Seeing Xandy enter her building, Lazarus exited his Impala and jogged over to Officer Jenkins's car.

"It's taken you long enough to catch up. I thought I lost you back there on Patterson," Jenkins said with a hearty laugh.

"Yeah, thankfully, I knew where you were headed from the radio transmission." Lazarus rubbed his hands together, wishing for the long-forgotten warmth of September. "How long are you going to be here?" He rubbed his hands together and blew into them. "I'm thirsting for some hot coffee."

"Now you're being stereotypical."

"I didn't say doughnuts," Lazarus snickered. "There's a Starbucks not far away. I could be back in a couple of minutes with something to make this more pleasant. How many creams and sugars do you want?"

"Sugar is for wimps. I take mine black."

"I'll treat since you are counting down the end of your service. I can't believe you are going to retire on me."

"I'm not done yet. Just thinking about what's best for me and my family. Patty has always wanted to head to the Caribbean for Christmas."

"It's not even Halloween yet."

"I know, but by putting in the paperwork early, I know how much I'll get out of my pension and what I can afford. She's going to be amazed when I tell her about it."

"She doesn't know?"

"Nah. I have to have some surprises."

Lazarus looked at his watch. "All right, I'll be right back with something to knock off this chill."

Xandy walked through the front door of her apartment with her mail in hand and cringed. She placed the neat stack of mail on the kitchen counter. Her once-lovely chaise, sofa, and stuffed armchair were shredded. Black grit from her potted plants covered the carpet. Her paintings now hung crooked on the walls, while her framed photos lay torn, surrounded by shards of glass. Her television had been smashed; the cabinets emptied; lamps and tables tossed.

Xandy's apartment was its own obstacle course. She meandered her way through the mess. Peering into her bedroom, she noticed that it was even worse, if that were possible. The mattress lay tossed to the side, slashed vertically; the bed's frame also lay on its side. Turning, she looked at her closet, where everything lay in a heap on the floor.

Everything had been rummaged through. Nothing was untouched; what was considered to be of little value was simply destroyed. Black and red spray-painted anarchy symbols littered her walls, as well as the words 'murderer' and 'killer.' Reaching out to touch the paint, she heard the squeaking of a floorboard behind her. She turned.

Feeling the needle's prick, she collapsed on the floor, seeing only black shoes and the hem of navy blue pants.

He'd finally come to get her.

Thanks to a short line and speedy preparation, Lazarus arrived back at the apartment complex after mere minutes away. Pulling into the parking lot, he saw a gray Ford Expedition roll out into traffic.

He carried the black gold over to the patrol car.

"Okay, Jenkins, you didn't specify a size, so I got you a–"

Lazarus dropped the hot coffee. It splattered over the cold cement. Steam rose as its last warmth escaped. Seeing his friend leaning back, and the fresh blood run from the large incision across and down his neck, on to his once crisp uniform, Lazarus reached for his cell phone. "We have an officer down!"

After spurting off all the details he could think of, he

bolted to Xandy's apartment to see if she was still there. Climbing the stairs three at a time, he immediately noticed Xandy's apartment door wide open. "Ms. Caras," he bellowed repeatedly. There was only silence. He checked each of the rooms, the closets, any place she might have been, searching for her. If he hadn't seen her walk into her building, he never would have thought she was ever there, except for a stack of mail neatly stacked in the chaos.

Pain shot through Lazarus's head. The room swam before him until he toppled over unconscious.

The searing stitch to his side told him something wasn't right. Lazarus felt battered and bruised. Opening his eyes, he stared at the mess in which he lay. It took a moment for it to come back to him. He was at Xandy's apartment. He'd been looking for her when someone attacked him? That didn't make sense. He moved to push up from the floor. His hands felt heavy. It was then that he saw the long blade which he grasped, covered in crimson, as well as his hands. He tossed the knife away from him. "No. No. No," he muttered.

Scurrying away, he rushed toward the front door, which was still ajar. He couldn't be found like this.

It was then that he heard the not-too-distant sirens and muffled sound of combat boots climbing the stairs up toward her apartment.

"Freeze!" One of the officers pointed his handgun at Lazarus's chest. Lazarus fell to his knees and placed his hands behind his head.

Damn, someone had just set him up!

Victor climbed the stairs to Xandy's apartment, taking them two at a time. He noticed the hallway lights leading to her apartment had been knocked out. Broken glass covered the carpet. Walkie-talkies squawked, alerting him to the other officers already securing the scene. Her apartment door was open.

After a cursory glance of the living room and the kitchen, Victor saw the damage, the struggle that must have ensued. The lights flickered. Turning on his flashlight, he moved toward the master bedroom and paused.

The light from his flashlight caught the movement of something dangling from the ceiling. He flipped on the overhead bedroom light and looked up. Watches with broken faces spanned across the ceiling. Each was different from the others in color and make, but all were encrusted with red stains.

Blood.

"We've checked everywhere, sir," said a uniformed officer. "There is no sign of Ms. Caras."

Victor nodded his head. One officer dead, one suspended cop in custody, and the key to it all gone.

Victor's face remained set. He couldn't come apart now, wondering if she'd be found– alive; wondering if he'd get a chance to make things right between them; wondering if…. Victor shook his head to be rid of the mind web weaving its way from one question to the next about her and him.

He couldn't afford another complication, not when literally, her life could be depending on him.

If he ever needed to be a hero– he hoped he had the strength to be one for her now.

The killer drove onward. Blending into traffic, he followed the cars on to Interstate 64 and headed east. He had such great plans, and they could only be accomplished at the place he'd planned for: the Pump House. His excitement simmered under the surface. He glowed from the pure excitement.

Now it could all begin.

<u>Chapter 28</u>

October 22

Xandy's breath caressed the killer's flesh as he carried her. Her skin felt like silk. Having her in his clutches, he ached to feel Pia again, to hear her laugh, to feel her sisterly love. He longed for a future that would never, could never exist.

He shook his head. He needed her. He longed to be closer to what she was, his midnight, and his aching soul. Taking the knife in his hand, he placed it against her clothes allowing its sharp blade to cut through, ever so gently as not to slice Xandy's skin. His heart hammered in his chest like a beating drum. His hands jittered like an adolescent boy's.

Electricity coursed through him. He knew what he was, just as he knew what he had to do. He was drowning in his own sea of blood. He needed to change her violently. There was no other way. Her scent pushed him over the brink of no return. He craved her.

All he wanted was to purge her. There was no other way.

She'd awoken the demon dwelling deep within.

Sleep wanted to drag Xandy back into its calm grasp, but something didn't feel right. She lifted her head and surveyed her surroundings. Strung up to a wall, standing with her arms stretched out above her with cold metal chains, a chill rushed through her from more than the cold stone. The only light was coming from the array of flickering candles in the medium-sized room with a stone floor, exposed timber beams and covered windows. A dead lamb lay strung out on the table. Its blood drained into a chrome mixing bowl. She was unsure of where she was but she recognized the shape of someone off to the side.

A ski mask covered his face and he stood naked before her, covered only in a thick crimson paste. Dark triangles covered his torso, arms, and legs. His hair hung limp in an odd Caesar cut, plastered with a mixture of what she could only imagine as blood and sweat. Her scream died as she stared at him. He closed the distance between them.

"You're finally awake? Good. There is no turning back."

"Why are you doing this?" Xandy asked, confused. Her brow furrowed.

"I see inside of you. I know. I know." He pointed an accusing finger at her.

"What? Who are you?" she asked, perplexed. "Why am I here?"

"You know the answer to that, Alexandria. The key to redemption is penance. You have suffered so much and caused so many to suffer. That is why you are different."

From his intonation, Xandy could hear his awe as he gushed over her. *Stay awake. Breathe. Listen.*

"'Let he without sin cast the first stone' was so simple to follow until you. You've created a sort of quagmire for me, you know. I don't know if I should purge you or applaud your malicious efforts."

"I don't know what you are talking about."

"Yes, that is the way of things with pathological liars. After a while, they believe their own tales. See,

Alexandria, I know the truth about your role in Thornton's death, and I know about the money he left for you if anything went wrong with his plan. Too bad he trusted you too much. I know about your leverage against Blackwell; your promises for protection while in jail, and even the lies you spewed to save yourself."

"Where am I?"

"Questions that are irrelevant will not be addressed," he sneered. "I offer you a solution. A sort of penance!"

"I don't care what you say!"

"Is that how you felt when you waved goodbye to her, leaving the poor sheep in a cage of ravenous lions?"

Xandy gulped.

"You are just like the others, but she liked you. Trusted you, didn't she? How much did it cost for you to sell her out? How much did Blackwell want to rescue her– have her charges erased, like yours?"

"She was my friend." Xandy heard her voice quiver at that admission.

"She waited for you. You told her it was all going to be okay, but it wasn't."

"Where is she? What have you done to Pia?"

"Now you act like you care, but if you truly did, you'd know the answer to your own question." He tilted his masked head to the side. His hand moved up her naked body, lingering.

Her skin crawled where he touched her. Xandy gulped, cringing at the idea of being sexually assaulted by him.

"Don't! Please! Stop!" She tried to move away from his touch, to kick him away, but the shackles hindered her flailing feet.

"Yes, beg. Beg and then pray. And pray harder. I might listen," he said, chuckling.

"What do you plan to do to me?" she demanded.

"You know, deification has entitled men to too much

over the centuries," he stated matter-of-factly. "Human or animal sacrifices, virgins, the spoils of war. Now, the greatest apostasy stands before you. Religion is worse than the strongest heroin. It has created wars, famines, hatred. We are all gods, able to create, destroy, bestowing this world with our curses."

Removing the lamb's head from the table, the killer placed its brain in a stainless steel bowl, along with the gathered blood from the chrome bowl. "You shall rise anew."

"You're full of bat shit," Xandy mumbled. Terror brewed below the surface. She needed to keep a cool head.

Xandy looked up at her chains. The metal cuffs were strong and the chains secure. He had to get close enough, she reassured herself, or she would lose more than what she was willing to sacrifice.

"You can be happy. But first we must dance in the blood of the wicked." Wild eyed, he stared at her, awaiting her response.

Xandy cackled. Her stomach ached from nervousness and well-hidden fear.

"Stop laughing!"

She laughed harder, her complexion reddening at the spasms.

Raising back his arm, with his gloved hand clenched, he swung, punching her. She laughed even harder.

In spite of the pain, she couldn't make herself stop. "Is that all you got, my lord?" she asked defiantly, as blood trickled from her nose.

He hit her again, knocking her unconscious.

Brennan fixed his tie just right, eyeing himself in the mirror. He could only grin about his surprise for Xandy. Tonight he'd have a chance to dote on her and maybe, just maybe, their friendship could evolve into more, he hoped. She was single and being around her brought life into his lonely existence. He could almost imagine a relationship with her.

Xandy should be walking through the door soon, and then his great evening could begin, he mused, as he walked away from his reflection and into the dining room, awaiting her arrival. Tonight he would tell her how he felt; tonight maybe he'd kiss away any lingering fear; tonight they'd celebrate what could be between them – their hearts.

Xandy could hear the water rushing in the distance. She came to in yet another room, still chained. But this time, her masked kidnapper was nowhere to be seen. She moved her head from side to side. With each movement, pain shot through her temples. Her jaw felt stiff and her nose ached. Only a distant light allowed her squinting eyes to peer into the tunnel. She was in a storm drain, or something similar, she realized from the drain's curve.

"First comes blood, then water," she heard him say from above. Looking, she saw him roosted above her, peering down into the chamber. "I need to clean that mess off of you. Let's see if this test proves your worthiness as well."

"Show me your face, you coward," Xandy said. "Soon the police will be here. You don't know who you're messing with!"

"Of course I know, for I am the police." With his chest stuck out, the killer shone a light on his face, a face she recognized.

"You? You're doing this to me?" Xandy said.

"No, I'm doing this for her!" Officer Bob Thomas said. "She was my sister; she trusted you; I trusted you, and you betrayed it all. Without my help, tampering with your evidence, manipulating, you'd still be behind bars."

"Why couldn't you help her?" Xandy muttered.

"No one cared about a young girl making a mistake. I had nothing to bargain with. For you, there was money in the bank and a kingpin who would do anything to make sure he got access to it again. With you, though, I have it all. I'm untouchable now. You're a liability, one that the police can't wait to be rid of. Now that they know where the money is, no one needs you anymore."

"People love me."

"Such drivel. They all were using you to locate the millions Thornton stole." Bob stared at her. He watched her lip tremble.

"You lie! I am somebody."

"It doesn't matter how many times you tell yourself that, it changes nothing. Now enough with the chit-chat, it's time to proceed. I'm sure you're aware that water has been used as not only a cleansing power but also a symbol of new life. Baptism, at least in Christian tradition, was an outward symbol of the internal change."

Xandy yanked on the chains as Bob continued his theology lesson. She hoped for a miracle, godly intervention, when the sound of rushing water started her way. It sounded like a waterfall crashing, and flowing forward, like the special effects of the water used with the *Titanic* movie, but this was no movie and there was no Leonardo DiCaprio there to transcend time and space to save her.

"In fact, there is still a large discussion over which way a baptism should be held– a small sprinkle as a child or full immersion as practiced by so many within the Christian community."

The first trickles of water seeped into the small room, first creating puddles and then quickly rising. With only her feet free, there was not much she could do. Images of her new life danced in her mind. She couldn't afford to cry, be sentimental. She needed to keep her wits about her.

"For me, I thought it better to do it slowly. To allow the water to rise, and quench any lingering sin you may have."

The cold water rose faster, now covering her ankles and calves.

She shivered.

"Do you have any confessions to make before you leave this world?"

Xandy remained silent, holding in the tears she refused to shed. Her teeth chattered. The water was now at her waist.

"Church history teaches that baptism also admitted one into the congregation of believers, and even though the Bible suggests immersion, history shows that most knelt in water until the third century and then water was poured over them. Since there are so many choices, I came up with my own way."

Xandy gulped as the water rose higher. "Why are you doing this to me? Just let me go."

"All religions have their ceremonies for inundating their believers. I've just been blessed to create my own. With all of my indoctrination, what was there left for me? I poured everything into my craft, my creation and then the answer. If God is indeed a reflection of man, then we are all doomed, but if men are a reflection of God, then I am a deity, just like the other more evolved are."

"You're making no sense," Xandy uttered. The water was now under her raised arms.

"Of course I am. The fittest and strongest survive in the wild. I am the newest demigod, half man, half deity. I am the new way of salvation on earth. For sin, there must be recompense, punishment. The dead cry out for justice, which I have delivered." Looking down at her plight, Bob leered. "May your soul now be cleansed." Rising from his squatting position, he removed himself from her sight.

Xandy stared at the water. It covered her chin and continued to gush into the room. She tilted her head back, trying to keep her nose and mouth above the liquid death. She kicked her legs to stay above the water's surge. She kicked and kicked, until the water almost covered her face. Taking one last breath before she was submerged under the water, she tried to float to the surface, but the chains pulled her down. With her eyes open, she tried to wrestle with the heavy metal, but that too was unfruitful, wasting her energy and oxygen.

Her chest started to burn, as bubbles escaped. Her oxygen was running out, and so was her time.

Lazarus knew what was going on behind the scenes, as he sat in the interview room. The officers had been nice enough to uncuff him, considering what he was being charged with: murder. Not just any murder, but he was suspected of being the serial killer. How the hell did that happen?

He heard the door unlock. They'd try to break him, get a confession out of him. He knew the routine because he'd done it numerous times himself. They wanted him to pin himself into a corner by trying to explain how innocent he was. He couldn't risk that. When his ex-partner walked in, he knew they were bringing out the big guns. The conflict of interest in the case should have been enough to keep Hobbes away, but his gut told him something was foul about the entire situation.

"Peter, what were you doing there?" Hobbes asked.

"You're a cop, man. I can't talk to you until I talk to my attorney. I'm innocent no matter what your evidence against me says. I'll give you a bone, though. When I arrived in her apartment complex after a coffee run, I saw a vehicle leaving."

"It's me, Pete. I'll try to help you anyway I can."

"You want to help me? Take me to see the Captain. Then we can straighten this all out.

"I need the feed from the traffic cameras," Victor said. "We are looking for a gray 2006 Ford Expedition."

"This city is filled with Ford Expeditions," Hobbes muttered. "How are we to know which one?"

"Just look for the one with the girl in it," Victor retorted. "If there are any calls about an SUV or whatnot," Victor said, "I want to know about it. Our guy does not play with his victims."

Brennan waited in his favorite black tuxedo. The candles were lit, soft music played in the background.

His phone rang.

Answering it on the first ring, he heard Victor's voice.

"Brennan, I have some news," Victor said. "It's Xandy. She's gone."

Chapter 29

October 22

Hearing a loud knock on the door, Brennan threw it open, hoping to see Xandy on the other side. Instead, Aden stood there looking disheveled– abnormal for his usual suave self.

"We need to talk." He entered and closed the door behind him. "I thought you'd show up for Emily's party. Since that wasn't the case, I knew I'd find you here."

"I can't right now!"

"I need you to listen to me. To what I have to say."

"I am not going to put your bull before what's going on. Right now, the woman I was supposed to protect is missing. I was supposed to be man enough to keep her safe; to keep her out of harm's way."

Brennan paced. He glared at the clock and paced some more. He kept trying her number. He'd hoped they could triangulate the call, but so far the police could not locate her. The fear of losing what could be was pushing him over the edge.

"The police are looking for her," Aden said

"There is nothing you can say right now." He didn't want to be patronized. He wanted to be out hitting the streets.

"I'm here to talk to you, and it can't wait. We need to talk about Jocelyn."

"You brought this shit to my house!" Brennan yelled. His face contorted into sheer agony. His hand clenched. Fisted. He advanced toward Aden, forcing him back toward the door, and ripped it open. "Get out! You left me with nothing."

"Hit me if it makes you feel better," Aden said. "It still won't change anything."

Brennan turned away and focused on the city's lights.

"Don't you get it?" Aden asked. Tears flowed down his face. "I just wanted to be you! You have it all, and for one minute, I wanted to feel that high. You had a trophy wife, a big shot career, money. And me? All I had were the name and the scraps you gave me. I wanted what you had, and if I couldn't have it, I needed you to lose it."

"Now you only have the broke trophy wife. I'm finished with the both of you."

Xandy felt a liquid splash into her face, waking her from the darkness. She sputtered trying to clear it from her face. Whatever it was, some had gotten into her mouth, metallic tasting. She coughed up the water she swallowed and inhaled. Her lungs hurt from the rush of oxygen. She wasn't sure of how much more she could take. But she understood his goal. It was to break her through her own mental anguish, placing her in situations that were too real with danger.

"Hmmm. And here I was thinking you wouldn't come back this time," he said.

Xandy opened her eyes and saw that blood-like liquid covered her, dripping from her hair, on to the stones. She was again chained to a wall, her arms still stretched above her. She could barely feel her arms anymore, due to their positioning, but that was the least of her worries.

She didn't know how much time had passed since the last conversation with him. Time was irrelevant, as she'd been intermittently lucid since she became aware that she was being held. But she was sure that he was ready to proceed with his plan.

"You're getting to experience some of what Pia went through because of you. Her angst, fear, pain." She stared at him, seeing that he, too, was doused in the fresh red goop. The only thing visible was his eyes, his face once again masked.

She could see the crazy in him.

"Taste the blood of the wicked, bathe in their transgressions," he chanted. "Aren't you going to speak, my child? Do you see their sins, like I see them, like I see yours?" He moved closer, taking her chin in his large hand.

Xandy remained silent.

Walking away, he turned on the light, allowing her to see a little more of the room. She stared into the distance, refusing to acknowledge his presence. The lights above them dimmed. She could hear a generator's high hum.

"Well, it would appear that you want to play games. I bet I can make you scream." He moved out of her line of sight.

She gasped.

He'd moved her to another room, but this one filled with animal corpses.

"Is that all you have for me? Stuffed animals," she croaked. "What an amateur. And here I was thinking you were diabolical. Any nine-year-old with a grudge against the world could do that."

"Oh, how dumb you are. I kill people. I watch them die. But I wanted you to see where it all starts, before we progress to the other stages."

Xandy could only hope that her four-legged friend wasn't there. Shaking her head free of that thought, she concentrated on the beast in front of her.

"With corpses come the rats. I will release them soon and leave you in their torment. They will want to hear your screams, as will I. Scream loudly so I can record you like the others."

Stepping away, he darkened the room again. She heard a door snap close behind her, and the creaking of metal as the unseen cages came unhinged. Then they started to come.

Squeak.

She could hear the scurrying coming closer.

Panic rose. She tried to move her legs away, but where? She pulled on the chains. There wasn't any leeway, nothing that could help her. Then she felt something brush against her. She jumped from one leg to the next.

Squeak.

She screamed.

With what sounded like a tape recorder's click, she started hearing the screaming of others. It echoed off the walls.

Unbearable pain rose up her leg. She continued to scream until her voice was raw. She couldn't stand it anymore.

Squeak.

She passed out.

Lazarus followed Hobbes, allowing the old atmosphere to pump him up even more. At least he'd left the handcuffs off, letting Lazarus walk without problems. For that simple kindness, Lazarus was grateful.

The threat of being in an orange jumpsuit, and hearing the hooting and hollering from those he'd locked up within the last few months gave Lazarus clarity. The precinct's noise was what he knew, what he understood. Even with all of the squawking, buzzing with the hint of unadulterated laughter, it was his precinct and where he belonged.

He knew the journals gave him the upper hand in dealing with Victor. For him, this was going to be like a poker game– he was playing with a royal flush. With this information, he was not only going to get reinstated, but he'd also pinpoint the reason Victor was so evasive when it came to Xandy. After all Lazarus had read and seen, Victor would have to give him more than a brush-off. He'd have to give him the truth.

Hobbes knocked on Victor's office door.

With a nod and wave to those he saw near and in the distance, he strode cocksure into Victor's office and took a seat.

"Leave us," Victor said to Hobbes and turned his attention to Lazarus. "Where is she?" He pounded on his desk and rose to his full six foot height.

Lazarus blanched. If Victor were a dog, he was close to being rabid. He almost foamed at the mouth. "I don't know where your woman is, like I told Hobbes. What I do know is you have the wrong person locked up in here. Is there something you want to tell me, *Captain*? Do you have me in here because I was getting too close to the truth?"

"Your truth."

"What of Blackwell?"

"I have no dealings with Blackwell, Lazarus," Victor cautioned.

"But if my evidence is correct–"

"–which is only circumstantial, from the diaries of the dead. I don't care about Blackwell. I care only about the dead bodies piling up that have a connection to you!"

"The Commonwealth will have to listen to what I have to say!"

"That was always your problem Peter, even as a beat cop. You thought it was okay to chase something down without taking the time to understand what was happening. It's the same thing here."

"My sources say that Blackwell was behind the hit on Thornton Gage and that Alphonso Henderson was paid to be the gunman. Thornton was to leave and head off with Lauren Donovan. How did Alphonso know Thornton was there?"

"Are you trying to interrogate me? I can only tell you that there were several 911 calls about shots being fired. As to what, how, why, you will have to ask the deceased."

"Cut the bullshit, Victor. What do they have over your head to keep you quiet?"

Victor's left eye started to twitch. He clenched his teeth and in a low almost growl, he said. "It's not your job to question me. My only concern is Ms. Caras and not some cockamamie story you've thought up!"

"I know there are only two ways out of Blackwell's clutches: death or continual running. The question is what will you choose to do? Out of respect, I will sit on what I have to give you a chance to decide, but decide wisely. These trumped up charges aren't going to stick."

Victor ran his fingers through his hair. "At least you have hope."

"Just remember my choices."

Chapter 30

October 23

Metro News

A suspect has been arrested in the string of murders attributed to the Thou Shall Not Killer, who has terrorized this city. Detective Peter Lazarus is currently being held at the Jail. Robert Humphries, the Commonwealth Attorney, said he believed that the city and its legal system would help to show the world that Richmond is no longer the Murder Capitol of the World, but a vigilant city, where murderers are captured, tried and sentenced.

The preliminary hearing for Lazarus is scheduled for January 2 in the John Marshall Courts Building. Chief Zimmerman is being praised for his assistance in making sure that our streets are safer, since the alleged killer has been caught. "With the Thou Shall Not Killer behind bars, we can all rest a little safer and the community is now aware of what we do to ensure public safety," he said. "We are a big city, but still have the feeling of a small town. If you do wrong, we will catch you." He is expected to receive the highest commendation from the governor and mayor later this month.

Peter Lazarus, a seven year veteran of the Greater Richmond Police Department, homicide division, is being accused of masterminding the slaughter of several people throughout the city. At this time, a motive has not been confirmed, although a confidential source has said that it was *to provide justice for those who were unable to receive it through the courts system. The legal community and his fellow officers were astounded to hear the official complaint and the city is in a state of outrage at such heinous crimes. There have been further murmurings of civil litigation against the Police Department, the mayor and its designees since Detective Lazarus was an agent of the city.*

Calls to Lazarus's attorney have not been returned.

Xandy glanced around, trying to get her bearings. Squinting, she stared at the cracked and water-damaged ceiling. She could only tell that she was lying in a deep wooden box. She tried to move but couldn't. She could still hear the screams instead of the eerie silence. She moved her arms and found them shackled to her feet in manacles.

Bob silently approached. "Finally. You're awake."

With pressure on her jaw, he stuffed a cotton bandana into her mouth. She tasted the dry cloth. The sound of duct tape being unfurled caused her to squirm.

He stared down at her, clothed in only a loincloth. Picking up the large clear plastic container that contained his snakes, he removed the lid.

"Many think that 'thou shalt' is only contained in the laws of the Old Testament, like Exodus and Numbers, but those words can even be found in the Book of Psalms. My favorite scripture, outside of the ten of course, is Psalm 91: 'Thou shalt tread upon the lion and the adder.' I cannot take the risk of you so easily walking away, so I chose to modify this. I could continue ad nauseam, but what fun would that be?"

He turned the container over, emptying the snakes on her naked body. He emptied three such containers over her.

Xandy released a soft muffled scream, as she felt them slither across her skin. "That may be your last scream," he said, closing the coffin-like enclosure.

She tried to yell again and again, as the snakes moved over her legs, torso and face. Her breathing caught.

The resonating sound of the nails being pounded into the wooden box crashed upon her. She screamed some more. She heard his retreating footsteps, as her heart hammered in her chest. Her stomach churned. Trapped in a small confined space, barely wide enough for her shoulders, every feeling was amplified. Her nostrils flared, sweat pooled, and anxiety mounted.

Then she heard it again and again and again. Blood curdling screams combined with something else familiar, too familiar. It was her voice. "You killed them. You killed them all."

Johnson Howell, manager of the James River Park System and the city park naturalist, had finished overseeing his small section of land between Powhite Parkway and Route 161, which included Pump House Park. The sun was setting and a frigid breeze off the river seeped in between his layers of clothing. He rubbed his gloved hands together.

With booted feet and visible breath, he broke free of the growing underbrush, panting from the exertion. He walked back toward the road, across the concrete and rusted iron bridge and up the small incline to the cold city vehicle that awaited him. Grabbing his clipboard, he checked off his approval of the day's tasks and turned the key in the ignition.

As his car moved forward, he noticed a gray Ford Expedition parked along the road. Pump House Park closed at sunset and with the sun's dying twinkle, it was time for the vehicle to leave. After careful scrutiny, much patience and seeing that the vehicle was not leaving, Johnson exited his truck and trudged over to the SUV. The driver sat behind the wheel.

Johnson tapped on the driver's window. As the window was rolled down, and after identifying himself, Johnson said, "You are going to have to move your car. The park's closing." He pointed to the sign.

Bob glared at the man and clenched his hands tighter around the steering wheel. "There's still a bit of sun. I only want to capture a few shots."

"Sorry. You'll have to come back tomorrow. Please leave or I will have to have you towed, buddy."

Bob frowned. "I just want to take a couple of pictures, and then I'll be on my way." He then rolled up his window, dismissing Johnson's attempts to make him do anything. When he heard the scanner's squeak, he knew his time had run out. He wanted to finish with Xandy, to make sure she perished at his hands, but now, with the cops potentially coming, he had to make a hurried change of plans.

Johnson stalked back to his car. The day had been long; he was cold, and the thought of staying out in the cold even a little longer for a man who wouldn't listen was beyond him. He'd reached his limit today of fools and idiots, but rules were rules. Although he could not make the SUV driver do anything, he knew the police could. There had been enough vandalism of the Gothic style building.

Johnson noted the SUV's license plate number and drove away. With his phone in hand, he called the local precinct. "I have another one for you. The SOB won't listen to me."

"No problem, Johnson," said the dispatcher, "Go ahead; give me the location, license plate, and make of the car."

"The license plate is Virginia tags: XTW-635. It's a gray Ford Expedition SUV."

The dispatcher, recognizing the SUV's description fit

the BOLO, contacted the alerting officers.

"Monroe," Hobbes called. "Dispatch just got a call about an SUV fitting the perp's description over on Pump Drive."

"Tell the Captain," Monroe said, grabbing his coat and heading toward the door. "Let him know what's going on. I'm getting there as soon as I can. We're going to need every hand available for this."

The snakes' movements had slowed. Their slithering shifted from an abominable intrusion to a caress. With every passing minute, Xandy's hope of rescue diminished more. She could taste death.

In the darkness, she mentally recited her favorite poems, haikus and monologues. She thought of math problems, history, grammar, and when she was too tired to think any more, she drifted into a peace that she'd long forgotten. Instead of seeing Thornton's face, she saw her own, her life and joy.

She heard the floorboards creak and a muffled voice.

The lid of the wooden coffin lifted. For a moment, hope surged.

It was squashed when she saw it was him again, but clothed. She didn't know how much time had passed, but seeing him almost human, sent rockets of fear through her.

"Change of plans. It's time," Bob said. He reached in and removed one snake at a time, placing them in a plastic container. He removed the vial of pancuronium from his pants pocket and filled the syringe. Inserting the needle into her neck, he pressed down on the plunger, and slowly dosed her.

It was time to move her paralyzed body.

Monroe stood outside the metal chain fence. The

place was abuzz with the crime scene investigation unit, dressed in white, and regular detectives making sure the scene was safe. This area was supposed to be peaceful, as the James River was only a couple of feet away. But instead, all he saw was a crime scene that needed his attention. Whoever was here was long gone, but so far they'd discovered a hidden bloody chamber, a holding cell and even a storage room for trophies. It wasn't a clean place: old and fresh blood spattered the grimy walls. The murderer's tools were set out, across from a soiled mattress. Fresh and dried droplets of blood were noticeable. Rope lay tied to the frame of an old brass bed.

Monroe walked into the trophy room. He found pictures of the victims tacked to the wall, and copies of files neatly organized. Picking one random file up with his gloved hand, he flipped the file open and read the ranting and railings against Gentry Walker. Words were highlighted. At the back of the file, he felt something more rigid. Flipping to the back, he found a small cassette tape taped to the back. Placing it in the evidence bag, he then moved on to see what other evidence he could locate.

Then he saw it, a memorial alight with a grainy color picture of a woman in her early twenties dancing on a beach. He recognized the woman as being Pia Spencer.

"Detective Monroe," said one of his colleagues. "We might have a problem."

Monroe followed the investigator, only to find another trophy room. This one had pictures plastered to all four walls of the room, pictures covering pictures, as well as newspaper articles, prosthetics and hair pieces. Seeing the pieces, Monroe quickly understood. The reason they could never pinpoint who he was, was because he was always changing his appearance.

"Bag all of this up. Let's see if we can get some usable

prints off of this."

"Sir, I meant that." The investigator pointed to the top of the high ceiling. Dangling there was an encased human heart. Watches hung from the bow of the ceiling, circling the heart in a winding pattern.

Detective Monroe took his flashlight, squinted and stared at the watches. Just like all of those collected from Xandy's apartment, they were broken and bloodied.

Mementos of death.

Then looking away, disturbed by what he saw, Monroe caught sight of vials and syringes filled with a clear liquid on a metal table.

Everything that he saw pointed to this place as being the haven for the Thou Shall Not Killer.

As Monroe followed the corridor, he opened a door to discover a room with a coffin lying in the middle of the floor. The wood was unfinished, the bearings rough. It had every appearance of being homemade, as splinters stuck out, and nails were hammered into the wood, sealing the lid on top of the base.

"Ms. Caras," Monroe called out. They'd looked almost all over the building for Xandy, and had not been able to find her. He couldn't take the chance that she could be right under his nose, literally.

"Give me a hand with this," Monroe called out to one of the men in white roaming the premises. Returning with a crowbar, Monroe then jammed it between the wood's edges, splintering the wood.

The wood groaned as he attempted to remove the lid.

Finally, it clattered to the floor, revealing a hodgepodge of snakes but not a human body.

They were too late.

With her arms tied with twine in front of her, Xandy's limbs slowly began to tremble. The drug was wearing off. Her eyes searched the dark. She could feel the space closing in around her, as she felt movement. She tried to stretch out her body, despite that pain that tore through her. She could feel the weight of some sort of gown now covering her. Something with long arms. Her feet were still bare. It shattered any chance that what she'd experienced was a nightmare. It was now all too real.

She could hear music blaring above her, but it wasn't until she saw the glow-in-the-dark lever that she knew she was truly in a trunk. If he was moving her, it was to kill her. With the grace of a beached whale, she rolled closer to the t-cord. She didn't know how long she had, but she needed to get out before the car stopped or it would be too late.

With her bound and sweaty hands gripping the plastic, she yanked on the cord. Her hands kept slipping. Shaking now and hyperventilating, she wiped them on the gown and tried again and again.

Only to fail.

Think, Xandy, think, she admonished herself. She needed a better grip. Taking one last deep breath, calming down, she focused on the task at hand. With everything she had, she pulled until she heard a click.

Xandy peeked out the trunk at the blurring landscape. Her heart gunned in her ears. Nothing looked familiar. The car had slowed from its previously high speed and drove up an incline, which she recognized as a highway exit ramp. She saw no one in sight.

When the car came to a full stop, Xandy bolted out of the trunk with everything she had. It was as if her feet took flight. She raced toward the lights of a nearby gas station, yelling at the top of her lungs. "Help!"

She heard the car's tires squeal behind her. With her wrists still bound, she flagged down an old pickup truck. Seeing the two soldiers inside made her cry. "Please call 911!"

Xandy finally allowed herself to turn around. She saw

nothing of the car she'd escaped from, not even its taillights, but he knew who she was and where she lived. How could she truly escape from someone who knew everything about her and was willing to kill her for it?

Xandy convulsed. EMTs rushed in, lifting her on to a gurney, covering her in the warmth of a sheet. She felt a needle's prick, heard her name being called.

"She's been given something. We have to get her to the hospital," she heard someone say. She felt swaying movements as she was carried to the ambulance, but she couldn't say anything.

The ambulance's door slammed shut behind her and an oxygen mask was pressed upon her face. She tried to stay awake until they reached the hospital, so she could tell them all what happened, but the promise of peace was too inviting until she remembered he knew all about her.

Suddenly, she heard the once low-beeping heart monitor peep as her heart walloped against her chest.

"She's going into cardiac arrest," the EMT announced to the driver. The oxygen mask was ripped from her face. With the EMT's hands placed over each other, he began chest compressions.

Then, all she heard was stillness.

Chapter 31

October 23

"Captain, we've found her," Monroe said, as Victor pulled up to the Pump House. The area was lit up with flashing blue lights, and officers swarmed everywhere.

"I'm very happy to hear that. How is she holding up?"

"She's on her way to the hospital in Williamsburg. She was located off of Route 33 in New Kent County."

"Any sign of the perpetrator?"

"No, but there is enough evidence here. Surely, he left something for us to find."

"Stay here and make sure the scene is processed. I'll go ahead and take care of Ms. Caras. You should start seeing what you can piece together from this place."

Monroe wasn't happy about the decision, but it wasn't his call. Victor put his car in reverse and drove away.

"You'll be fine, Ms. Caras," said the attending doctor. "You're lucky you escaped such an adventure."

Xandy looked up at the doctor, barely able to see his white lab coat. Her face had started to swell and black and blue marks covered her body, and her feet and ankles were bandaged due to the rat bites. Lying in the cool bed, she shivered. She felt every inch of her bruised skin. The black and blue welts that crisscrossed her body appeared like plaid. She didn't want to think of the hands that had beaten her, grabbed and tortured her, or the eyes that belonged to those terrifying hands. Instead, she concentrated on the IV, the beeping of the heart monitor, and then the sound of metal scraping metal as the curtain was drawn back to reveal Detective Hobbes.

"Ms. Caras," Hobbes said. "If you have a moment, I'd like to ask you a couple of questions." He flipped open his pad, ready to jot down the information he needed.

"Is there any possibility that this can wait, detective? I really am not feeling up to answering any questions," Xandy said. Each word hurt coming out, just as each breath.

"I know that you may be experiencing some discomfort, but we need to catch the guy who did this to you. Can I get a statement of what happened?"

"Not right now, Hobbes," Victor interjected, as he placed his hand on Hobbes's right shoulder. "I'll take it from here."

"Not a problem, Captain." Closing his pad, Hobbes walked away.

"So this is where I find you. I'm happy to see that you are okay, Xandy," Victor said, pulling up a chair to sit next to her. "You scared me there for a while."

"How long have I been out?"

"Long enough." He held her hand. "Do you know who did this to you?"

"I wish it was that simple, Victor," Xandy croaked. "Yes…it was Bob. He knows all about me."

Victor glanced back at the door to make sure no one was there listening. He placed his finger up over his lips to shush her.

"What did he say?"

"He went on and on about sacrifices and resurrection. About the money." He knew who she was, where she lived. He knew her life. Everything that made her Xandy. The heart monitor beeping increased. Panic choked her, stealing another moment.

"Calm down. You're safe now," Victor said. He patted her blanketed leg.

She touched her face and winced. "The bruising is just a nice reminder then of what I've been through," Xandy said. "Where's Brennan?"

"He's on his way. I'm sure he would have been as close to your bedside as possible, if he could have ... I called him and let him know we found you and you were conscious again."

"I made it out alive, but I can't stay here." Xandy started to pull out her IV and rise from the hospital bed until he stopped her.

"What are you doing?"

"Bob knows everything. I have to get out of here. I'll never be safe here with him after me. It's time for plan B. You told me, if things went downhill, we'd have to go, and you'd come with me."

"I can't leave yet. Not now. I'm already facing pressure from this investigation and have to see it to the end. I have to keep you safe. I've protected you so long, but this has helped me realize that your protection has to be my top priority."

"And us...what about us?"

Victor leaned in closer to her. "My job has always been exciting, and I lived off of that adrenaline until you walked into my life. When I saw you come undone and heard everything you had to say, I knew I had to help you. But it wasn't until you were free and I saw your smile – that genuine grin that comes out on rare occasions – that I knew what you meant to me. I've been a fool for taking you for granted, but it wasn't because you are not worthy of my love, but because I'm not worthy of yours.

"These last few days have been the worse of my career. It's pitted the two things I care about the most against each other. You and my badge. Once I know he's gone, I'll willingly walk away from the badge, but never you. I haven't done anything wrong or broken any rules until now."

"Now?" Xandy asked.

"I wasn't supposed to fall in love with you, Buttercup, but I did." Victor clenched his hands open and closed. "I've been with the force for what feels like forever. You're right. Under the circumstances, it's probably time for me to seek early retirement. If I leave now, I don't risk losing anything." Retrieving a card from his pocket, he scribbled a number on its back. "Here is the number you can reach me if ever anything happens. I want you to get out of here and go somewhere safe."

"You want me to leave you behind?"

"I'll find you. The thing about buttercups that I've always appreciated is that they bloom even in harsh terrains and brackish water. They are lovely flowers that many see as simple weeds, but for me, they've always been a wonderful wildflower." Victor leaned in and placed a gentle kiss against her lips.

Taking the card, Xandy tucked it into her hands. "Come with me. What better way to protect me than to be by my side?"

"I'm not going to run from this situation. If you're safe, then I only have one concern: catching Bob. You're not safe here, and this proves it." Rising from his chair with a staunch official pose, he turned to walk away.

"Victor," Xandy called behind him. He continued to walk away. "Captain Hawthorne!" she called out, stopping him in his steps.

"I love you, too."

A smile was his answer as he disappeared into the bustle of the hospital corridor.

Brennan caught his breath when he saw Xandy. As he approached, he could feel her trepidation. Without words, he walked over to her. He saw the pain on her bruised face. Even with all of his skills, he'd lacked the common sense of ensuring that she was watched, taken care of. Her eyes, which used to look at him with such tenderness, now spoke words of worry, framed by black and blue bruising. He gently cupped her face in his hands, waiting for her to resist. Focusing all his attention on her, he said, as his voice shook, "I could live without my toys, without my wealth, without my status, but not without you."

Xandy slowly pulled away. "You're going to have to. What I want, you can't give me." She stared at the wall, unwilling to see the hurt on his beautiful face.

"I love you, Xandy! It's taken me until now to see it."

"You have been a wonderful friend, but there cannot be more between us. Please go." Xandy pressed the button in her hand. Hearing the beep, her voice wavered. "Nurse, can you please have Mr. Tal escorted from my room?"

The tears she had attempted to hold back streamed down her face. Brennan grabbed Xandy's hand. "Why? What's wrong? What happened to you?"

Reaching out, he tried to wipe away her tears, as he pulled her into his warm embrace.

Breaking the hug, Xandy said, "I can't be a replacement for the wife you lost. You have to land on your feet, find yourself and then, then you'll find the woman who can complete you. And I'll be cheering you on from the sidelines, as a dear friend should."

An orderly entered, followed by Detective Hobbes. "Is there a problem here?"

"Just go, Brennan. Please." Xandy mentally pulled herself together, straightened and turned away from him. "Believe me. This is for the best." She turned and stared out of the window into the night sky. He made her vulnerable and that was something she couldn't be.

Brennan stared at her profile. Disbelief warred with what she'd said. He waited for her to turn back to him, to say she didn't mean a word of it. Hobbes's hand on his arm yanked him back to the present. "Get your hands off of me! I heard the lady." He snatched his arm out of Hobbes's grasp and turned away. "One day you're going to regret this," he said, as calm as the wind before a storm. Without waiting for a response, he left.

After she heard him leave, and the room was once again filled with the sounds of the heart rate monitor and the IV drip, she released her pent-up breath and whispered, "Losing a friend...I already do."

Chapter 32

October 24

With a metallic buzz, the thick safe door slid open, allowing Xandy to limp through. With three keys in hand, she placed the first into the lock and heard the magical click. The other two in her purse were needed to open the treasure they'd packed away a little over two years prior. She set the large titanium briefcase on the marble counter. Removing the two keys needed, she inserted them. Each key opened one lock on the briefcase– a briefcase custom made for them. The suitcase couldn't be jimmied or broken into.

Inside she found what she expected. Everything she needed to start over: cash, identifications, a handgun and the packet of Blackwell's illegal business activities.

Xandy grinned and walked out of the bank and into the new chapter of her new life.

Removing the three packages she prepared, she dropped them into the blue mail receptacle. Now lighter, she headed back toward her car, parked in the parking deck.

Who said starting over wouldn't be easy?

Outside Bob watched and waited. He'd given her a second chance. A second chance to prove to him that she could and would do better. Seeing her stroll through the bank's doors and out toward her car with a whimsical smile, he discerned that she'd learned nothing.

With each step she took, his thoughts started to whirl. Nothing could hold him, neither this world nor the next. He only needed time, to wait. Then he would show the world what he really was. Not just a killer, but a god, and he knew with whom he'd start.

Her.

Excerpt from NUMBERS
(*The second book in the /eks/series*)

"We've already had this conversation! What do you want from me, Victor?" Alexandria "Xandy" Caras crossed her arms and secured her grip on the titanium briefcase. She could hear Richmond's downtown traffic buzzing by them. Her face still showed signs of her assault, but her disposition had changed.

Victor Hawthorne was a police captain for the Greater Richmond Police Department, and although having already proclaimed his love for her, he'd walked away, leaving her in a hospital bed alone and unprotected. He stood six feet tall and towered over her, but his size did nothing to intimidate her. She'd have to find a way to live without him, because he'd already made it clear he could live without her.

"I wanted to make sure you're okay," Victor said. He closed the space between them, and reached out to touch her face. She winced and stepped back. "I mean, I know what I said in the hospital, and I know you need to get out of here." His honey eyes twinkled in the sunlight.

"I have to be fine," Xandy said. Her voice echoed off of the gray concrete walls of the parking deck. She turned away from him and walked towards her parked car, clicking on her keyless entry remote. "I can't make you choose me; one thing I've learned is love is not always a two way street. Sometimes it's just a cul-de-sac. I have– "

Suddenly, her car exploded knocking her off her feet and into the concrete wall. Red, blue and orange flames engulfed her Mini Cooper.

Lying on the hard concrete, blood gushed from her nose and mouth.

"Xandy!" she heard her name called as if in slow motion. She stared up at Victor as he held her close.

Then she saw nothing at all.

If you enjoyed **THOU SHALL NOT**

Recommend it – Please help others to find this great story by recommending it to your friends, family and all other suspense lovers.

Post it on Facebook and Tweet it on Twitter

Review it – Please tell others why you liked this book. You can review it at Amazon and/or Goodreads, or any other review site. If you do write a review, please don't give away the mystery; let them be surprised. ☺ And please copy me via email at Tina@TinaGlasneck.com so that I can personally express my heartfelt gratitude.

Connect with me – As an indie author, there is nothing like hearing about the different elements that readers enjoy and I hope that you will enjoy the time you spent in my twisted world. THOU SHALL NOT is the first book of a series, which is continuing to develop, and your feedback can help to shape it. Therefore, please feel free to send me an email and let me know what you've enjoyed – was it the romance, the mystery? Was there ever a point that gave you chills? I love hearing about what readers have enjoyed about this book, and new series, and look forward to hearing from you!

Coming Soon – THOU SHALL NOT is the first of several books coming soon. Please stay tuned to the continuation of this wonderful series as well as other great books!

About the Author

TINA GLASNECK lives with her family in Central Virginia. An avid reader and writer, she enjoys coming up with crazy ways for people to die.

To find out more about Tina, please visit her at www.tinaglasneck.com

A Message from Tina

Dear Reader,

I am honored that you spent your free time reading THOU SHALL NOT, and hope you enjoyed it as much as I enjoyed writing this story.

Writing is my great passion and my goal is to provide my readers with tales filled with murder, mystery, suspense and romance, highlighting that an absolute good or evil does not exist. Maybe this is part of the theologian in me or maybe it is just a result of working in the legal field, but I feel that story requires not only conflict, but also intrigue.

Thank you for supporting me on my journey to fulfill my dream. I am forever grateful.

Keep Smiling,
Tina Glasneck

Made in the USA
Charleston, SC
02 May 2013